NATASHA NGAN

HOT
KEY
BOOKS

First published in Great Britain in 2013 by Hot Key Books
Northburgh House, 10 Northburgh Street, London EC1V 0AT

A CIP catalogue record for this book is available from the British Library.

ISBN: 978-1-4714-0152-7

1

Typeset by Palimpsest Book Production Limited, Falkirk, Stirlingshire
This book is set in 11pt Berling LT Std

Printed and bound by Nørhaven, Denmark

www.hotkeybooks.com

Hot Key Books is part of the Bonnier Publishing Group
www.bonnierpublishing.com

*To my parents, who have always encouraged
me to chase my dreams.*

And to Callum, who chases them with me.

Prologue

There is a rumour that the Elites don't bleed.

As the boy stands in the corner of the small, shadowy room, his whole body trembling, he thinks, *If only I could be an Elite*. Clenching and unclenching his hands, he tries to stop the shaking. *An Elite wouldn't feel anything*, he thinks. Then: *But I will feel it all*.

His mother is talking to the doctor by the operating table. They have their backs to him and are almost whispering, but he can still hear the insistence in their voices, the tension. Their murmurs rise over the room's electronic ticks, the muffled throbbing of a generator nearby. The boy tries to focus on the shapes of their bodies, bent over like trees in the wind, but his eyes keep getting pulled away to the rest of the room.

The room and its contents scare him. Twists and coils of wires hang from the low ceiling, their ends feeding into strange machinery the boy does not recognise. Here and there he spies a familiar piece of technology; the round face of an air-tram light hanging above the operating table, casting a pool of liquid yellow in the darkness. And there, built into the wall, is a mosaic of screens that look as though they have been ripped from tablets.

Though their screens are blank, every movement his mother or the doctor make sends a slice of light across their dark surfaces. It makes the boy feel as though the room is alive, watching him.

Then he spots a case of sharp metal instruments on a tray beside the operating table; the blade of a scalpel gleams in the low light. A shiver runs down the boy's neck. Breathing slowly, he focuses on the conversation between his mother and the doctor, trying to block out the horrible room and its ominous metal instruments and its rotting smell of death.

'What about two forty, *sensei*?' his mother asks.

'No,' the doctor snaps. 'Three hundred. Lowest.'

The doctor's voice has a curl of an accent in it, but the boy isn't able to trace it. Afronese? New Indian? *Things are so muddled in the Limpets*, he thinks. *Even blood*.

The boy's mother shakes her head. 'Two sixty –'

'Two eighty.'

'Two sixty-five.'

'Two seventy. Last offer.'

The boy's mother hesitates for a second, then nods.

'Good.' The doctor holds his hand out. 'Pay now.'

'N-now?' she asks. 'Can't it wait until *after* Sauro's operation?'

He shakes his head. 'No guarantee. Must be now. What if it not work, then afterwards you don't want to pay?' He waves his open hand. 'Must be before.'

Sauro's mother glances back at him. He has a sudden urge to shout out to her, to ask her not to make him do this. To grab her hand and run out of the room. But then his mother pulls out her purse and turns back to the doctor, and all too soon, Sauro is strapped down on the operating table, his face pushed through a hole and his head clamped tight in the jaws of the metal.

The doctor prepares for the operation. Sauro hears the pings and clangs of sharp metal – the noises make his teeth ache – but all he can see is the warped linoleum lining the floor of the room. It is covered in dark smudges. *That must be* . . . he thinks, then pushes the thought away. *I am an Elite*, he tells himself firmly. *I am an Elite, and I don't bleed. I can't bleed.*

His mother has been sent to wait outside. Sauro wishes she could stay with him for the operation. He feels stupid for wanting it; a twelve-year-old boy shouldn't need his *mummy*. But suddenly he can't help it, and suddenly it's all too much, and he's struggling and trying to get his head out of the clamp and the doctor is holding him down, hissing at him with sour, stinking breath, 'Stay still! Stay still! Do you want me to cut your head off?', and he feels a hot, sharp bite in the side of his neck and he screams.

Part I

NEO-BABEL

1

The Banquet

Silver was standing outside her own bedroom, one ear pressed against the door. She couldn't hear anything apart from the thudding of her heartbeat, which hadn't calmed since finishing that afternoon's training session. Her whole body ached – even her hair seemed to hurt – and she wanted more than anything to take a nap before the banquet that night, but she couldn't bear facing Ember, her Elite senior. She pressed her ear harder against the cool metal of the door, listening for sounds that suggested Ember was inside.

As soon as they began the training programme, all juniors were paired with an older Elite to be their mentor. Silver had moved into the bedroom she shared with Ember when she was thirteen years old. She was fifteen now. Two years of living with her Elite senior had taught Silver enough to know that if she found Ember waiting in their bedroom now, she'd end up feeling even worse than she did already.

Silver pulled away from the door. She hadn't heard a thing. Sending a quick prayer to the gods that Ember was elsewhere – and ignoring the thought of what her parents would say if they knew she'd asked the gods for help with such a trivial matter – she unlocked the door by touching her hand to the panel at its side. Then, carefully, she pushed it open.

The room was empty.

'Thank you, gods!' Silver smiled, stepping inside.

The room was just as she'd left it that morning. To the right, the shutters of her and Ember's bedpods were open, and at the far end of the room the blinds for the plastiglass outer wall were pulled up, letting in a wave of pale light from the setting sun.

Silver shut the door behind her and dropped to the floor. She lay spread-eagled on her back, grinning widely. It felt so good not to be on her feet. Training had been intense that afternoon; five hours of stamina, stealth and fighting sessions. She could already feel the bruises forming on her body where the blows of her trainer had landed. Now, lying on the floor in the warmth of the sunshine, she felt her muscles relaxing, her limbs softening. Fighting had never been Silver's strong point. She was quick and agile, which suited her to the covert assignments Elites were given by the Council, but even after years of training her combat skills were poor.

'I'm not moving *all* night,' she announced out loud to herself. 'I'll just have to miss the banquet. No one will care.' She snorted. 'And Ember will be thankful that she won't have to sit next to me, pretending to be nice –'

'Oh, is that right?'

Silver scrambled up so quickly she banged her forehead into the door.

'Careful now,' said the voice behind her. 'We don't want you injured for your big day tomorrow.'

'I'm fine,' muttered Silver, getting to her feet.

Ember was leaning in the bathroom doorway. She had changed out of her uniform and was wearing a silk kimono tied loosely at her waist, slipping off one shoulder to reveal a curve of white skin. Her flame-red hair was wet and dark from the shower. Even without make-up she was beautiful, and Silver felt the familiar pang of jealousy as she took in Ember's womanly figure, her large green eyes bright and sharp as jade stones.

'It doesn't look like you're fine.' Ember crossed her arms, the corners of her lips curled in a sneer. 'After that pathetic performance at training today, I'm amazed Senior Surrey didn't remove you from the Elite programme right away.'

Silver ignored this. She went to move towards her bedpod.

Ember stepped in her way. 'But then,' she said, leaning her face down to Silver's, 'maybe he's finally realised how irrelevant you are to the Council.' The orange blossom fragrance of her perfume was sickly sweet, clogging in Silver's throat.

'Look, Ember –'

'Perhaps he's working out who to replace you with tomorrow.'

Swallowing down an angry retort, Silver tried to push past her, but Ember grabbed her shoulders, leaning her face so close to Silver's their noses almost touched.

'You know,' Ember whispered coldly, 'I always ask him

3

how it came to be that a *Red* would have the exceptional DNA needed to be streamed into the Elite programme –'

'Don't *call* me that!'

It came out louder than Silver had expected. For a few breathless seconds they stared at each other. Ember's wide eyes were unreadable. Then, slowly, her mouth tightening, Ember straightened.

'I will call you a Red, Silver,' she said, 'because that is what you are.'

Silver hung her head, her cheeks burning. She didn't look back up until she had heard Ember move away, slamming the bedroom door as she left.

Every year, a banquet was held the night before the parade. It took place in the Ebora Building, the main offices of the Council and home to the Elites. It was nicknamed the Stacks due to its hollow centre criss-crossed with walkways and jutting prayer gantries. The preparations for the banquet had been underway all day. Enticing aromas wafted up from the east-wing kitchens as the city's best chefs created an elaborate menu featuring dishes from every kind of cultural cuisine, while geisha maids in pretty kimonos ritualised the banquet space.

By the time Silver arrived, the hall was filled with the buzz of voices. Hundreds of Council members milled around, sipping sake and commenting on the performance of the musicians playing on a stage at the far end of the hall. Some Council members had their heads bowed deep in conversation, perhaps discussing the parade

4

taking place the next day. Would the president stumble in his speech? Would there be a repeat of last year's minor disturbance? Protestors were common at these events. There were low sniggers as many imagined the punishments awaiting troublemakers.

Silver hovered near the doorway. She tugged at the neck of her cheongsam, a traditional dress of the Chinese cultures of the Red Nations. She hadn't meant to wear it, but after Ember's comment earlier about her nationality – Reds was the derogatory term for the Chinese ethnicities of the Red Nations – she'd put it on in a little act of defiance. Silver was now starting to feel like it was a bad idea. The bright red colour of the dress and the slit hem which exposed the olive skin of her thigh was drawing looks from some of the male Council members, and she regretted wearing her long black hair loose. It made her look older than her age.

A Council member nearby caught her eye, smiling. As he started towards her, Silver rushed off into the crowd. *Your fault for wearing a dress like this!* she thought angrily to herself. She was just turning to check whether the man had followed her when she walked straight into someone, her head thumping against their chest.

'I'm so sorry!' Silver gushed, stepping back, but she broke into a smile when she saw who it was. 'Butterfly!'

Though he looked smart in a fitted silk shirt and slim black trousers, Butterfly's messy brown hair still fell into his blue eyes as it always did, and he was holding himself a little stiffly, as if he was uncomfortable in his clothes too. He was tall for his sixteen years. Unlike

5

Silver, who was as slim as she'd always been, years of Elite training had defined the muscles in Butterfly's body. She caught a couple of pretty female Council members nearby watching him hopefully, their eyes trailing over his broad shoulders, his defined cheekbones and freshly shaved jaw.

Silver's grin widened.

Butterfly raised an eyebrow. 'What?'

'Nothing,' she said quickly, stifling a giggle. She gestured at his clothes. 'You just look nice, that's all.'

Butterfly smiled; only a second and then it was gone. Having been best friends with Butterfly since she'd joined the Elites training programme a year after him, Silver was used to that. He didn't smile very much, and when he did it was a fleeting thing, gone as soon as it had come. She remembered a time when Butterfly had smiled easily, but that was before the explosion.

'Have you seen any of the others?' Silver asked, changing the subject. She and Butterfly were close friends with some of the other Elites.

'Not yet.'

She glanced round the crowd to see whether she could spot any of their friends. 'I can't wait for this to be over,' she murmured. 'Three hours stuck with Ember isn't going to be fun.'

Butterfly nodded. 'And this shirt is so uncomfortable. It's really irritating my wings.'

Silver knew that if she reached a hand round his back, she'd feel two raised wing discs and the folds of his wings beneath his shirt. The Council had implanted the discs in Butterfly when he was a year into his Elites training to assess the practicalities of developing aerial surveillance. His wings were a secret kept within the Elites and their associated Council members, and Silver was one of the only people who had ever seen him in the air. Flying was still a contested subject after the Red Nations made the planes come down all those hundreds of years ago.

'It's a shame you still can't fly on assignments,' Silver said. 'Where are they stationing you tomorrow?'

'I'll be on the stage with Ember,' Butterfly replied. 'And you?'

'Hemmingway House rooftop. Right across from the stage.' She hesitated. 'I'm . . . I'm the only one that's going to be there.'

Surprise registered on Butterfly's face for a split second before he composed himself, flashing another quick smile. 'That's great! Senior Surrey must really be starting to trust you.'

Silver scrunched up her nose and looked away. 'I doubt it. We all know I'm the worst Elite. Gods know why he's given me such a big responsibility.' Ever since she'd found out about the assignment, she'd wondered whether it was a challenge from Senior Surrey and the Council to see whether she really had the skills and confidence to be an Elite. She swallowed nervously. She didn't like to think what would happen if she *didn't* prove herself to them tomorrow.

'Hey,' said Butterfly, touching her shoulder. 'Don't doubt yourself. He's given you the responsibility for a

7

reason. And just think – after tomorrow, you won't ever have to take Ember's abuse again. She might even be *proud* of you.'

Silver let out a bark of laughter. She was about to say exactly what she thought about *that* when a gong sounded.

The clamour of the hall hushed immediately. On the stage, the musicians put down their instruments as a man in a brilliant blue tunic and slim metallic trousers stepped out in front of them. A man Silver had only ever seen from afar at events such as this; the city's president, Tanaka.

Tanaka gave a deep bow. He was a kindly faced Japanean man, with greying hair and small, almond-shaped eyes similar to Silver's own. Though there was nothing particularly striking about his appearance, there was something about him that gave the impression of a calm assuredness, and despite his slender frame and average height, he commanded attention.

'Council members!' Tanaka beamed. 'I am delighted to be President of Neo-Babel for yet another year, and to celebrate our Council's leadership with you all one more time. But tonight is not the time for speeches. You will all have to sit through one tomorrow, and I don't want you to fall asleep before having the chance to sample the fine food our chefs have prepared for us tonight!' There were twitters among the crowd. 'Now,' he continued, gesturing at the tables spaced round the hall. 'Let us take our places, and enjoy the finest food and company Neo-Babel has to offer!'

'Good luck,' said Butterfly, brushing Silver's arm as the room burst once again into noise and activity.

'For what?' She gave him a grim smile. 'The parade tomorrow or three hours with Ember tonight? I'm not really sure which I'm dreading more.'

He didn't return her smile. 'Don't worry about it,' he said, turning to leave. 'You'll be great tomorrow. Tanaka's in safe hands with you.'

It didn't take Silver long to find her seat in the busy hall; Ember's shock of fiery red hair was easy to spot. As she sat down, Ember's eyes travelled slowly over her, taking in her loose hair and cheongsam.

'Well, don't you look nice,' Ember said acidly before turning back to the Council member on her other side.

Ember stayed in that position for the entirety of the banquet, for which Silver was thankful. With no one else to talk to, she was left alone with her thoughts. Her mind wandered to the gift she'd bought for her father's birthday in a few weeks' time, an antique musical instrument from before the Great Fall. It had cost her the best part of her yearly salary, but with little else to spend the money on, she hadn't minded. Silver was close to her parents, spending much of her free time outside of her Elites schedule with them. She smiled, imagining how delighted her father would be with her gift. Hopefully, he'd not try and play it though; she doubted the strange string instrument sounded much better than the ear-splitting Chinese opera her mother and father were so fond of.

But as nerves at the next day's assignment settled in,

Silver could soon think of nothing else, and she picked listlessly at course after course, drinking far too much sake than she ought to to ease her anxieties. *Less than twenty-four hours to go*, she kept thinking. *Just one more sleep, and then I'll be up on that roof, responsible for keeping Tanaka and the others safe from danger.* She was so caught up in going over every little detail from her training sessions and briefings that the banquet passed in a whirl. Before she knew it, it was past midnight and she was standing to leave.

Ember grabbed her arm. 'Not so fast,' she hissed. 'No late-night trip to boyfriend Butterfly tonight, I'm afraid.'

Silver felt her cheeks redden. 'He's *not* my –'

'I don't care. You need all the rest you can get if you're not to screw everything up tomorrow.'

Ember steered her roughly across the banquet hall towards the line of senior Council members waiting by the door. Having grown up in the Stacks, Silver was used to the customs of the Council, whose members were mainly Japanean like Tanaka, or of Mainland ethnicities, as Butterfly and Ember were. At the door, she bowed deeply to each member in turn. Just as she turned to leave, the person at the end of the line spoke.

'Silver. A word, if I may?'

She spun round to see Tanaka smiling at her. Immediately, her throat went dry.

He pulled her gently aside so they were out of earshot of the Council members still milling around. 'You are one of our junior Elites, am I correct?' he asked.

Tanaka's kindly expression did nothing to settle Silver's surprise at finding herself talking to Neo-Babel's president. 'Y-yes, sir.' She nodded. 'My senior is Ember, sir.'

He smiled. 'Ah, yes. Ember is one of Senior Surrey's favourites. Well, I just wanted to tell you personally how pleased I am at having you on assignment tomorrow. I understand it is your first time working the parade?'

'Yes, sir.'

'Enough with the sir!' he laughed. 'Tanaka, please. Now, I must see our other guests out, but let me say once again how much I appreciate the hard work you – and all the Elites – put in to protecting and serving the Council. Your input is vital to making our city the success it continues to be. I hope you remember that, Silver, as I give my speech tomorrow.'

'I will, sir,' she said, bowing as Tanaka left.

Later that night, lying awake in her bedpod, still warm with a glow from Tanaka's words, Silver made a promise to herself that tomorrow she would be the best Elite out there, smiling at the thought of how pleased Tanaka would be, and the look on Ember's face as he told her how well Silver had performed.

2

Silver's Mistake

The parade began at midday at a dock on the Outer Circle of the river. Since dawn, a flotilla of boats had gathered. Large commuter ferries sat patiently on the water, while floating shisha cafes – engulfed by clouds of sweetly smelling smoke – and delicate little plastiwood dhows jostled against their sides. River vendors squeezed their boats through the busy waterway, shouting out their wares.

'*Teh*, sweetened with honey!'

'Beer-soaked sausages, made with top-quality grade-three meat!'

'Mango rice and coconut sauce, hot or cold!'

The streets along the dock were just as packed as the river. People from the nearby Limpets and residential condominiums haggled with merchants offering shishas and handmade trinkets out of grubby metal cases strapped to the sides of their bikes. Groups of men, already tipsy from drink, stumbled through the crowds. Their crude language drew faceless stares from the masked police patrolling the thoroughfares in silence. At the street edges, children ducked the railings to sit with their feet dangling over the water, daring each other to jump across to nearby boat decks.

For now, the atmosphere in the city was one of celebration, moods buoyed by the free food being handed out from the Council tugboats. Intoxicating cooking smells wafted across the streets, tempting the people who watched the proceedings from tiny balconies studding the walls of nearby condominiums. Music drifted out of open doors and windows; the city anthem, old pop songs from before the Great Fall. From some rooms came chanting as their residents recited morning prayers.

At one o'clock, the gongs rang. Slowly, stretching out like a lazy caterpillar, the procession went on its way. It moved through the city waterways until reaching the Council District four hours later. There, on a stage in Pantheon Square, stepped out the Council officials, resplendent in their grey tunics and silver robes which fluttered behind them in the growing wind.

And up in a building at the corner of the square's southern edge, above a sea of heads bobbing to hear the president's speech, a hunched figure edged out onto a balcony and raised its gun.

Silver was dreaming of swimming; a clear sea, open and vast. Sunlight slanted into the water, dappling the blue with trembling puddles of light. Her long black hair fanned like seaweed from her head. She smiled in her sleep, enjoying the coolness of the water, the openness of the ocean.

Then the water began to churn. Huge currents came out of nowhere. They slammed into her, rolling her body to and fro. She twisted against them, trying to get out of their grip, and in her sleep she punched her arm straight into her bedpod shutters.

Silver snapped awake with a cry. She lay still, cradling her throbbing hand and staring at the metal that encased her bedpod. The sea's roaring from her dream lingered, and as her brain began to wake, she realised it was not just an echo from her dream but that there was actually a muffled rumble coming from somewhere nearby.

She slid open the shutters and stepped out of her bedpod. Sunshine poured into the bedroom from the plastiglass outer wall, casting a slice of shadow across the empty bedpod beside her own, the shutter half open. *Strange*, Silver thought as she ducked into the bathroom to make sure Ember wasn't in there; she hadn't forgotten her lesson yesterday. *I'm sure I was meant to go with Ember for training today.*

She wandered over to the glass wall, yawning and stretching her arms above her head. Her eyes were adjusting to the light, and she could now see clearly the broad avenue of Noda Parkway stretched out below. An elegant strip of trees ran down its centre, city flags billowing from light posts. As one of the main streets in the Council District, Noda Parkway was usually fairly busy, but today it was packed with people, a sea of rippling heads bobbing by.

For a moment, Silver couldn't understand why there were so many people. Then, with a sickening jolt, she remembered –

The parade.

'Oh gods!' she groaned. 'Oh gods! Oh no, no, no, *no*!'

Still cursing, Silver stumbled into the bathroom, where she undressed, popped a mouthwash tablet between her teeth, and splashed her face with water. Back in the bedroom, she pulled on her Elite uniform – black jumpsuit, flexivinyl boots and gloves, her comms cuffs, her stungun – before hurtling out of the room, down the corridor and onto the floor's landing platform at the hollow centre of the Stacks.

No one was around. Silver took a plastiglass lift down to the atrium, tying her hair into a ponytail. The pathways and prayer gantries lining the centre of the Stacks like a vertical maze were empty. She checked her comms cuff and groaned again; it was seven minutes past five. Tanaka's speech was due to begin in just twenty-three minutes, which meant she should have been at Hemmingway House over an hour ago.

Silver squeezed her hands into fists. How could she have let herself be so late on the biggest assignment she had ever been given? *Especially* after what Tanaka had said to her last night. It must have been all the sake she'd drunk at the banquet.

Thanks for waking me, Ember, she thought sarcastically, scowling. *I can always count on you.*

By the time the gongs were sounding, signalling the start of Tanaka's speech, Silver had made it to Hemmingway House. It was a squat, ten-storey building on the southern edge of Pantheon Square, built with the same granite-blend material as most of the buildings in the Council

15

District. Its polished surface shone in the sun. Two masked policemen stood outside the building, and Silver threw them an apologetic look, touching her hand to the panel beside the door.

Just as she slipped inside, she heard one of the policemen grumble under his breath, 'Stupid Red. They can't do anything right.'

A statement like this would have usually hurt her, but today she was in such a rush she barely noticed. Besides, she'd not forgotten the promise she'd made last night. She was determined to be the best Elite at the parade today for Tanaka, Red or not.

Silver took an elevator to the roof. As soon as the doors opened, wind hit her. It buffeted her small frame as she ran bent over to the northern edge, her ponytail flapping wildly about her face, her eyes watering. She reached the parapet lining the edge of the roof and knelt down, taking her lookout position, just as Tanaka began to speak.

'Welcome, dear citizens, to our annual parade. A celebration of our fine city, Neo-Babel!'

The square erupted into cheers. Silver grinned, feeling a flush of excitement at the energy of the crowd. Down below, Pantheon Square was packed. Pockets of colour from city flags flecked the crowd, and there were vendors selling balloons with the faces of popular Council officials on them. Tanaka's was there, and even Senior Surrey's, who was the Council's Head of Security, as well as being in charge of the Elites.

The real Council members were on the stage at the

opposite end of the square, guarded by a row of masked police. Tanaka stood at the front. His hair was hidden beneath the official broken-winged cap all the Council members were wearing. As he looked round at the crowd, his silver robe fluttered in the breeze.

'Once, our great city was just the seed of an idea,' Tanaka began, his voice magnified by the small microphone strapped to the collar of his tunic. 'A seed born from the riots that spread through the three great continents – the Mainland, Afrika and the Red Nations. A seed that was planted in the late twenty-fifth century, when what was left of the Global Council agreed upon the build of a city in the deserted lands of the former Eastern Europe. They dreamt of a place where civilisation could continue and flourish, where the disastrous effects of the sea-level rises, economic collapse and cultural dilution could be forgotten. A fresh start made.' He raised his arms, his voice growing louder. 'A city where history could be outrun, and in time, overcome. A city of hope, of sustainability, of unity. A city, dear citizens, named Neo-Babel!'

The cheers of the crowds drowned Tanaka's voice. The atmosphere of Pantheon Square was electric, as though their leader's words were charged with some fantastic energy that danced in the air, slipping into people's veins. Even alone on the rooftop, Silver was getting caught up in the speech, forgetting her job as lookout.

'Yes,' Tanaka said, dropping his arms. 'Neo-Babel was born. But then came the Great Fall.'

The crowd hushed, listening eagerly.

'We were a young city, not yet equipped to survive alone, and the wars were savage. We saw the deaths on our tablet screens – whole cities and countries obliterated under the touch of nuclear weapons. We watched as the oil ran out and the planes came down. We hoped that would mark the end of it, but we all saw with horrified eyes as countries continued to fight without their aerial armies, using bioweapons and foot soldiers instead.'

Tanaka paused, and the crowd was so quiet in its eagerness to hear their president's words that Silver thought she heard a click from somewhere nearby. She turned. The rooftop was empty.

'But though the Great Fall destroyed the rest of the world,' continued Tanaka, his hands in fists at his sides, 'it only made Neo-Babel stronger! We lived up to our motto – *A Place for Everyone* – and not only the Council but every single citizen worked hard to ensure that our city remained fair and just. To this very day, we strive to maintain our legacy as a city of hope, of sustainability, of unity. The legacy our Global Council fathers envisioned for us.' His voice grew suddenly low, dangerous. 'Yet despite this, there are those that challenge our system. There are those that fight *against* us, disrupting the routine that has kept us alive and well, that has supported us all these years. And it is my duty as our city's leader to tell those individuals that *this* is the year they are stopped.'

There was a tense silence now at the turn Tanaka's speech had taken, but Silver wasn't listening any more.

18

She was sure of what she'd heard a minute before; it *had* been a metallic click. Quietly, lightly, she crouched and skirted the perimeter of the rooftop. Nothing. She went back to her original position, paused for a second, thinking, then leant forward over the parapet, gripping the edge tightly, and saw –

A man knelt on the balcony below, clutching a gun aimed straight at the stage.

Silver swung back behind the parapet, stifling a gasp. *Oh gods, oh gods!* she thought desperately. *An assassin, here in my lookout zone, and I was late, and I didn't find him, and now he's got a gun pointed at Tanaka!*

She shook her head, pushing her thoughts away. It was no time to panic. She thought about calling Ember on her comms cuff, but the man was just twelve feet away with a gun in his hand. Any second now he could shoot. There was no time. And, though she didn't want to admit it, there was the thought of how catching the assassin alone would prove to everyone – to Ember, to Senior Surrey, even to Tanaka – that she was every bit an Elite as the others.

I can do this, thought Silver, nodding to herself. She took out her stungun. A deep, slow breath. Then –

She flipped herself over the parapet. Her legs jarred as she landed on the balcony below. The man swung round at the noise. His arm arced towards her with the gun, but he didn't shoot, and she charged at him, firing her stungun.

He danced out of its range. In the second it took for the stungun to recharge, the man lunged – his face a blur of stubble and bright brown eyes – and wrestled the stungun out of her hand, pushing her to the floor. She jumped up, ready to fight with her fists, but the man was stepping back from her, holding out his hands.

'Silver!' he said, in a low, urgent voice. 'Please understand. I have to do this!'

But she didn't understand. How did he know her name?

For the first time since Silver had landed on the balcony, she had time to take in his appearance. The man was a Red, like her. He had a weather-beaten face, skin darkened by the sun and etched with lines and scars. There was a shadow of stubble on the lower half of his face, and more shadows under his small eyes, as though he hadn't slept in days. He wore simple, factory-worker clothes; khaki-coloured shirt, trousers and boots. He looked just like any other worker in the Industrial District, but there was something about his eyes that drew her attention. She saw flecks of gold in them and felt a strange stirring of memories.

'I have to do this,' the man repeated, stepping towards her. His eyes were wide, pleading. Silver could smell shisha smoke on his clothes, and, beneath it, a scent she almost recognised. A scent that somehow seemed *familiar*. They looked at each other for a moment and she could feel the man's name on the edge of her tongue, curling and solidifying into –

Then he darted forward and pushed her down and crouched back in position at the balcony ledge, raising his gun. Silver jumped up, running to him just as he pulled the trigger.

The sound shocked her into stillness. She jerked to a halt at the edge of the balcony, but she could still see what had happened, what *was* happening, and a single thought: *No*.

It was as though the bullet froze the second it hit Tanaka's forehead. There was no explosion, no spilling of brains. Even his eyes stayed open, gazing blankly in front of him at the horrified crowd. As Silver watched, too stunned to move, the ghostly half-smile on his face seemed to twist into a snarl. Then his head disappeared in a cloud of red. The smell of wet metal hit her like a wall, and the screaming began.

3

The Head of the Elites

That evening, the streets were silent. Still. Across the city, celebrations had been planned for after the parade; paper lantern-lighting parties, late-opening hours for bars, dances and meals and floating arcades. But they had all been abandoned. Instead, people huddled in their homes, watching the footage of Tanaka's assassination on their tablets, his head disappearing into a cloud of red again and again.

Silver was in her bedpod in the Stacks. After Tanaka's shooting, all Elites and Council members had been called back to the Stacks. Police had checked everyone upon entering. Senior Surrey's assistant Miss Apell had recorded a short statement from each of them. Silver recounted the day's events as though she'd never left the roof. Then she and the rest of the Elites and police had been sent to search the city.

They covered every street, every house, every inch of Neo-Babel to find the assassin. The colourful decorations from the parade had not yet been taken down, and still painted the city a rainbow. But they seemed garish suddenly, and hollow, and as Silver moved through Neo-Babel the colours stung her eyes.

No one had found anything. Not a trace of the assassin, no trail to follow, no witnesses to his flight. It seemed as if he had vanished, just melted away into the air like a coil of shisha smoke. Now, the Council's forensics team were modelling the bullet's trajectory. *And,* Silver thought, *when they trace the assassin's position to Hemmingway House . . .*

She closed her eyes, trying to squeeze away the image of Tanaka's shooting. Yet no matter how hard she stared, the image of his head disappearing flashed in her mind like a light being flicked on and off; head, no head, head, no head. Silver couldn't quite grasp it. It didn't feel real.

But Tanaka's head *had* disappeared, he *had* died, and that was all on her.

After the search, the Elites had been ordered to their rooms to await further instructions. Ember had not returned to their bedroom, but that was typical of her, ignoring orders. Strangely, Senior Surrey seemed not to care when it was Ember who disregarded his instructions.

Silver was glad to have the room to herself. She had some time now to figure out what to say to Senior Surrey, to decide how to lie. Because of course she couldn't be honest about what had happened up on Hemmingway House. How could she, when she had been right next to the assassin and it was only his strange, familiar smell and some funny look in his eyes that had prevented her from stopping him? When after he'd shot Tanaka, she'd let the assassin escape back into the building, too shocked and stunned to follow him?

Silver couldn't believe she'd been so careless. All her training had led to this. Elites knew their first time working the parade was a challenge from the Council to prove their competence. To show that they could live up to their DNA, which had streamed them at birth into the Elite training programme due to superior levels in their genes of intelligence, adeptness, healthiness, loyalty, and other such characteristics. Butterfly had been assigned his first job at the parade when he was fourteen. Ember at thirteen. Because of her poor fighting skills, Senior Surrey hadn't trusted Silver until this year when she was fifteen, and now she'd failed him. Worse –

She had failed Tanaka.

Over the next hour, Silver watched the night drain from the bedroom, the slow brightening as the room was pulled out of shadows and into soft morning sunlight. At some point, she must have dozed off, for the next thing she knew she was jerking upright as a loud beeping filled the room. She tossed aside her blanket and rushed to the comms panel beside the door, touching it to answer the call.

'Silver,' came Miss Apell's crisp voice. 'Please report to Senior Surrey's office immediately.'

This is it, Silver thought, swallowing anxiously. She took one last look around the room, as if the answers to what she should say to Senior Surrey would somehow pop out at her. But they didn't, so she just smoothed down her clothes and hair – her hands shaking – before nodding to herself and heading out of the door.

*   *   *

The Head of the Elites' office was in the east wing of the Stacks. It was a large room, furnished to the highest standards, with an ornately carved maple-wood desk and leather chaise longue. In one corner stood a small acer, its slender trunk disappearing into the floor. Sunlight streamed into the room from tall glass doors set into the furthest wall.

Senior Surrey stood up from behind the desk as Silver entered, gesturing to the chair opposite him. 'Please, sit.'

She took the seat he was indicating, watching him carefully. He was a handsome man, youthful for his forty-two years, with white-streaked black hair and a broad chest. Once, he'd been the best Elite the Council had, and she could sense that strength and sharpness in the way he carried himself.

'I'm going to be frank with you, Silver,' Senior Surrey said, leaning forward in his chair and wrapping his hands round a cup of *teh*. 'It's been a long night, and an awful thing has happened. You're the last Elite I'm talking to. Let's make this quick and easy, shall we?'

'Yes, sir,' she said, hoping that would be true. She could feel her nerves like a hand squeezing her gut, and she struggled to try and appear calm.

Over the next fifteen minutes they discussed everything that happened the day of the parade. Silver oversleeping and being late for her assignment; she knew there was no point lying about that as the policemen outside had seen her, and luckily Senior Surrey didn't seem too angry about it. Her journey to Pantheon Square, Tanaka's speech. In fact, Senior Surrey was being *so* easy on her that Silver almost wanted to tell him the truth about what happened. She imagined him coming round the table as she dissolved into tears. He'd hold her in his large, fatherly arms and say, 'There, there. You did as much as you could. You did your best.'

Just as her own father would.

But Silver wasn't that naive. Despite his calm, pleasant manner, she knew how tough Senior Surrey could be, and the serious repercussions on her life as an Elite something like this would have. So she kept lying. It was all going well until Senior Surrey asked whether she'd heard any unusual noises on the rooftop.

Silver had let herself relax so that, without thinking, she said, 'Yes, sir. A sort of clicking sound.'

The truth was out of her mouth before she could stop it. Her heart began to race as she realised what just she'd said, but she forced herself to look calm as Senior Surrey leant back in his chair, looking at her carefully with those dark, granite-flecked eyes.

'A clicking sound?'

Silver nodded. 'About halfway through Tanaka's speech, somewhere to my left.'

'I see. And then?'

'I . . . I went over to have a look.'

'And what did you find?'

'Er . . . nothing,' she answered weakly. She fiddled with the underside of the desk. 'There wasn't anything. It was probably just the wind knocking something over or –'

'Which side of the building was this?' Senior Surrey interrupted.

Silver thought quickly, tracking back through her lies to find the answer. 'The west side.'

'What happened next?'

'Well, I . . . I was looking around when I heard the . . .' Images flashed in her mind; head, no head, head. She swallowed. 'When it happened.'

'Tanaka's assassination?'

No head.

'Yes,' she said quietly.

Senior Surrey pressed the tips of his fingers together. 'I see.' He said the words slowly, drawing them out like he really didn't see at all.

Silver held her breath. She tried to prepare herself for what was about to happen; Senior Surrey pulling apart her lies, pushing her until the truth came out. But the next words he spoke were so completely the opposite of what she had been expecting that she didn't hear them properly at first.

'That is all,' Senior Surrey repeated.

Silver blinked. 'That's all?'

'You must be tired, and after everything that has happened I'm sure you need time to grieve and pray for President Tanaka. There will be no assignments or training tomorrow. Work will continue as normal on Thursday.' He gestured at the door. 'You may go.'

Silver almost jumped out of her seat in her haste to leave. Once in the corridor, she stopped to lean against the wall, breathing slowly to calm her heart. She couldn't believe what had happened. She'd been prepared for an intense interrogation, and yet Senior Surrey seemed to have accepted her story with barely any question at all.

She started heading back to her bedroom. Flushed and happy with relief, she didn't notice someone move out behind her as she passed a shadowy corridor.

A hand clamped across her mouth, stifling her scream, and an arm locked round her neck, dragging Silver from the corridor through a nearby door and slamming it shut.

4

Confrontations and Confessions

Silver's captor twisted her round, keeping a hand tight against her mouth, and slammed her up against the wall at the back of the room. The coldness of the concrete shot up her spine. Her body stiffened with the shock of it, the shock of Ember suddenly here right in her face, a hand clamped over her mouth, the crazed look in Ember's eyes.

Even in the dim light, Silver knew her captor was Ember. The sweet orange blossom fragrance of her perfume danced in the air as she moved, her red hair bouncing around her face like an excited flame.

'I've been waiting for you,' Ember hissed. 'Wanted to have a little interrogation of my own.'

Silver struggled against Ember's grip. She could see they were in some kind of storage room, and the door out to the corridor wasn't too far away. But it was impossible to move. Ember had an arm pushed hard across her chest and a hand squeezed so tightly over her mouth, Silver could feel Ember's long, tapered fingernails pinching her cheeks.

'Don't bother,' Ember snarled. 'You know that won't work. You're my junior after all. Just a baby. What can you do against me? Now listen carefully.'

Silver ignored her. She wriggled one arm free to scrabble at the wall behind her, but there was nothing she could use to defend herself. She squirmed, reaching out for the shelf to her right.

Ember sprang back and whipped her hand across Silver's cheek, slapping her so hard that she barely had time to realise she was free before Ember was pressed back up against her.

'What did I tell you? Now shut up and listen.'

Ember dipped her head to the pocket in her shirt. When her face lifted, there was a small, slim blade gripped between her teeth. A man's shaving razor, by the looks of it. Ember let go of Silver's mouth to take the blade in her hand, and Silver knew better than to try and scream for help. The next second, the cold point of the blade was pressed to her neck.

'Oh gods,' she murmured.

'What are your gods going to do?' Ember laughed, her bright green eyes flashing. 'They're a useless bunch – I don't know why you Reds bother. Kitchen god going to come at me with some spaghetti? Monkey god getting ready to swing down from the heavens and shove a banana in my face?'

Silver didn't say anything. She stared at Ember with silent hatred.

'There you go,' Ember smiled nastily. 'Isn't it easier to just do as I say rather than to try and think for yourself? We all know Reds don't have much brainpower.'

Silver couldn't help it; she felt the blush spread across her cheeks. The same thing she felt every time that word

30

was directed at her. But this time, alongside the shame rose a hot, hard feeling –

Anger.

'Must be why they assigned me as your junior,' Silver snarled. 'A Red was all *you* could handle.'

She got another slap for that. This time the blade in Ember's hand nicked her skin, drawing a line of blood along her right cheekbone.

'I'm warning you,' Ember growled. 'Now, tell me what happened at the parade. What *actually* happened, not whatever lies you fed Surrey. Or I'll paint your other cheek red too.'

'I told Senior Surrey the truth,' Silver answered, trying to keep her voice steady. 'During Tanaka's speech, I went to investigate a sound on the west side of the roof. There wasn't anything there, but it meant I missed what actually happened when the shot –'

'Liar,' hissed Ember. 'You forget I was on the stage. I saw everything.'

Silver pushed on with her fake bravado. 'Then why are you asking if you already know?'

'All right,' Ember said, her eyes narrowing. 'I'll tell you what happened. After the shot, I looked up to see *you* on a balcony on the north side of the building. The side facing the stage. Care to tell me what you were doing there?'

Silver did not.

'What I believe happened,' continued Ember, 'is that either you personally delivered the shot to Tanaka, or you aided the person that *did* to get into the building and onto that balcony.'

This was so far from the truth that Silver couldn't help but laugh. 'That's crazy! Why would I –'

Ember pressed the blade harder against Silver's neck. 'Why indeed? That's what I asked myself. But I think the answer is clear.'

Silver stared at her. 'I suppose you believe I'm working for an anti-birthchip group? That I actually harbour a secret hatred for the Council and am helping bring them down?' She spoke almost jokingly, half rolling her eyes, but to her shock Ember let out a growl of anger.

'I knew it!'

Silver's mouth dropped. 'I was joking, Ember! I'm an Elite! I've been working for the Council my whole life.'

But Ember didn't seem to be listening. 'You're probably not even an Elite by nature,' she murmured, speaking as though to herself. 'An anti-birthchip group must have gene-hacked your DNA to get you streamed as one to act as an inside informant for them.'

Silver couldn't believe what she was hearing. She had spent the entirety of her life as an Elite fighting *against* anti-birthchip groups. She understood their cause; they wanted to do away with the compulsory DNA streaming that dictated the jobs every Neo-Babel citizen had, as well as the birthchips the Council implanted in the back of everyone's necks at birth, which tracked movements. If a person was arrested for a crime, their birthchip records could be used as evidence in their case. But although she could sympathise with their arguments, that didn't mean she supported the anti-birthchip groups. In fact, her experiences as an Elite had shown her that birthchips were vital to maintain the efficiency and safety of their city, and the laws surrounding their use kept the system fair.

'You've known me since I was a baby,' Silver said. 'You're with me half the time! When would I get the chance to meet with an anti-birthchip group?'

Ember ignored her. 'I'm going to prove it. I can get those records, you know – your birthchip records. The Council will make an exception. They'll release them for me, and when they find out you were there on that balcony . . .'

Silver felt a surge of panic. If Ember did manage to get the Council to release her birthchip records, she would be placed right at the scene of Tanaka's shooting. Nothing could then stop a full-blown enquiry into her as a suspect of assassination. She groped frantically for something to say that wouldn't implicate her further, some way of making it seem like this was all some big misunderstanding.

'They wouldn't do that,' she said eventually. 'The Council won't look up my birthchip records without an arrest warrant. They *wouldn't*.'

Ember let go of Silver, backing away towards the door. 'You think you're untouchable?' she laughed. 'You think that because you've got the other Elites wrapped round your little finger and have somehow made Surrey believe your lies that the truth won't come out?' As she opened the door, she added coldly, 'You might be an Elite, Silver, but remember that in the end you're nothing more than a dirty Red.'

*   *   *

The Stacks were busy as Silver rushed to Butterfly's room, but she barely noticed, weaving her way past Council members through narrow walkways and corridors, her mind unable to escape the events in the storage room. She could still feel the pressure of Ember's arm against her chest, the feel of the cold blade on her skin. Silver forced back the tears that were threatening to fall. She told herself she was stronger than that. When she reached Butterfly and his senior Cobe's bedroom, she let herself in quietly through the unlocked door and slipped into her friend's bedpod, where he was sleeping.

'Butterfly?' She crouched beside him in the dark curve of the bedpod.

'Huh?' Butterfly murmured. His eyes were glassy in the dim light. He went to sit up but she pushed him back down gently.

'I'm sorry I woke you,' she whispered. 'Go back to sleep.'

Silver lay down beside Butterfly, their bodies inches away from each other in the small space. She tried to stop the tears that were filling her eyes, focusing on the comforting, soft smell of sleep that filled the bedpod and the familiar warmth of Butterfly lying near her. But she couldn't help it. It was as though everything that'd happened over the past two days suddenly hit her at once, and her whole body shook with the awfulness of it all.

Butterfly seemed to have realised she was crying. He sat up, pulling Silver with him. His fingers brushed the smudged line of blood across one cheek. 'You're hurt,' he said. 'Did someone do this to you?'

'It's nothing,' she mumbled.

'No, it's not.'

Silver saw the concern in his eyes, and she realised she couldn't lie to him. She'd not lied to Butterfly once in all the years they'd been best friends. Even though speaking the truth out loud would make it feel more real, would make it impossible to escape, she had to tell him. Wiping her face with the back of her hand, she began to explain what had happened at the parade, then Senior Surrey's interrogation. Ember's own private interrogation after.

'She's gone too far this time,' Butterfly growled when Silver had finished. He touched the scar on her cheek again. 'Does it hurt?'

She shook her head. 'No, it's fine. There are more important things, and they're not like a cut. They can't . . .' Her voice broke. 'They can't be fixed.'

'Don't say that.' Butterfly dropped his head and ran a hand through his hair, his frown deepening. 'There's got to be something we can do. Are you *sure* you know the assassin from somewhere?'

'I'm sure. I just can't remember where.'

'Maybe if you can remember, we can tell the Council about him,' he suggested. 'Then they'd overlook the fact that you didn't get him on the day.'

Silver raised an eyebrow, smiling ruefully. 'You really believe they won't be angry that I let Tanaka get shot, *and* lied to Senior Surrey about it? Butterfly – saying they won't be happy about any of that is an understatement.'

35

He fell silent for a while. 'You're right. We can't let them know you were there.' He hesitated, then added gently, 'And we can't let any of the others know.'

'I know,' she murmured. Silver felt her stomach tighten at the thought of keeping this a secret from their friends. Even though she was closest to Butterfly, she cared deeply for their Elite friends, and it felt wrong keeping this from them. She shook her head. 'But what if despite all of this, the Council *do* manage to find out? They might work out where the bullet came from. Then they'll want to question me further, and if Ember tells Senior Surrey about her suspicions and what she saw, and they look up my birthchip records . . .' The tears came again then, hot and fast, blurring everything away until Silver couldn't see anything clearly, and she wished for a moment she could live the rest of her life like that, always looking at the world through a mask, never having to face up to what she had done.

Butterfly wrapped his arms round her gently. 'Don't worry,' he said. 'We'll work out what to do. Everything will turn out fine.'

Silver didn't reply. She'd lied enough that day herself to recognise the lies in his words.

5

The Wink

The next few weeks were a whirlwind of training sessions, lessons and restless nights as Silver lay awake in her bedpod, expecting Ember to come at her again with a blade between her teeth and a crazy glint in her eye. Yet Ember seemed to be avoiding Silver now, just as much as Silver was avoiding her. And as the days went on without any sign that Ember had acted on her words from their confrontation in the storage room, Silver started to feel hopeful that Butterfly had actually been right – everything *was* going to be fine – and relaxed back into her everyday life as an Elite.

But there was still one aspect of her life that was yet to return to normal. Since the parade, Silver hadn't been given any assignments. She started to worry it was because Senior Surrey knew the truth about her. She began to whisper to herself, in the middle of the night when it was so quiet even the gods must be sleeping, or during training as she looked around at the other Elites surrounding her: *I'm useless. I'm a useless Red.*

Barely any other Reds worked in the Stacks, and certainly no other Elites were Reds. With DNA streaming deciding everyone's place in society, this was to be expected. They had all been taught since young how Red blood had been proven by scientists to be naturally inferior, so it was remarkable that Silver had been streamed into the Elite training programme; a fact Ember took constant job in reminding her. Yet there was another side to this that Silver held onto, keeping it safe and solid inside her like a secret made real, a stone of truth she could turn over and over in her mind. That to be an Elite meant *her* blood – her tainted, dirty *Red* blood – was still superior to most people's in the city. Even Ember couldn't take that away from her.

Three weeks passed without Silver receiving any assignments. Just when she'd started to convince herself that it was because Senior Surrey was planning on dropping her off the Elite training programme, and she was getting ready one morning for a trip Butterfly had planned to cheer her up, her comms cuff started beeping. Her heart leapt. That particular low beep was only used to notify Elites of an assignment. Tugging a shirt over her head, she grabbed her comms cuff from where she had thrown it to the floor before her morning shower and touched its screen.

'Hello?'

'Good morning, Silver,' said Miss Apell. 'Please check your tablet. Senior Surrey has an assignment for you this morning.'

'Yes, miss,' answered Silver breathlessly, unable to contain the delight from her voice.

Feeling a flush of excitement, she picked up her tablet

to check the details Miss Apell had just sent her. The assignment was to oversee an information exchange at the Spotted Elephant, a chai bar in Little New India. It would take just over an hour. Butterfly wouldn't mind her being slightly late for their trip. She could just imagine how happy he'd be for her and she couldn't wait to tell him and their friends the good news.

As the assignment didn't require her to wear her uniform, Silver dressed in a floaty green shirt that was more like a dress on her slender frame, with thin leggings underneath to keep cool in the heat. She pulled on her flexi-vinyl boots, just in case there was any trouble and she needed to be quick on her feet. She slipped her stungun into the belt around her waist, its shape hidden under the loose shirt, before heading down to the galley.

The galley was one of the eating areas in the Stacks for Council members. As usual, it was busy, full of noise, delicious aromas and the heat from the cookers. Sunlight poured in through the long slatted windows that striped the ceiling, filling the large hall with light. Food stalls serving a variety of dishes and cuisines lined the walls. In the centre of the hall were dozens of benches for seating.

Making her way down the steps into the hall, Silver spotted Butterfly and their Elite friends at the bench where they always sat. She picked up a plate of food from a stall on her way over to them and sat at the end of the bench next to Butterfly.

'Are you all right?' he asked, dipping his head towards her so his hair fell into his eyes.

She smiled. 'Yes,' she answered, and for the first time in weeks it didn't feel like a lie.

Just then, a deep voice with a strong Afrikan lilt boomed down the bench. 'Baby Silver! Always under Butterfly's wing, hey?'

Silver looked up to see Allum laughing. She grinned back; it was impossible not to. Allum had the sort of laugh that when you heard it, you couldn't help but fall into it. His smile was shockingly white against his smooth brown skin.

'Sorry!' She smiled down the bench at her friends. 'Morning, everyone.'

To Butterfly's right was Cobe, his senior Elite. Cobe was a pale, slim boy, always slightly nervous, with a clean-shaven head shining like a polished egg in the sun. He had dark eyes and thin lips that like Butterfly's, were slow to smile. Opposite him was Allum, who as usual sat beside his junior Taiyo. They made a funny pair. Allum's huge Afrikan figure dwarfed little Taiyo, who was tiny not just due to her small Japanean frame but also because of her age. Most Elite pairs had an age gap of under ten years, but with Taiyo just ten years old, she and Allum had fourteen years between them. That didn't seem to matter though. They were by far the closest pair out of all the Elites Silver knew.

A memory flashed into her mind then; Ember's snarling face close to hers, the glint of a blade in the dim light of the storage room. Silver shivered. She and Ember were only six years apart, but they may as well have had whole worlds orbiting between them for how different they were.

Talk at the bench had settled into their plans for the day. Taiyo was chatting excitedly about swimming, her cropped black hair bobbing around her face as she talked. Allum had promised to teach her the butterfly stroke, which he was taking obvious delight in joking about.

'You must always make a pouty face when doing it,' he instructed. 'Oh, there you go – brother Butterfly is showing you how to do it right now!'

'I'll have to meet you all there,' Silver said when everyone had stopped laughing. 'I've got an assignment this morning.'

Butterfly flashed her a concerned look, but Allum and Taiyo looked delighted.

'Oh, baby girl, that's great news!' said Allum. 'You haven't had one in a while. The last time must have been . . .'

'Before the parade,' Silver answered quietly.

Allum nodded. 'Yes, the parade.' The playful tone in his voice disappeared. 'You know, I've been hearing rumours about what happened.'

'I've heard some things too,' Taiyo said eagerly. She leant forward across the bench, almost sticking her elbow in Allum's plate. 'I overheard one of the forensic team talking to Senior Surrey yesterday.'

Allum grinned at her. 'You didn't tell me. Sneakier and sneakier every day.'

Taiyo jabbed him in the ribs. '*Shush!* I'm telling everyone what I heard.' She glanced round and lowered her voice dramatically. 'This man was telling Senior Surrey that

41

they'd finally traced the bullet's trajectory. Guess where it came from.'

Silver didn't have to guess. For one horrible moment the world seemed to spin to a halt, the noise and activity of the galley freezing as she stared at Taiyo, her stomach dropping.

'The History Museum!' exclaimed Taiyo.

The world started spinning again. Silver felt as though she were tipping with it. She reached for Butterfly's hand under the table, dizzy with relief, barely listening as the others debated this news. The History Museum was on the eastern edge of Pantheon Square. Nowhere near where the actual assassin had been, up on a balcony of Hemmingway House with Silver. She couldn't believe the forensic team had got it so wrong, but she didn't want to waste time thinking about that when she was out of the clear.

Beside her, Butterfly smiled. He held it a little longer than usual.

An hour later, Silver was in a first-class air-tram carriage on her way to Little New India. She enjoyed riding in the fast trams that hung high above the ground from reinforced strong wires strung between buildings. From high up, it was difficult to tell people apart. Afrikans, New Indians, Japaneans, Mainlanders, even Reds, all blended into each other, until they were just people, all the same, living day by day in their amazing walled city that had stayed standing even as the rest of the world fell around it.

When the air-tram reached Little India, Silver alighted at a station that overlooked the district's famous Brick

Lane. It was a sinuous street paved entirely from red bricks to recreate a famous street from an old Mainland capital, London. As soon as she was at street level, she was swept up by foreign sights and smells. Street vendors shouted out to her, holding up brightly coloured saris and sandals, and the air was filled with exotic smells of curry vats and spices, the wind picking up the scents from the coloured mounds of the spice market. Usually, Silver would have taken her time, enjoying the atmosphere. Today, however, she rushed down the street, her mind focused on the assignment she was about to undertake. She could feel the adrenalin already pumping through her, setting her on edge. This was her chance to prove herself after everything that had happened at the parade.

The Spotted Elephant was empty when she arrived ten minutes later, slightly flushed from having jogged up the rickety stairway nailed to the side of a building. The chai bar was large and low-ceilinged, the space sectioned into smaller areas by wooden panels. Filigreed lanterns hung from the ceiling, creating ornate-looking shadows on the floor below. The whole placed smelt of spices and sweetened milk.

Silver took a seat near the door. A waiter in a brown waistcoat took her order, returning a few minutes later with an engraved ceramic cup of chai. She had only taken one sip when the bell above the door to the bar jingled.

A bearded man whom she recognised as a senior Council member from the Intelligence Department hovered in the doorway. He caught her eye and gave the barest hint of a nod before taking his place at a table on the opposite side of the room. A few moments later, the bell above the door sounded again and another man entered, whom Silver guessed was the contact for the information exchange.

The man was a Mainlander, white-skinned and tall beneath his sweeping grey robes. He walked hunched over, but his middle-aged face looked too handsome and bright for its broken body. A sweep of golden brown hair fell into his eyes. Without looking at Silver, he took his place at the table where the Council member sat. The faint scratches of their voices rose a moment later.

Silver ordered another cup of chai. She kept her ears focused on the men's table, listening for sounds of conflict in case she needed to step in. She wished she could hear what they were saying; she was curious about this strange Mainlander. But that wasn't part of her assignment. All she had to do was intervene if there was any trouble. As she waited, she brushed her fingers across the handle of her stungun, still hidden underneath her shirt. She felt nervous at the thought of having to use it. Luckily, the information exchange came to an end twenty minutes later without any trouble at all.

The senior Council member left first, not acknowledging Silver as he went. When the hunched man passed her table, she expected the same treatment, but as she raised her eyes to look at him she realised with a jolt that he was looking back at her. His bright green eyes twinkled. Then, so quickly she might have missed it if she'd blinked –

The man winked.

Silver looked down at the floor. She didn't look back up until she heard the bell above the door jingling as the man left the bar. She sat for a while, confused. What had that wink meant? Was it just the man's way of saying hello? Or was he indicating that he knew she'd been there to oversee the information exchange? A thought came to her: *Maybe he just thought I was pretty.* But she pushed it down. How could he? She was a Red.

Once she had paid the waiter, Silver left the chai bar, her eyes squinting as they adjusted to the bright light outside. The exotic atmosphere mixed with the sunshine into a heady concoction, pushing away the unease that had stirred in her stomach. As she made her way back down Brick Lane to the air-tram station, she started to think less and less about the strange man and his wink. She was just happy she'd undertaken her assignment without anything going wrong. Perhaps now everything really *would* be all right. The forensic team hadn't traced the bullet back to that balcony on Pantheon Square, and she'd completed her first assignment since the parade faultlessly.

By the time she was back above the city, the midday sun blazing down from the blue mirrored sky, Silver had forgotten about the wink completely.

6

At the Beach

Nestled in a curve of the western path of the river's Outer Circle, next to the premium fishing farms and meat labs, was the beach. Originally designed as a public park where all could enjoy its artificially warmed sands and enclosed sea created by triple-filtered river-water, the beach had since been bought by a private investor. Now it was open only to those who could afford its annual membership fee. The Council had bought memberships for all the Elites, and it was one of Silver and her friends' favourite places to go in the city.

After the hectic atmosphere of Brick Lane, Silver felt a rush of calm overtake her as she stepped out of the lobby into the bay of the beach. It was as if the city had disappeared. Holoscreen-mounted walls ringed the whole enclosure, so that it looked as though the sea went on forever and ever, its deepening blue reaching out to a distant, hazy horizon. Rising behind the sloping stretch of golden sand of the beach were fake cliffs.

The holoscreens had not been kept well. The Council's rationing of energy had been stricter over the last few years, and here was the evidence. Black specks dotted the cliffs where the illusion of white clay was meant to be. In several places the image shivered slightly, as though the technology was tired, feeble. Despite this, the illusion of the beach was still irresistible, especially with such a bright, shameless sun blazing in the sky. Its golden light glittered on the water's surface like wet diamonds.

Silver kicked off her boots and stepped from the decking. Her feet sunk into the hot sand. Holding her boots in one hand, she walked towards the shoreline where she'd spotted her friends.

'Baby Silver!' Allum waved at her as she approached.

Both he and Butterfly were in their swimming shorts, though Butterfly also wore an unbuttoned shirt to hide his wings, which folded almost flat against his back. They leant back on their elbows, faces tilted to catch the sun. Cobe sat a little way from them. He was fully dressed in a tunic and metallic grey trousers.

'Where's Taiyo?' asked Silver.

Allum grinned, shrugging.

I know that look, she thought, and no sooner had she gone to sit down when she jumped back up, laughing, as Taiyo exploded out of the sand beneath her. Taiyo's pink bell-bottomed swimsuit made her look like an upturned strawberry ice cream.

Giggling, the two of them scuffled until Taiyo squirmed out of her grasp. Taiyo ran away, squealing and holding her arms up high in mock terror, and Silver lunged after her, grabbing her round the waist and carrying her towards the sea.

'No, no!' Taiyo pleaded, her voice bubbling with laughter as she squirmed in Silver's arms.

Silver didn't let her go until they reached the shore, where – Taiyo kicking her legs frantically now – she threw the little girl into the water. Allum roared with laughter as Taiyo jumped out of the sea. Her hair was plastered to her head like soggy seaweed.

'Yeah, yeah,' Taiyo pouted. 'You won this time.' She smiled suddenly and threw herself back into the water. 'Allum, come teach me swimming now! It's so warm.'

Allum flashed a smile as he passed Silver. 'Nice one.'

Back on the beach, Silver nodded a hello to Cobe before sitting next to Butterfly. Her eyes slid over his taut, softly muscular chest, the line of hair leading down from his bellybutton. She was so used to him that some-times it surprised her to see him so grown up. *He's sixteen now*, she thought. *He might get a girlfriend soon*. She felt a twinge of jealousy at the idea. An image of Butterfly leaning across to kiss her jumped into her mind, but he only turned his head to greet her.

'Hey.' He was squinting against the sun. 'How was the assignment?'

Silver smiled. 'It went really well. How long have you all been here?'

Butterfly turned onto his front and laid his head on his arms, closing his eyes. 'Just an hour or so.' He laughed. 'You missed Taiyo's impression of Ember falling into the sea. It was pretty funny.'

'I can imagine.' She grinned, lying back on the sand.

The heat of the sun made Silver feel lazy, with the steady sound of the sea lapping the shore, rustling softly across the sand as though whispering secrets to it, and soon she began to doze. They spent the rest of the afternoon drifting in and out of sleep as the sun arced in the azure sky above, Taiyo and Allum's laughter reaching them from the sea like distant bird calls. The events of the parade felt like a whole lifetime ago. Silver felt safe and happy again, the image of Tanaka's head bursting open a blurred memory, distant and unreal. There was a nagging thought at the back of her mind that wondered why the forensic team had made an error about the bullet's trajectory, but she did her best to ignore it. Instead, she tried to feel lucky that they'd made a mistake.

They stayed at the beach all day until the sun slipped down low in the sky. The air picked up a chill.

'Time to go?' Butterfly asked. 'It's getting cold.'

She nodded. 'I'm getting hungry too.'

He smiled, raising an eyebrow. 'When are you not?' He helped her to her feet before buttoning up his shirt.

'I'll tell the others,' Silver said.

Taiyo, Allum and Cobe were all in the sea, sitting in the shallows and talking. Their chests and heads poked above the silvery water, bobbing in the swell and push of the tide; another man-made fabrication by the beach's engineers. Silver started towards them when a low beeping made her stop. She looked down. The noise was coming from a comms cuff half buried in the sand.

'Someone's got an assignment,' Butterfly said, picking it up. He turned it over in his hand. 'It's Allum's. I'll bring it to him.' But he must have accidentally touched its screen, for the next moment Miss Apell's voice sounded.

'Good, Allum. I'm glad I've got you.' She spoke so quickly they didn't have a chance to tell her it wasn't Allum. 'I need you to secure the scene of what appears to be an abduction. Do not tell anyone about this – I'll only be sending you and Ember. You'll see why later. The police are already there. Senior Surrey will be joining you once he's finished with a meeting here.'

'This isn't –' Butterfly started as soon as Miss Apell stopped for breath, but she cut him off.

'Just get there right away. The address is Flat Seven, Lucky Dragon Condominium, Zhangdong Street. You might recognise it.' There was a beep as she hung up.

Silver felt sick. She stared at Butterfly in horror, her heart racing in her chest, her throat going dry.

You might recognise it, Miss Apell had said, and it was true. Silver *did* recognise the address –

It was her parents' apartment.

7

The Message Under the
Moneyplant

It had grown dark by the time Silver and Butterfly arrived at Zhangdong Street. White moonlight shivered on the surface of the ornamental fish pond outside Lucky Dragon Condominium, the red and orange scales of the koi inside brilliant in the inky blue light. Past the gardens, the tall building stood silent. Only shadows moving behind latticed windows revealed anyone was home.

'What if they *are* gone?' Silver whispered as she and Butterfly passed through the gate into the condominium grounds.

She hadn't spoken for the whole journey. After hearing the message from Miss Apell, she had pulled on her boots and ran across the beach towards the lobby, stumbling as the sand shifted beneath her feet. Behind her, she was dimly aware of Butterfly's voice, but it sounded distant, as though the air was thick, as though she was in a dream and he was reaching through it, trying to wake her. He'd caught up with Silver in the lobby, where she had been forced to slow to show her membership card to the reception staff in order to leave.

'I'm going to my parents' apartment,' she had said. 'I don't care what Miss Apell says. I'm going there.'

'I know,' Butterfly had said. 'Come on, let's go before the others realise we're gone.'

Now, standing in the quiet condominium grounds, Silver's voice shook. 'What if . . . what if they're . . .' She couldn't bring herself to say the word.

Butterfly took her hand. 'Don't.'

They walked quickly through the gardens. In the deepening blue light of dusk, every tree and bush seemed to move, and the darkness that pooled across the ground was as thick and dark as blood. Nearing the open condominium foyer, they saw a policeman standing on the entrance steps.

Butterfly stopped. 'They'll be expecting Allum and Ember.'

'Do you think Allum would've found the message about the assignment by now?' Silver asked. She felt guilty at the thought of getting Allum in trouble, but right now she was too anxious over what had happened to her parents to worry about him.

Butterfly nodded. 'Probably. Let's tell the police for now that Allum sent us as he's been held up. Our birth-chips should see us through.'

They approached the policeman. Like all of Neo-Babel's police force, he wore a mask stretched across his face like a pearly black shell. The masks protected the identity of the policemen, just as the identity of the Elites was a secret to protect them from attacks by anti-birthchip groups. Still, Silver had always found them unnerving. The policeman moved down the steps to meet them.

Yellowy light from the lanterns hanging above the foyer entrance slid across the surface of his mask like wet flames.

'There has been an incident in the condiminium,' he began, his voice slightly muffled by the mask. 'Only authorised personnel are being admitted –'

'That's us,' Butterfly interrupted confidently. 'We've been sent by our Elite seniors. They're currently busy with assignments. We're to secure the crime scene until they arrive.'

The policeman hesitated. Before he could say anything, Butterfly turned, brushing away the hair at the back of his neck to expose the skin beneath which his birthchip was buried. Silver was worried the policeman would want more of an explanation, but he just pulled out the scanner from the holster at his hip. Once he'd scanned both their birthchips, nodding in approval, they made their way towards the stairs at the end of the foyer.

Silver's parents' apartment was on the third floor. Police were stationed outside it too. Butterfly told them the same story, and after another scan of their birthchips, he and Silver were given the basic details about what had happened. Neighbours had reported suspicious noises coming from the apartment, and one had seen three people leaving through the living-room window.

'But aren't you here to secure the location?' asked one of the policemen.

'Yes,' said Butterfly. 'Just covering the basics.'

Silver had gone pale at the policeman's account. She walked as if in a dream towards the apartment. The policeman beside the front door handed her and Butterfly a torch each.

Silver hovered in the doorway, looking into the apartment with a growing sense of unease. There was a hush in the air that set her teeth on edge. The flat was strange in the dark. It did not feel like the place she had visited all her life, filled with her parents' laughter and the awful screeching music of Chinese opera and the sweet, smoky smell of jasmine tea brewing.

'Come on,' Butterfly whispered, stepping inside.

The white light from their torches sliced through the darkness and chaos of the apartment. The furniture had been upturned, trashed, her parents' things strewn everywhere as though some huge tide had swept through it all. Glass crunched underfoot as they moved. The windows were broken, and moonlight slid into the room, stark and white, catching on objects and lighting them with silvery flickers.

'They're gone,' Silver breathed, confirming what she'd feared ever since hearing Miss Apell's voice on the beach. With this realisation came the stirrings of despair, but she pushed it down. *Not yet*, she thought. *Not yet.*

'We don't know what happened,' Butterfly said. 'They could be fine . . .' He trailed off as she pushed past him.

Out of the window, Silver had caught sight of Ember and Allum running across the gardens towards the condominium. In a few minutes they would be in the apartment, and she and Butterfly would be thrown out. There was something she had to do before that happened.

She picked her way across the living room and into

her parents' quarters. On the far side she slid back the pretty, hand-carved shutters that hid the balcony. She searched its floor with her torch. For a moment, Silver thought that it too was destroyed along with the rest of the apartment, and she felt a twist of panic at the thought. Then her torchlight fell across what she'd been looking for and she sighed in relief. The money tree sat untouched at the end of the balcony.

'What are you doing?' Butterfly's voice came from behind her as he entered the room. He moved closer. 'They'll be here soon.'

Silver ignored him. She gripped the leathery trunk of the tree and pulled it out of its pot, roots and soil and all. There, at the bottom of the pot, just as she had hoped, was a slip of paper. She picked it out and replaced the plant.

At the same time, voices reached them from outside; Allum and Ember would be here any second.

'My parents always told me that if anything happened to them, they'd try and leave me a message,' Silver explained, turning to Butterfly. 'Underneath Dad's money tree.' Then, in a breathless voice full of wonder, 'Look.'

She held out the piece of paper. It was folded in half, and on the top side someone had written in a messy scrawl:

My mei li

'My *mei li?*' asked Butterfly.

'It means "my beautiful". It's what Dad calls me sometimes.'

Fingers trembling, Silver unfolded the piece of paper. She didn't know what she expected to find, but what was written there was more surprising than what she could possibly have imagined. Inside, were just two words:

Come Outside

Her heart slammed into her chest. Her stomach squeezed, and she had to reach out a hand to grab the balcony ledge to steady herself. She stared at the note, but no matter how hard she looked, those two little words didn't change.

Come Outside.

It could only mean one thing. The phrasing, the capital 'o'; any Neo-Babel citizen would read the note and know what it meant.

Leave the city –

Leave Neo-Babel.

Silver looked up. Butterfly was staring at her, the same mix of fear and confusion and wonder shining in his eyes. Then she was stuffing the note into the top of her leggings as Ember and a policeman burst into the room, shouting words Silver barely registered, and as they dragged her and Butterfly out of the apartment she felt the note pressing against her skin where she'd hidden it, burning, and beating almost like a heart.

8

A Secret Overheard

'Thank you, Ember. I'll take it from here.'

Ember paused, her mouth half open with more angry, hissed words about how Silver and Butterfly were going to pay for their complete disregard for orders when Senior Surrey emerged at the top of the stairs.

Silver's stomach knotted at the sight of him. The black office cape swirled round his body in the crisp night air like dark smoke. His eyes slid over her and Butterfly, who were sitting on the floor outside Silver's parents' apartment, their backs to the wall.

Ember straightened. 'As you wish.' She turned to Allum, who had been watching the events in silence. 'Come on.'

Allum gave Silver a sympathetic look as he left. She tried to smile in response, but failed.

Senior Surrey crouched down in front of them. 'Hello, Silver, Butterfly. It seems the two of you have already been reprimanded by Ember. I will spare you the humiliation of another lecture. But know this. You have failed to follow orders from your superiors. I will not accept either of you doing so again.'

'Yes, sir.' Butterfly nodded.

'Can you promise me the same, Silver?'

She looked back at Senior Surrey as he turned to her. She'd expected him to be as angry as Ember at discovering two of his junior Elites had acted outside direct orders, but this bland impassiveness was somehow worse. Her parents had been abducted. Yes, her and Butterfly had lied to get access to the apartment. But could he really blame her for wanting to know what had happened to her parents? She felt a jolt of anger that Senior Surrey had offered no sympathy at all.

'Yes, sir,' she answered dully.

He nodded. 'Good.' He leant closer and dropped his voice to a low growl, so the policemen standing nearby couldn't hear his next words. 'Or I'm afraid there will be serious consequences. As you know, it is illegal to look at any Neo-Babel citizen's birthchip records unless they are suspected of criminal activity. But perhaps I should make an exception for you two. I wonder what I might find, where you might have been.' He focused on Silver, his eyes dark as stones. 'The day of the parade, for instance.'

Silver couldn't help it. She let out a small gasp. The awful events of that day up on Hemmingway House resurfaced in her mind; a weather-beaten face, stubble, the flash of metal as a gun was raised. *Senior Surrey knows*, she thought, staring into his cold eyes. *He knows.*

'Well,' Senior Surrey said after a long pause, straightening. 'There is a rickshaw waiting to take you back to the Ebora Building. You will resume your normal duties tomorrow.' And without waiting for a reply, he strode off into the apartment, his cape billowing behind him like a second shadow.

As soon as they were back at the Stacks, Silver and Butterfly took a lift up to the roof garden. There was an unspoken agreement between them that this garden was where they could talk. Not the rickshaw on their way back from Silver's parents' apartment, nor Butterfly's bedroom, where Cobe might be waiting. Although all Council members were permitted to visit the rooftop garden, senior staff preferred their private ornamental pleasure gardens in the east wing, and most of the other members and staff did not reside in the Stacks, so at night the roof garden was almost always deserted.

When they reached the roof, they found the garden empty, just as they'd hoped. The leaves of the trees and cropped bushes rustled in the wind that lifted off the top of the building. Silver started down a path, heading to a corner of the garden where a daybed was half hidden under a rose-covered archway. They climbed onto its mattress under the privacy of the low, rosebush ceiling, the sweet smell of the flowers pungent in the air. One side of the daybed had a brilliant view of the Council District. Silver usually loved looking out at it. It was so different from the rest of the city, with its wide, straight boulevards and elegant sparseness. Tonight, however, it just looked flat and empty. Moonlight slid across the lacquered concrete streets like black ice. Silver turned her back on the view and sat facing out towards the garden, hugging her knees to her chin.

'I don't know where to start,' said Butterfly gently after a minute's silence.

'I do.'

He turned to look at Silver, brushing his hair back from his face so his blue eyes flashed in the darkness. 'You *do*?'

She nodded, tears springing to her eyes. An image of her father's note came to her; *Come Outside*. The truth was she'd known what she was going to have to do ever since reading those two words back in her parents' apartment. Those two words were a cry for help from her parents. She couldn't ignore them.

Butterfly's eyes widened as he realised what she meant. 'Oh,' he breathed. 'You want to leave Neo. Look for them in the Outside.' He moved closer to Silver on the daybed. 'Are you sure?'

'Yes,' she said firmly. 'I can't find a note like that from my parents and not do anything about it. They wouldn't say something like that unless they really needed me. They *have* to be outside the city.' Her hand found Butterfly's on top of the mattress. 'I need to go, but you don't have to.'

He shook his head. 'Of course I'm coming.' He said it fiercely, and Silver felt a rush of relief and guilt at the same time.

She wiped her face, nodding. 'Do you think Senior Surrey meant what he said?' she asked. 'That if we went against orders again he'd look up our records?'

'Yes.'

Silver began to shiver. Suddenly, the magnitude of

leaving the city hit her at full force. She felt the weight of the consequences of doing such a thing pressing down on her, solid and impossibly heavy. Her tears flowed faster.

'They won't let us back in!' she cried, clutching her hands to her chest. 'If the Council see my birthchip records, they'll know I was there when the assassin shot Tanaka. You heard Senior Surrey – he suspects me! Maybe Ember told him her suspicions about me working for an anti-birthchip group. And even if my parents can explain what happened and that I was only leaving the city to save them, I might be locked away for killing Tanaka –'

Butterfly took her hands, squeezing them tightly. 'Silver, calm down! Look. You've got to decide. Is finding your parents the most important thing to you? Forget about everything else for a while. Just think about your parents. Do you want to find them?'

She nodded.

'Then you can go find out what happened for yourself,' he continued, 'or you can ignore what you found in the letter and let the police figure deal with it.'

Silver shook her head. 'I can't do that,' she said, her voice thick with tears. 'I have to go. The Council won't do anything about it if they think my parents have left Neo, and they won't let us go. We have to leave without them knowing. Without *anyone* knowing. I know it's wrong, but I just can't stay here knowing that my parents might be . . .'

She jumped up, terrified at finishing the sentence. Her hair tangled in the thorns of the rosebush overhead, and she cursed, tugging it free. A wild feeling had come over her, and suddenly she couldn't just sit here talking about her parents when they had been abducted and taken to the Outside, and gods knew what else.

Butterfly stood up and tried to pull Silver into a hug, but she struggled away.

'No!' she shouted. 'I let the assassin shoot Tanaka! I let my parents get abducted! What kind of an Elite *am* I?'

Sobbing, she turned to run, and crashed straight into someone who'd been hiding in the darkness of the line of bushes beside the daybed. They both fell to the ground. The other person cried out as their head smacked against the floor. Silver scrambled to her feet. She saw that the person was a boy, and he was kneeling now, his head bowed between his legs.

A white, shaven head, bright in the moonlight.

'Cobe,' she breathed.

9

Aiming to Kill

'How long have you been there?' Butterfly's voice was low as he helped Cobe up.

A drizzle of blood snaked down Cobe's right cheek from where he had hit his head on the ground. His dark eyes shifted nervously. 'Long enough,' he said.

Silver felt her stomach drop.

Cobe held up his hands. 'Look, I didn't mean to listen in on your conversation. Taiyo told me what happened to Silver's parents, and when you didn't come back to our bedroom, I guessed you'd be up here. But then I heard shouting and . . .'

Silver eyed him carefully. She liked Cobe, but there was a part of her that was wary of him. He'd always been slightly distant with her, and she could never tell what he was thinking. Could they trust him?

'Well, you've heard it all now,' said Butterfly. 'All we can ask is that you don't turn us in, and maybe . . . maybe you can help us.'

Cobe brushed a hand over his shaved head. 'Help you?'

Butterfly nodded. 'We have to leave Neo to find Silver's parents.'

'But –'

'Please.' Butterfly grasped Cobe's shoulder. 'We need your help, Cobe. You've always been there for me, through everything. And I need you now more than ever.'

Cobe stared back at Butterfly, his cheeks flushing. Silver was convinced he was going to refuse them – she could see the fear in his eyes, the questions on his lips – but then he dropped his head and let out a long sigh, nodding. 'All right,' he said. 'I'll help.'

Butterfly smiled and lowered his hands. 'Thank you, Cobe.'

'Thank you.' Silver said.

Cobe didn't turn to her. He looked hard at Butterfly. 'You need a way out of the city?'

'Yes.'

Cobe licked his lips, hesitating. 'What do you know about the Limpets?'

Butterfly turned to Silver. She shook her head. She'd never been to the slums of Neo-Babel. Only senior Elites were given assignments there.

'Ember's talked about it a little,' she said. 'She says it's awful. Well, "disgusting" was her exact word, but . . .'

Cobe nodded. 'It *is* horrible. But it's also different from what most people think.'

'What do you mean?'

'Well, most people think it's complete chaos, but . . .' Cobe lowered his voice. 'Much of it is organised too. They're smart, some of the slum rats. They've got businesses down there, social structures. The place operates almost like its own city.'

'I've heard that from Allum,' said Butterfly. 'There's a black market too. Is that what you think could help us?'

Cobe shook his head. 'There's something much *more* than that. The Council don't like to admit it, but I've heard Senior Surrey talking about it, and I once had an assignment to do with it. An exit,' he breathed. 'A way out of Neo.'

Silver's mouth fell open in surprise. 'An exit?'

'Just one tunnel out, we think,' said Cobe. 'But many entrances, constantly changing so the Council can't find them.'

She felt numb with amazement. She wasn't sure how she had thought they were going to leave the city. Silver had always imagined there was some sort of gate you could walk through, but she felt stupid for thinking that now. Why would there be a gate in and out of a city no one ever left, and no one ever entered?

They fell silent. Wind rustled the leaves of the bushes and small trees, and sounds of the city – rickshaws honking, air-trams rushing through the air, tinny strands of music – reached them from a distance. Silver felt removed from it all. She couldn't believe the city was still out there, carrying on as though nothing had happened, when in one night her whole world had come crashing down.

Butterfly broke the silence. 'How do we find the exit?'

Cobe shifted uncomfortably. 'Well, it's not that easy,' he admitted, 'or we'd have found it and shut the system down years ago.'

'But there has to be a way,' Silver urged.

Cobe looked at her, and she could see something shining in his eyes. Excitement? Hope? She couldn't place it exactly. But she felt a sudden rush of trust as she looked back into his deep brown eyes.

He nodded. 'There is. But to get to it, I only have a name – *Xiao* Mae, Little Mae. That's all we know. It seems she's the contact, but we've never been able to find her.'

'How do you know this Little Mae can deliver?' asked Silver.

Cobe paused, glancing away. 'I know she's done it before.'

Before she could ask how, Butterfly spoke. 'I don't know how to thank you, Cobe.'

Cobe focused down at his feet. 'You're my junior. I've got to look out for you.' He looked up, his face hardening. 'I just wish I could do more to make sure you get out safely,' he added darkly. 'It's not going to be easy, and if the Council find out what you're doing, you're both as good as dead.'

There was no right moment, no perfect time to leave the city, Silver knew that. Though she wished there was. It would have been so much easier if there had been some sign from the gods to tell her, *Yes, now is the time – go.* But the gods were silent, and in the end she and Butterfly just had to gather up the courage to pick a day and leave. They decided the coming Saturday would be their best chance, just over a week after Silver's parents' disappearance. Every Council member would be at Tanaka's funeral. Once they realised two Elites were missing Silver and Butterfly would already have a few hours' head start.

Those last few days before leaving were tense. Saturday crept up so slowly Silver had to keep checking her comms cuff to make sure time hadn't actually stopped, and she felt a building sense of dread at the thought of leaving the city. But when she noticed it rising, she forced her fear down. She was an Elite. She could do this. And thinking about her parents in the Outside would give her a surge of courage, of determination, and then suddenly Saturday couldn't come soon enough.

'When you progress to senior Elite status in three years, you'll be issued with an N70 pistol, just like this one. I'd like to see how comfortable you are with it.'

Every two weeks on a Friday afternoon, Silver had training at the indoor shooting range at Central Police Command, a building on the northern edge of the Council District. Usually, her lessons were taken by one of the policemen's own training officers, but today when she stepped into the range's entrance hall it was Senior Surrey who greeted her, a gun held in his outstretched hand.

Silver took it. 'Where's the training officer, sir?'

'I thought I'd oversee your training today,' he replied, smoothing down the black tunic he was wearing. His dark eyes were as unreadable as always. He gestured at the plastiglass panel to the range beyond. 'Shall we?'

They put on their earplugs and went into the hall, walking to a booth at the far side. Senior Surrey pulled the door shut behind them. The noise of guns firing from the other booths was loud in the small space, even with earplugs in, the air filled with the metallic *clink* of spent cases hitting the floor. Silver waited for instructions on how to proceed, but Senior Surrey just sat down on the bench lining one side of the booth and looked expectantly at her, a thin smile hovering on his lips.

'I'll just get started, then!' she shouted.

She took position at the firing line, propping her arm on the top of the barrier. Lowering her head, she looked down the barrel through the sight. The standard range target – a life-size cut-out of a human silhouette – was set halfway down the lane. Silver aimed at its head, knowing with absolute certainty she'd hit it. Even though she'd only been training for four months, she had exceptional aim. Every officer who oversaw her training said so. It was the one time when she truly felt she belonged with the Elites.

Silver took a deep breath before exhaling slowly. Then –

Bang!

She jumped, the gunshot loud in her ear. She spun round to see Senior Surrey standing beside her, his arm extended, smoke curling from the barrel of his gun.

'Practising with a support leads to laziness,' he shouted over the noise of the hall. 'Try again. Standing upright this time, no support.'

Silver turned back to the target, raising her arm, which

was shaking slightly. She felt on edge all of a sudden, her heart sent thudding by the sound of a gunshot so close to her. Memories of the assassin at the parade rushed back.

No, she thought, forcing herself to keep calm. *You can't let Senior Surrey see you panic.* And she pulled the trigger, hitting the target right in the forehead, the gun only kicking back in her hands for a fraction of a second.

Senior Surrey nodded. 'Not bad.' He touched the control panel in the wall of the booth, running his finger along an electronic dial. In response, the target in the lane slid back a metre. 'Now try.'

This time, Silver's arm was steady. The bullet punched the target square in the forehead again. Before the empty shell even hit the floor, Senior Surrey moved the target back another metre.

'Again.'

It went on like this for half an hour. When the target had reached its furthest point near the receiving wall and Silver's aim was still perfect, Senior Surrey made the target move, zigzagging up the lane as she shot. Then he got her to shoot while he held her left arm behind her back.

'Whatever the situation,' he shouted, his mouth close to her ear, 'you have to be able to keep your focus. Tell me, Silver – when you shoot, what do you think about?'

Tanaka's face came to her mind in an instant, his head bursting into a dense red mist.

'Nothing,' she lied.

Senior Surrey reached for the control panel, touching

in more instructions. A moment later, the lane fell into darkness, strobe lights flashing on, dancing down the lane in a dizzying array of colours. Senior Surrey pressed closer to Silver, twisting her arm so hard she bit back a cry.

'When aiming to kill, you need to move with accuracy, with purpose. With a clear, hard objective. You hold it in your mind until you are thinking of nothing else. It will give you focus. It will keep your arm steady. Understand?'

'Yes, sir.'

'Do you have an objective in mind now?'

Silver thought of her parents' laughter, of how she'd felt that day on the beach when she'd heard Miss Apell's message that they'd been abducted. She thought of how she'd do anything to get them back.

'Yes,' she said.

'Then shoot,' growled Senior Surrey.

And even with her left arm twisted painfully behind her back and the target zigzagging down the lane, only visible in quick snatches when the strobe lights flashed on, Silver's bullet found its mark right in the centre of the target's forehead.

10

The Limpets

Silver slipped out of her bedpod at six thirty the next morning. She was fully dressed, having prepared for leaving the previous night, and had barely slept, counting down the minutes until she and Butterfly were to meet. As she crept across the room to the door, she heard a voice from Ember's bedpod. Hesitating, she tiptoed over.

Ember was crying softly in her sleep. 'Please, Quoma! Please, no!'

Silver didn't dare to breathe. She had heard Ember saying things like this before in her sleep, in a voice Ember would never have used when she was awake. Silver didn't know who Quoma was, or what he could have done to give someone like Ember such terrible nightmares. She waited to hear more, but Ember had fallen silent. Shaking off a momentary rush of pity for Ember, and wondering whether she'd ever see her again, Silver crossed the room and headed out of the door.

The Stacks were respectfully quiet that morning, the preparations for Tanaka's funeral just beginning. Silver left the building and headed down Noda Parkway towards Achebe Bridge Station. She climbed up the steps to the platform and saw Butterfly waiting for her, two backpacks at his feet. He wore a white top, the sleeves rolled up to his elbows, and slim blue trousers. He had on the boots from his Elite uniform, but to an untrained eye they looked just like any black worker's boots. Silver was also dressed in plain clothes to avoid raising suspicions in the Limpets. A grey jumper hung loosely off her small frame, and dark green trousers were tucked into her boots.

'This is it, then,' she said as she joined Butterfly.

'This is it.' He handed her one of the backpacks and swung the other onto his shoulder, glancing round at the station guard to make sure they were out of earshot. 'Ready?'

Silver nodded, pulling her backpack on. 'I am. But it's not too late to change your mind.' She touched his arm, hesitating. 'You don't have to come with me. You can go back now, and no one will ever know.'

'You're my family, Silver,' said Butterfly. 'I'm coming with you. Besides, what's here for me? Years on end working for the Council, assignment after assignment, following orders?' He glanced away, his eyes focusing on the buildings of the Council District behind them. 'After the explosion, this place stopped feeling like my home.'

'But it is,' she said, watching his face carefully. 'And once we leave, we might not be able to ever come back.'

Butterfly smiled tightly. 'I know that.'

As they waited at the station platform for the air-tram, Silver looked out over the Council District. She could just make out the Stacks in the distance, morning sunlight glancing off its polished black exterior. City flags that had been put up for the parade still hung from some of the windows, unmoving in the still air. Usually she would have smiled at this view, but today all she felt was a sickening sense of unease. Over the last few weeks, her feelings towards the Council District – and the Council itself – had begun to change, lurking inside her veins like a poison. Now she looked at the Council District and saw not only the place that had been her home for nearly all her life, but also memories she'd rather forget. Tanaka's head bursting into red, Ember's sneering face in the darkness of the storeroom, Surrey's threats about looking up their birthchip records. So much of her life in this place had gone sour.

Silver turned away from the Council District. She didn't look back as the air-tram arrived and they boarded an empty carriage, nor as it slid away from the station, rising up to meet the taller buildings of the inner city. She didn't look back even once.

After forty minutes of travelling, the city began to fall away around them, first exposing the grubby graphene solar sheets covering the roofs of buildings, and then leaving empty sky, punctured only by the stilts of the air-tram supports and the shaggy circular silhouettes of the derelict skylungs, long destitute and now wreathed with moss. As the air-tram approached the eastern reach of the river's Outer Circle, it started its descent. Silver could make out the faces of factory workers sitting by the riverside, smoking shishas and eating snacks. Their faces and clothes were grubby with dirt. None of them glanced up at the air-tram descending above their heads.

She was glad. She didn't want them to see her looking down from the pristine first-class carriage.

Silver and Butterfly finally left the air-tram at Industrial District East Station, a dilapidated platform just past the river. They chose one of the unlicensed rickshaws waiting outside the station and climbed into its passenger bench. It took them down shadowy roads between squat factory buildings, all the while heading towards an enormous mass ahead of them protruding from the city walls; the Limpets. The slums were tiered, with five or four levels stacked upon each other. Sheets of tarpaulin and rain-stained canvas were strung over its bulk, rusty pieces of corrugated iron in place of walls.

Silver felt a thrill of excitement as the rickshaw pulled up to a wide hole in the Limpets' side. This would be her first time inside the slums. Even though she'd rather they didn't have reason to be making this trip, she was still eager to see what the place was like. After paying the driver, they headed into the shadowy opening. In the dim light, they couldn't see very far, but further in there were clusters of lights strung across the ceiling, melting away the darkness, and as they turned a corner, Silver let out a gasp.

They stood at the edge of an enormous cavern. Like the central hallway of the Stacks, the main chamber of the Limpets was criss-crossed all over with walkways; plaited ropes and wooden bridges, pathways made entirely from metal sheets stapled together. From many of the larger bridges hung hammocks and strings of clothing, and even what looked like little shacks, ladders running from their porches up to the walkways above. The cavern went five storeys into the ground. Ringing it above were the different floors that Silver had seen from the outside, though here their ledges hung open to the chamber, as though a huge piece had been scooped out of a giant wedding cake.

The whole place was alive with activity. People scurried across walkways. Groups shouted orders to each other. Small children with no shoes shimmied down the ropes and ladders and precariously balanced staircases that led from floor to floor. Pungent odours mixed with the stink of excrement, and the acrid taste of smoke bit the back of Silver's throat.

'We should start looking for Little Mae,' Butterfly said. 'Tanaka's funeral is about to begin. We've only got a couple of hours before they realise we're missing.'

Silver threw open her arms. 'But *look* at this. Little Mae could be anywhere!'

'Exactly. So we'd better start asking around now.'

But asking around proved of little use. Over two hours later, they were deep in the Limpets, no closer to finding Little Mae than they'd been when they arrived. Silver was not just frustrated at that; the atmosphere of the Limpets was getting to her too. People shouted and spat at her and Butterfly when they tried to approach them, and she felt as though she were being buried alive in a sea of grime and poverty. Even in their plain clothes, Silver and Butterfly were by far the most well-dressed. Their healthy bodies stood out like new buds in a field of dying flowers.

'What are we going to do now?' Silver moaned as

they came to another dead end. 'We've asked and asked and *asked* –'

'And we'll ask some more,' said Butterfly calmly. 'Let's go back and try another floor.'

They'd just turned round when they heard raised voices echoing down a narrow alley to their left, the dull thuds of flesh being kicked.

Silver glanced at Butterfly. She saw the flash of concern across his face. 'It's not our problem,' she said, but he ignored her, heading down the alley. Reluctantly, she followed. The corridor opened onto a ledge overlooking the Limpets' huge main cavern. Silver was disorientated for a second; she hadn't realised they were so close to where they had started their search. Then she saw Butterfly had followed the sound of the shouting voices to a small ledge to the right that perched over the edge of the floor. She inched her way across the ledge and was almost bowled back by three young boys. They ran past her, just a blur of tatty clothes and grimy faces, cursing as they disappeared into the alley. Suppressing a curse herself, Silver regained her balance and started back along the ledge.

Ahead, Butterfly was hunched over something. A boy around twelve years old stood beside him, shouting and gesturing angrily. The boy had the caramel skin of an Afronese and was dressed in the cleanest clothes Silver had seen on anyone here all day.

'What d'you do *that* for?' he cried. 'I had them fine before you came. Now they'll think I'm easy meat next time they see me!'

Butterfly ignored him, tending to the thing he was crouching over. Silver moved closer and saw that it was another boy. He was a Japanean like Taiyo, and though he looked of a similar age to the Afronese boy, his clothes were filthy, little more than rags. He lay unmoving on the floor.

Butterfly felt the boy's pulse. 'He's alive, but he's not speaking or moving.'

The Afronese boy had stopped shouting now. 'Oh, don't worry,' he said. 'That's normal.'

Butterfly turned to him. 'Normal? How is not speaking or moving *normal*?'

The boy shrugged. 'It is for him. He's been like that for ages – a birthchip op gone wrong.'

Silver looked back at the Japanean boy on the floor. She felt sick. She'd heard how criminals would try to get their birthchips removed to avoid tracking by the Council. But the operations rarely worked. Birthchips were connected to the spinal cord in such a way that only a few highly trained surgeons knew how to remove them without permanent damage to a person's neuro-logical functions. The Limpets was the last place a surgeon like that would be found.

'Poor boy,' Silver breathed. She reached out to touch his cheek, his wide, terrified eyes following her every movement. 'Why did he risk the operation?'

The Afronese boy crossed his arms. 'His mum used him in her DNA hacker business, but there was an undercover policeman who managed to scan his birth-chip, and so his mum had to get it out or he'd be captured next time. She abandoned him here after the op went wrong. Easier to avoid him being found. Anyway,' he said, his voice brightening, 'it's not that bad – one of our people found him. He makes a great lookout. We've got this blinking system with him, see, since he doesn't speak. Only annoying thing is when he lets himself get beat up, like just now, and one of us has to come help him. Look where that got me.' The boy pointed at a bruise darkening his right cheek, an indignant look on his face.

Butterfly ignored him. 'We need to get this boy some help,' he said, an edge of anger in his voice. He looked up at the Afronese boy. 'What's your name?'

The boy hesitated. 'Akhezo.'

'Akhezo, does this boy have a home here? Someone who can help?'

Akhezo shrugged. 'He lives in a bridge-house nearby.'

'Can you take us there?'

'But I'm late for an appointment –'

'Take us there,' said Butterfly, reaching into a pocket and holding out a sliver of grey notes.

Akhezo's eyes widened greedily. 'Sure.' He grinned, grabbing the money. 'It's not too far from where I'm going actually, so Little Mae won't be too –'

'Little Mae?' Silver interrupted, her head snapping up at Akhezo's words.

'Yeah. Little Mae. What's it to you?'

Silver exchanged a quick look with Butterfly. She didn't dare to believe it. 'You know where she is?' she asked, turning back to the boy.

He rubbed the notes in his hand. 'I might . . .'

Butterfly pulled out a few more notes and held them up. Akhezo reached for them but Butterfly jerked his hand back. '*Only* if you'll help us take this boy back to his house first.'

'Oh, all right,' sighed Akhezo. 'I don't know why you want to meet Little Mae, though. She's a horrible witch of a Red.'

Butterfly handed the money to Akhezo. His face was harder than Silver had ever seen it, and she could tell that he was pushing down the anger that she felt rising in *her* too.

'Just take us to this boy's house first,' he said, lifting the Japanean boy in his arms.

They followed Akhezo back along the ledge. Silver looked at the boy in Butterfly's arms. His eyes were wide, scared. She ran a hand across his brow. 'You'll be home soon, don't worry.' She looked up and called ahead, 'What's his name?'

'Who?' Akhezo glanced over his shoulder. 'Oh, him. That's Sauro. Anyway, what does *that* matter?' He turned, hurrying up the path. 'We need to get going or I'll end up just like him. Little Mae hates it when I'm late.'

11

Little Mae's Last Hours

It turned out Akhezo was right; Little Mae *did* hate it when he was late. Butterfly barely had time to straighten after ducking through the entrance to her hideout – a curved dugout guarded by two boys clutching metal poles – before what looked like a small fireball flew at him, spitting and screaming.

He raised his hands to protect himself, then stopped when he realised what looked like a fireball was actually a tiny old Red woman dressed in bright pink and red clothes, teetering on platform clogs almost half as tall as she was. Her wrinkled face was sagging and liver-spotted with age, but her eyes were alert, shining like the coins dangling from the trimmings of her hat. They narrowed as she spotted Akhezo.

'Fifty minutes, *xiao zhu*!' she snarled, swooping over to the boy and striking him with the back of her hand. 'Fifty minutes Little Mae has been sat here waiting for your news!'

Akhezo cowered. 'Sorry, Little Mae. But I ran into these two, and they wanted to meet you . . .'

Little Mae's head twitched, setting the coins on her hat tinkling, as her eyes followed his pointed finger to where Butterfly and Silver stood. Shoving Akhezo out of the way, the woman shuffled over to them, tottering on her huge clogs so quickly that Butterfly was amazed she didn't fall flat on her face. She leant in towards Butterfly. He could smell her sickly perfume and see the flecks of food stuck between her rotten teeth.

'You do not have an appointment with Little Mae, and Little Mae has never seen you before, white boy.' She snapped her head round and shuffled over to Silver. 'Little Mae hasn't seen you either, Red. You are not from the Limpets, and you dress so fine for a Red girl. Look at these clothes, *xiao zhu*!' the old woman shouted back at Akhezo. 'When you grow up, you might have clothes like this. Unless you continue to keep Little Mae waiting. Then Little Mae will make her own clothes out of your skin, *xiao zhu*!' She cackled, leaning towards Butterfly and Silver, a sharp glint in her eyes. 'Little Mae calls him little pig because he squeals like one –'

'Little Mae,' interrupted Butterfly. 'We need your help with something.'

The old woman's wrinkled face crinkled even more as she smiled nastily. 'Oh, Little Mae knows what you want.'

Out the corner of his eye, Butterfly saw Silver shoot him a worried look. 'And what's that?' he asked, trying to seem indifferent.

'What everyone wants from Little Mae,' the woman chuckled. 'A way out.'

Butterfly nodded. 'Can you give us one?'

She burst into a shrieking laugh. 'You ask if Little Mae

81

knows how to leave Neo? Of course she does! Little Mae knows everything!' She stopped laughing suddenly, edging forward on her clogs. A cruel smile curled the corners of her lips. 'Though Little Mae does not know who you are . . .'

'We have money,' Butterfly said quickly. 'If you can get us birthchip blockers, and show us the exit, we'll pay you. But no questions.'

The woman nodded. 'Little Mae understands. She does not like questions either.' Her beady eyes still trained on Butterfly's face, she screeched loudly, '*Xiao zhu!* Tell the guards outside to not let anyone in. Little Mae has business to take care of.'

Half an hour later and 550 dollars lighter, birthchip blockers hung round Butterfly and Silver's necks as they followed Little Mae's tottering form down winding corridor after winding corridor towards the exit's secret location in the depths of the Limpets. Butterfly knew how lucky it was they were paid well as Elites. Five-hundred dollars was a small fortune to many people in Neo-Babel.

'Are you sure these will work?' Silver whispered.

Butterfly touched the little metal cube on the end of the long piece of cord looped round his neck. He didn't know the answer to her question, and there wasn't a way to test the birthchip blockers either. But he kept reminding himself birthchip tracking was supposedly limited within the walls of Neo-Babel. Why would birth-chips need to work outside the city if no one was allowed to leave?

'I think they're good,' he answered eventually. 'Don't worry about it.'

She shook her head. 'I can't help it. This is crazy.'

Butterfly touched her arm. His body tensed slightly, as it always did when he touched Silver. 'There's nothing crazy about it. We're just going to find your parents. So it involves leaving Neo. There used to be a time when people came and went from cities without any thought at all.'

Up ahead, the passage widened. Twists of metal tubing hung from the bare-earth ceiling, wires spouting from their ends. Little Mae slowed.

'Are we here?' Butterfly asked.

'Not yet, not yet.' She rubbed the rings on her fingers, the coins on her hat tinkling as she glanced round. 'Little Mae just thought she felt eyes on her.'

Silver looked round nervously. 'Eyes?' she whispered.

There was no one around, but distant shouts and sounds reached them from the rest of the Limpets.

'Don't worry,' said Butterfly. 'We're almost there. And remember what Little Mae gave us? I've got it right here.' He touched his trouser pocket.

For an extra 100 dollars, the woman had given them directions to the nearest settlement in the Outside. Having that little piece of paper tucked into his pocket seemed amazing to Butterfly. Just a few words and scribbled lines, and the world outside of the city had been made real, tangible. He wasn't sure he believed it. A settlement so close to Neo-Babel? Surely they'd have heard about it. But unlike most people, he'd never thought the Council's insistence that they were alone in the world was true. The Great Fall had broken the civilisations of the Mainland, Red Nations and Afrika, but it hadn't destroyed them completely. He was sure of it.

They followed Little Mae for another few minutes until she stopped at a junction, the corridor fraying into a tangle of winding pathways that disappeared into shadows. Noises seemed to echo out from them; shouts and calls and crashes, and even something which sounded like a scream. Butterfly felt a shiver of nervousness. The Limpets had been filled with noise since they'd arrived, but these sounded different.

'Is something going on?' he asked.

Little Mae waved a hand at him. 'Of course not!' she replied, heading down one of the pathways. 'The tunnels are just playing tricks with you.'

But after a few more minutes, Butterfly felt sure the noises were closer. They'd grown so loud he made out some of the words in the half-barked shouts and jeers; *don't belong here* and *leave* and *your precious Council District*, and he swallowed, realising with a sickening jolt what was happening –

They're here.

Silver turned to him, her eyes widening. 'Butterfly –'

'I know.'

'Our headstart?'

He checked his comms cuff. 'Gone. They must have noticed we were missing from the funeral.'

'But how do they know we're here?'

'It's the first place they'd look.' Butterfly pulled off

his backpack and reached inside, taking out a stungun. 'I packed these just in case. Get yours.'

He slipped his backpack back on. Little Mae had disappeared ahead of them round the corner of the tunnel, and he jogged over to her. The noises and voices seemed louder now, and he felt them seeping into his veins, turning his blood cold.

'Not long now, white boy,' the woman called over her shoulder as she heard him approach, still tottering quickly up the corridor.

He grabbed her arm. 'Please, Little Mae. Give us the directions to the exit.'

Her lips curled. 'Only *I* am to know the –'

'They're coming!' shouted Silver as she ran over, her stungun clutched in one hand. She grasped Little Mae's shoulder. 'Please. I know it's a lot to ask, but this is our only chance. We need to get to the exit *now*.'

Butterfly could see the desperation in Silver's eyes. He knew that she was terrified they were about to be caught, and their shot at leaving the city to find her parents would be ruined. He felt that same urgency too. All around them, running footsteps and voices bounced off the corridor's tall walls.

The old woman pushed Silver off her. 'We will get to the exit when *Little Mae* wants.'

With a growl, Silver raised her stungun, pressing it to the woman's neck. 'Tell us how to get there,' she hissed, 'or you'll have to deal with the people coming after us. And trust me – they won't bother with stunguns. They'll just go straight for the real thing.'

Little Mae narrowed her eyes. After a pause, she answered. 'Down this corridor, first right, second right, then take each right turn you come to.'

Just then, stabs of light slashed the corridor. A group of masked police rounded the corner, guns held in front of them, Neo-Babel's flag emblazoned across their chests.

'We've got them!' shouted one of the policemen.

For one split second, Butterfly stared back at them. Then he spun round, grabbing Silver's arm and dragging her down the tunnel away from the police as gunshots screamed past their heads. He glanced back to see Little Mae's tiny body keel over, a dark bloodstain blossoming between her shoulder blades.

They sped down the corridor, bullets following them. He almost missed the opening to the right but remembered Little Mae's directions at the last second and they ducked through it, not letting up their pace. They passed one tunnel to the right before turning at the next.

Then take each right turn you come to. Butterfly repeated the directions Little Mae had given them in his head as they ran. The noises of the police were still at their backs – crashing footsteps, frustrated shouts, bullets skidding off the walls – but it all seemed quieter now. Distant. Still, they didn't dare slow.

The passageway they were travelling down shrank into a plain, dirt-walled tunnel. It became narrower and lower. It felt like they were being squeezed alive, both by the size and the darkness. The lights that dangled from overhead were spaced far apart now, offering just a few small pools in the blackness. After what felt like hundreds of right turns later, Butterfly and Silver slowed their pace to a jog. Only when the noises of their own footsteps and breathing had quietened did they realise the tunnel was silent, and they finally came to a stop.

Silver leant against the earth wall, panting. 'I think we lost them.'

Butterfly moved forward, looking up the passageway ahead. What he saw made his stomach clench. Round the curve, the corridor grew even smaller, but instead of disappearing into shadows he could see some reflective material across it –

A metal door.

He gestured Silver over. 'Look,' he said.

Together they approached the door. At first they had to crouch, and when the ceiling pressed down even further they dropped to their hands and knees. When they reached the door, it was too dark to see anything, so Butterfly felt the cold metal with shaking hands, feeling for a handle. He panicked suddenly at the thought that perhaps the door was locked and Little Mae had the key, but then his fingers touched a latch and he pulled.

The stink of dry earth rushed out as the door opened. Shadows hung in the tunnel beyond.

'Is this it?' breathed Silver.

Butterfly crawled in. He slipped off his backpack and took out a torch. Its white light was harsh in the darkness. He trained it on the door and both of them gasped as they saw the words daubed on the metal in white paint:

Say goodbye! You are now leaving Neo!

They were both quiet, staring at the sign. Then Silver turned from the door to look at Butterfly, her dark eyes shining.

'Let's go get my parents,' she said, and crawled past the door, pulling it shut behind them.

12

Inside the Skylung

Akhezo woke yet again with a mouth full of bitter moss and clumps of stringy vegetation. He leant over the side of the bed and spat them out, scowling. There was no point using a bin. The whole place – the walls, the floor, even the odd assortment of furniture, all stolen of course – was covered in tangles of rotting vegetation. Plants even crawled over the window, bathing the room in a green, underwater glow. It smelt something horrendous too, but for a boy who had grown up in the Limpets it was near enough heaven.

For four years now, Akhezo had been a runner for the Pigeons, the biggest anti-birthchip group in Neo-Babel. Their aim, like all anti-birthchip groups, was to stop DNA streaming and abolish birthchips. But they were more extreme in their methods, and their hatred for the Council was marked in everything they did. They'd been the ones behind the Council District Fire of 13 September and the murder a year later of two senior Council members. And unlike other anti-birthchip groups, they'd never been caught.

Akhezo got out of bed and picked his way across the vegetation-tangled floor to the door out of the room. He headed down the curving corridor, bright light feeling its way through gaps in the vine-wreathed plastiglass wall to his right. At the end of the corridor, he shoved aside the tangle of hanging vines covering the door and stepped out onto the tiny platform.

Cool wind hit him, bursting with morning freshness. The roar of the city was distant up here, over 600 metres from the ground, but he was still struck by the noise of Neo-Babel that the vegetation-muffled pods of the skylung masked.

The Pigeons were named after their secret set-up in one of the five derelict skylungs along the river's Outer Circle. The silhouettes of the skylungs' huge, wheel-shaped structures with glass pods ringing their edges was known to every person in Neo-Babel. They had originally been created to be organic air purifiers, each housing thousands of plants to oxygenate the air from the Industrial Districts to keep the inner city pollution free. But after being abandoned due to energy constraints, the plants had over-grown and the skylungs had become vertical forests.

Akhezo looked out at the city. Almost directly below was the Outer Circle of the river, its waters already busy with boats, and beyond it the buildings of the inner city rose up like flat metal mountains, growing higher than the skylung in the densest parts. It was a beautiful view, but what he registered was not its beauty; it was hatred for the Council who controlled it. He took a dark pleasure in looking at the city and knowing that the Pigeons were going to be the ones to bring the Council down.

'Watch out,' he sniggered to himself. 'You never know when Pigeons are gonna come and crap all over you.'

Akhezo had been abandoned by his mother at birth, and a Red forge-owner had chanced upon the crying baby and claimed him. Then, four years ago, Domino had found him in the forge in the Limpets' lowest floor. He remembered Domino leering at him through the flames of the furnace he was pumping, the man's old face all wrinkly and grey-eyed. Domino had bought Akhezo off the Red, and though Akhezo had been wary at first, the minute he set foot in the skylung he knew things were looking up.

Domino had handed Akhezo a pair of shining white trainers. He'd never seen anything so beautiful in his life.

'What're they for?' he'd asked.

Domino had grinned. 'They're for running.'

Akhezo never had much brains or patience, but you didn't need any of that for running. All you needed were quick feet and an eye for spotting trouble. Those were two things most Limpets kids had. He'd spotted trouble the minute he'd laid eyes on those two Council-type snobs; a skinny little Red girl and a tall Mainland boy.

Just wait till I tell Cambridge 'bout you two, Akhezo thought, sniggering.

He crossed the balcony and started down a ladder strung between the pod he was on and the one to its left. The outside of the skylung was covered in these ladders, slides and ropes, enabling Pigeon members to move between the pods, and from the ground they were invisible, hidden among the dark mass of tangled vegetation that wreathed the skylungs like green cobwebs. Razor-edged leaves cut into his skin as he crossed the ladder. At his sides the world yawned open, a mouth waiting for food to be dropped into it.

'Not this time,' he taunted. He reached the balcony of the other pod and had just pulled himself up when the door in its wall burst open.

'Dammit!' A thin girl stormed out, curses flying from her mouth. She had pale skin, an assortment of piercings on her face and short, silvery hair, spiky and shot through with pink. She flung the door so violently it bounced back in her face, making her swear again.

Akhezo laughed.

The girl whipped her head towards him. 'Oh, shut it, Akhezo!' she snarled.

He made a face at her. 'What's got you so angry, Neve? One of the women try and get you into a dress again?'

'Gods, that was awful,' she snorted. She shoved her hands into the pockets of her baggy canvas overalls, which were slung over a big white T-shirt. 'Nah,' she explained. 'I was just trying to spy on Cambridge's meeting this morning. Something top secret apparently – though isn't it always? Domino found me in the corridor outside and . . . well, here I am.'

'Something top secret?' Akhezo said excitedly. 'Maybe it's related to my news. I've gotta see Cambridge.'

He made for the doorway but Neve darted in front of it. 'What've you got?' she asked, her eyes narrowing.

'Mind your own business.'

She smirked. 'It must be good. You'd tell me if it

92

wasn't. Come on, let's share it! Let's tell Cambridge it was our find, he'll –'

Akhezo pushed her aside. He got hold of the door handle, but as he pulled it open and stepped inside she pounced, jumping on his back. He crashed to the floor. Neve sat on him, laughing, then crying out as Akhezo reared up and grabbed her hair, yanking it hard. They fought scrappily until a croaky voice shouted at them from down the corridor.

'You little rats! Get up at once!'

They stood up quickly, smoothing down their clothes and plucking bits of vegetation out of their hair as Domino waddled towards them in his hunched-over way, pointing his finger with one thin, shaking hand, the other clutching at the hems of his tattered robes. His wrinkled face was flushed with anger. They stood up quickly, smoothing down their clothes and plucking bits of vegetation out of their hair.

'I should fling both of you off this pod!' Domino grabbed them by the scruffs of their collars. 'An important meeting, that was, and you two decide to have a spat on Cambridge's doorstep. Insolence!'

Akhezo didn't know what 'insolence' meant but he could tell Domino was angry. It wasn't good to anger Domino. As Cambridge's most trusted finder – someone who found and employed talent for the Pigeons – he had the ability to say who stayed and who went from the skylung. Akhezo wouldn't go back to the Limpets. He'd been born in the dirt there like a maggot, but he wouldn't live like one.

'Sorry, Domino,' Akhezo said. He pointed at Neve. 'But she started it!'

'What! It was all you, Akhezo, you big fat liar –'

'Silence!' Domino croaked, as loudly as his old lungs allowed him. 'The meeting is over now. If neither one of you little rats has anything to report to Cambridge, then get lost.'

'I've got something,' said Akhezo quickly.

Domino nodded. He pushed Akhezo roughly down the corridor. 'All right, boy. Come with me.'

'Hey, what about me!' Neve spluttered from behind them.

The old man flapped a hand at her. 'Go away, girl! And don't let me catch you skulking out here again, or I'll throw you off the pod ledge for real this time.'

Akhezo grinned. He glanced back and could almost see the steam coming out of Neve's ears.

Cambridge's private rooms were the only place in the skylung where the plants had been cleared completely. The rank smell of rotting vegetation was kept at bay by incense and scented pouches hanging from the walls and ceiling. The place was almost homely; an assortment of furniture, piles of stolen books. Birds twittering in pretty cages.

Domino led Akhezo to a meeting room at the back of the pod and knocked on the door.

'Come in!' called a bright voice.

Inside, a man was standing on a table that took up most of the room. He was middle-aged, tall and slim, with a handsome face and floppy, golden brown hair. He wore a shabby tunic and robe that swirled round his ankles as he paced across the wooden surface.

'Ah, Domino, Akhezo!' He jumped off the table, flashing them a wide smile. 'Sorry about that. I find I think better *on* the table rather than at it. I, ah, thought the meeting was over?'

Domino made a grumbling sound. 'Akhezo has information for you, Cambridge. Please sit down and listen.'

'Of course, of course!' Cambridge made an apologetic face, though when Domino had shuffled past, he caught Akhezo's eyes with his own bright green pair and winked.

Once they had all sat, Cambridge leant forward across the table and said with childish eagerness, 'Speak up, Akhezo! What information do you have for me?'

Akhezo shifted, a little nervous at having the rapt attention of the leader of the Pigeons. 'Well, I . . . I was on running duty when I came across these two Council snobs. They wanted to find Little Mae, so I thought I'd take them to her personally. You know, find out what they wanted without asking.'

Cambridge clapped his hands. 'Good, good! You're a Pigeon through and through.'

Akhezo flushed with pride. He grew bolder, recounting his story hurriedly. 'Little Mae let me stay in the room as they talked, and I overheard them telling her they wanted to . . . to leave Neo! They wanted birthchip blockers, the directions to the nearest village in the Outside. Everything. Little Mae took me aside and said she wouldn't turn on the birthchip blockers until you said so.'

Cambridge jumped up from his stool. 'This is it!' he cried. He grabbed Akhezo and shook him, his eyes wide with excitement.

'Slow down, Cambridge,' Domino wheezed, but Cambridge just went and grabbed him too, laughing.

'Ah, this is it, my dear friends. This is what we've been waiting for!' And without another word, he hurtled out of the room, laughing and whooping all the way.

With an exasperated sigh, Domino grabbed Akhezo's arm and dragged him after Cambridge. They found the man bouncing around a large room covered in screens of all sizes, displaying complex map-like images in black and white. Red dots flashed on some of the screens. Their glow lit his laughing face as he turned to them, and for a moment he looked almost mad in the ghostly white light.

'Look!'

Akhezo followed Cambridge's pointing finger to one of the screens. Its image was less cluttered than the other ones. There were only two lines, marking some sort of tunnel, and he realised straight away what it was.

'The tunnel out of the city!' he gasped. Towards the edge of the screen were two flashing red dots. 'Are those the Council members?'

Cambridge nodded. 'I just checked the birthchip database and it's them all right. Though it's a shame I can't see her pretty face – she looked lovely in the chai bar. Just as they had described. Silver and her friend Butterfly, our little runaways. Our homing pigeons, doing exactly what we wanted.'

'What *we* wanted?' asked Akhezo eagerly.

Domino spluttered. 'Really, Cambridge! This is top-secret information. We should not be giving it to this child.'

'This *child* has brought us the news that we've been waiting for,' said Cambridge, ignoring Domino. He clutched Akhezo tightly by the shoulders. 'The news that will change everything! It's time, my dear boy. It's all begun. And I'll need you to help me – there is a lot to do.' He lowered his voice and said almost reverently, 'The time has come for the Pigeons to fly.'

13

The Tunnel

The tunnel out of the city was long and deep. After hours in the dim light, her senses clogged with the earthy smell of soil and the feel of dirt under her fingernails, Silver felt as though she'd been crawling there her whole life. By the time it grew tall enough for them to stand, both she and Butterfly were covered in soil. She stretched, sighing in pleasure as her muscles relaxed, her joints easing.

'A break?' asked Butterfly.

'Yes, please.' Silver pulled off her backpack and sat down against the bare-earth wall. 'What did you pack in these things? Never heard of the term travel light?'

He smiled wryly. 'It's hard to pack when you're going somewhere you know nothing about.'

'Sorry,' she said. 'I didn't think.'

'It's fine.' Butterfly sat down beside her and opened his backpack. 'Let's see. There's our Elite uniforms – we should probably change into them soon. Some medical equipment. A couple of knives. Our stunguns. Material for blankets and hammocks. And here.' He pulled out a box and passed it to her. 'The most important thing of all.'

Silver laughed as she opened it; the box was stuffed with food. 'Please tell me there's chilli rice crackers in there.'

Butterfly smiled. 'How could I not bring your favourite food?'

After a quick snack, they picked up their torches and set off again. Butterfly consulted the piece of paper with directions Little Mae had given them as they went. The old woman hadn't wanted to give it to them until after they'd reached the tunnel entrance, but he'd offered more money to have it right away. Silver couldn't believe how lucky they'd been for that. If Little Mae had refused, that piece of paper would have been left there lying in the Limpets with her dead body.

She shivered, remembering what had happened to Little Mae. Her small body keening forward with the momentum of the bullet, a patch of blood blooming across her back. It reminded her of Tanaka. She felt a fresh wave of shame then at how she'd failed the Council that day on Hemmingway House. Now, because of her, someone else was dead. One thing she was certain of was that the two people she couldn't afford to fail were her parents.

Silver pointed to the piece of paper in Butterfly's hand. 'How much longer?'

'There's a rest stop about three miles ahead. We can get some sleep there. After that, it's half a day's walk to the end of the tunnel.'

'So we'll be out of here in around twenty-four hours?'

'Hopefully.' He smiled.

Just like that, the thought of sunshine on her face and the fresh smell of wind and Butterfly's beautiful, fleeting smile made all the tiredness and fear disappear from Silver's body, and for one small, perfect moment, she felt like everything was going to be all right.

They spent the night at the rest stop, a small room off to the side of the tunnel with a couple of makeshift bedpods carved into its walls. Butterfly was so exhausted from the long hours of travelling that he fell asleep as soon as he lay down. But just as quickly as sleep came, so did the dream. The dream that haunted him most nights, half memory, half regret –

The dream about the explosion . . .

Butterfly left his family's apartment and went down the elevator to the condominium's foyer, just as he had done that day. He'd spent the afternoon with his parents and his newborn sister Emeli; just a small, soap-smelling, swaddled thing, ruddy cheeked and beautiful.

It was the first and last time he had seen her.

In the foyer. Watery light filtered through the glass doors. A motorised rickshaw waited outside. As Butterfly stepped out of the building, the driver spotted him and hastily stuffed the rest of the chicken-rice ball in his mouth, gave a little wave and ricey grin. Behind him, half hidden by a tatty curtain of material drawn across the opening, one of the junior Elite guardians sat on the passenger bench. Butterfly watched his shadowy outline, saw the tiny burst of flame as the guardian lit a portable shisha.

He felt that same hot flush of unease in his chest he had felt that day. Go back inside, *a voice in his head was urging him.* Something's not right. *So he turned and ran back into the foyer.*

He'd pictured this moment, dreamt of it, a thousand times before. What happened each time changed slightly. Sometimes he pulled off his shirt and opened his wings and flew up the stairwell, reaching the apartment door just as the explosion started. Sometimes he got inside first, and then it happened. Sometimes he ran, and halfway up the stairs he felt the shudder, saw the crack of white that split across the ceiling, debris punching his body. Sometimes he couldn't walk or fly up the stairs at all, and just stood at the bottom, looking up with a sickly taste of fear in his mouth.

But every time he was the teenage Butterfly, his current age, and not the young child of six he had been the day it happened. The child that had got into the rickshaw and, just as it began to move, had pulled back the curtain and saw the apartment burst from the inside out.

This time, he just stood at the bottom of the stairwell and waited for the shudder to come.

When he woke, Butterfly felt more tired than he had before sleeping. The burst of the explosion still prickled behind his eyelids. He pressed his thumbs against them, trying to get rid of the horrible image and the breathless feeling the dream always left him with. Silver had curled next to him while he had been asleep. Her burrowed face was turned towards him, soft in sleep. Her closeness calmed him, dimming the roar of the explosion and the bursting of the fire behind his eyelids until they'd drained away. Until the quietness of the cocooned space of the bedpod wrapped its arms round him, and the dream was gone.

Butterfly shook Silver gently. 'Wake up. We'd better go.'

They changed into their Elite uniforms and headed back into the tunnel. They made good time, walking steadily in silence, and Butterfly was so focused on putting one foot in front of the other, hour after hour, that when the beam of light from his torch hit something solid in the path up ahead, he didn't notice at first. Then he focused properly on what he was seeing and stopped still, touching Silver's arm.

'What?' she asked.

He pointed ahead. They squinted into the darkness of the tunnel, and saw something flat and metal; a door. As they approached it, their torchlight slashed across a line of words painted across the metal:

Welcome to the Outside!

This is it, thought Butterfly, feeling a thrill of excitement, his heart start to race. With Silver, he gripped the handle and pushed. The door opened into more darkness. Butterfly's heart fell, but a second later he felt a rush of air hit his face, cool and crisp. Up ahead, the tunnel seemed lighter too. He turned to Silver and they burst out laughing.

'Race you!' She grinned, and the words had barely left her mouth before she was off.

Butterfly ran after her, the light at the end of the

tunnel yawning open, turning blue as he got close enough to tell it was the sky. After what felt like days of darkness, he was overwhelmed by how blue it looked. He ran faster, panting as the incline got steeper, and before he knew it he was clambering out into sunlight, into the world –

Into the Outside.

Part II
OUTSIDE

14

Trapped

Silver and Butterfly stood rooted to where they had emerged from the tunnel, a gust of wind hitting their dusty faces and open land stretching out before them as though some god had unfolded a map at their feet and the world rolled out.

They'd exited the tunnel at the top of a long shoulder of hill. From their high vantage point Silver could see for miles; an emerald sea of grass and forests, the glittering snake of the river winding through it all. The grass was long and green. Pockets of flowers dotted the landscape, and even the dark swatch of trees at the closest forest border was coloured with more shades of green than Silver knew existed. Above, the sky was a flat lid of blue. The horizon shimmered in the distance, its pale grey slither like a mouth waiting to smile.

Looking out at the world, she felt a strange ache in her stomach. Having spent her whole life surrounded by walls, it was a scene she'd never quite been able to imagine. But now she was outside the city and inside the huge arms of the world, and its size lapped at her like a wave. She felt. dizzy. Then she turned, and saw Neo-Babel.

The city was unrecognisable from the outside. A wide grey-black scar across the earth, with the tall, blockish shapes of the inner city buildings rising up behind the walls and crowding the skyline with their beetle-shell skins. Windows glittered in the sunlight.

'Ugly, isn't it?' said Butterfly.

Silver shook her head. 'Can you believe this?' She swung her arms wide, laughing. 'We're outside Neo. *Outside Neo*. I never thought I'd say that!' She whooped. Her voice was swallowed by the space.

Butterfly grinned. 'Not loud enough.'

He jumped up, letting out a cry, and suddenly they were both punching the air, dancing, laughing and whooping and shouting out at the top of their lungs, giddy with the ridiculousness of it all, the two of them, here, outside the city, away from everything they had ever known.

When she started feeling light-headed, Silver dropped to the ground, smiling up at the sky. She took a long, deep breath. Now she was outside of Neo-Babel, away from the pollution and dirt and noise and people, she could smell the air's natural scent. It was clean, fresh, sweetened by the grass and trees and sunshine. It was perfect.

She looked over at Butterfly. He'd pulled off his backpack and was reaching an arm round for the zip that ran down the material of his jumpsuit between his shoulder blades.

'Do you mind?' he asked, catching her looking.

'Of course not,' she said, knowing immediately what he meant.

No sooner were the words out of her mouth when a

108

pair of knife-edge thin wings unfolded from his back. Two tall, arced wings layered over their smaller lower-half counterparts, which had the telltale teardrops of butterfly wings. They were stronger than they looked. Their silicone-aluminium blend gave them strength without sacrificing lightness, though looking at them now with the sunlight shining through them they looked more like a thin film of oil on water than wings.

Butterfly smiled, closing his eyes. 'I won't be long.' A quick crouch and beat of his wings later, and he was off.

Silver watched him fly through the air, getting smaller and smaller until he was just a flick of dust curling on the wind's waves. Then she lay back down on the grass. She thought how nothing would ever feel as good again as sunlight on her skin and grass under her fingers and the taste of summer in the air. For a while, everything else fell away. Tanaka was still alive. Her parents were still safe inside Neo-Babel. Being here in the Outside was as normal and natural as breathing.

A few minutes later, Butterfly returned. He sat down, running a hand through his brown hair. It was even messier than usual, ruffled by the wind.

'Good fly?' asked Silver.

'*Best* fly.'

She stared at him. She felt as though something was off, and sat up quickly, realising what it was. 'You're smiling,' she said, almost accusatory.

And he was. Not Butterfly's usual flash of a smile, but a slow, small one, hovering on his lips like a secret that tasted good.

'You don't know how good it felt to be up there,' he said. 'No walls, no buildings. No stupid flight director shouting in my ear. Just the rush of the wind and my own heartbeat.' He nodded at the city, miles away in the distance. 'It was weird though, seeing Neo from above. Did you ever think about how it would look from the Outside?'

Silver shrugged. 'I never really thought about it.'

Nobody inside could see much of the Outside. The huge wall encircling the city had no windows or holes. Even the waterfall where the river exited Neo-Babel was covered by it, the wall sitting across its surface like a tightly shut mouth. The tallest buildings in the inner city had a view past the walls, but they were too far away to see much; just the vast, dusty wastelands surrounding the immediate vicinity of the city, which had been chemically dehydrated to make surveillance easier, and the green swathe of distant hills and forests.

'Do you want to stay here for a bit?' asked Butterfly.

Silver shook her head. Looking at the city made her think of why they'd left it in the first place, and she felt anxious to find her parents now. She pushed herself off the ground and brushed down her clothes. 'Let's go.'

Following Little Mae's directions, they made their way to the nearby settlement. At first they made good time, and Silver found herself enjoying the journey. The undulating landscape of lazy, sloping hills, touched by the ribbon of the river at their bases was beautiful to walk through, and she felt excited about the prospect of finding her parents. Butterfly had estimated they would reach the settlement by nightfall, and that thought kept her moving. But the directions grew increasingly difficult to follow. After a few hours, the green hills and dark swathes of forest turned the landscape into an endless sea of green. Silver couldn't tell which direction was which. Even the wide black mouth of the city behind them disappeared as they descended into deep valleys.

It was worse when night came. Thick ochre shadows slid across the landscape like spilt oil, until the whole land was cloaked in darkness. When they entered a forest, the trees edged closer and closer. The leafy ceiling began to crowd out even the moon's light. Strange, night-time sounds cut through the darkness; screeches, rustling, the sudden flappings of birds erupting from resting places as they passed.

'Let's try our torches,' Butterfly said after Silver had tripped over something in the darkness for what felt like the millionth time. 'Little Mae didn't say how far out of the city the energy grid covers. We could still have been using it while we were in the tunnel, so they might have some reserve power left.'

But the torches didn't turn on no matter how many times Silver flicked the switch.

'That's just great,' she snapped, stuffing the torch back into her backpack. 'Now what?'

'Do you want to stop for the night?'

'No,' she said, walking on quickly. 'Let's just –'

The ground beneath Silver fell away.

She screamed, falling for a few seconds before smashing

into the hard floor of the earth, her shoulder jarring at the impact, her lungs tightening as they emptied of air. She gasped. Leaves and branches rustled and cracked as she twisted round in pain, clutching her side which had caught the fall. The loamy smell of damp dirt filled the air.

'Silver?' Butterfly's eyes flashed in the darkness. He helped her up. 'Are you all right?'

Tilting her head back, she saw above a circle of speckled sky, spots of moonlight winking through leaves. 'Yes.' She nodded breathlessly, rubbing her side. 'You?'

'I'm all right. Give me a second, I'll fly up and take a look.'

Butterfly pulled off his backpack and reached behind him. His wings whipped out, shiny and silvery in the dappled darkness. He flew up into the air. A moment later, he cursed loudly.

'What's wrong?' called Silver.

'There's some mesh material covering the pit.' He grunted with effort. 'I can't get it off.'

'Can we cut it?'

Butterfly flew down quickly. 'Good idea.' He got a knife from his backpack and flew back into the air, but came down after just a few moments. 'It's some rein-forced material. The knife can't cut it.'

Silver looked round at the pit. 'What *is* this, anyway?' she asked, walking to one side and pressing her hand against the earthy wall.

'Looks like some kind of trap.'

'*Whose* trap?'

'The villagers, maybe. To hunt wild animals.'

Silver felt like a wild animal then, trapped at the bottom of some pit with its claggy, earthy smell and the darkness so thick that she could barely see the broken face of the moon far above.

No, she thought. *I'm not an animal. I'm human –*
I am an Elite.

She refused to give up. 'Maybe there's another way out,' she said, running her hands along the side of the pit, searching for an opening. 'Help me check.'

But after half an hour of thorough searching, neither of them had found anything.

Butterfly sighed. 'Let's wait until morning. We'll be able to see better in daylight, and we need to rest anyway.' He settled down against the side of the pit and pulled out the fold of soft material inside his backpack to use as a blanket.

Silver sat next to him, slipping off her backpack. She brushed dried mud from her hands. 'Do you think we'll be all right?' she whispered. The sounds of the forest seemed to echo in the deep pit, making her feel exposed and vulnerable. 'Whoever made this trap might be coming to claim their catch.'

'Then we'll have to deal with them when they come,' Butterfly answered, his voice quiet. He paused. 'We've got our knives.'

Silver opened her backpack and felt around inside until her hand clasped the cold metal of the knife Butterfly had packed. She pulled it out. Moonlight caught on the long blade. Her hand tightened around the handle. In the morning, they'd find a way out of this trap. And if they didn't have until then, and someone came for them before –

She clutched the knife close to her chest.

Nothing would stop her from finding her parents.

15

The Temple of the Fat Wives

That night, Akhezo made his way down to one of the central slides of the skylung to the building at its base. He shot out of the bottom of the chute and crashed into the wall opposite it, his landing softened by a pile of old mattresses.

'You're late.'

Domino stood in the corner of the room. He wore his usual clothes; a greasy set of tunic and robes, moth-bitten and tattered, with worn leather sandals. Akhezo scrambled to his feet.

'As you were told yesterday,' Domino started, turning to leave the room, 'you'll be overseeing an information trans-action between Cambridge and a Council member tonight.'

Akhezo followed Domino quickly, eager to impress. A couple of days after reporting those Council snobs to Cambridge and he still had to keep pinching himself to believe everything that was happening. He'd expected a reward, but he'd thought it would be something along the lines of a new pair of trainers. Not a rank upgrade within the Pigeons to Cambridge's personal assistant on a top-secret project, the Pigeons' final flight, and jobs as important as the one tonight.

Neve hadn't been happy. She'd spent hours pleading with Domino for a part in the whole thing.

'Everyone will be needed soon, just be patient, you little rat!' he kept saying, and that would shut her up. But as soon as Domino's back was turned she'd send Akhezo a scathing look, her eyes dangerous slits.

The truth was, Akhezo *had* been meaning to tell Neve what'd happened after he returned from Cambridge's quarters, but when he'd found her waiting in his room, her face glowing with anticipation, something had stopped him. A slithering feeling in his stomach and a voice that whispered, *Why tell her? She doesn't deserve it.* You *found them.* You *reported them to Cambridge.*

Domino led Akhezo down a corridor to a large hall dappled with moonlight. When the skylungs were still running, this building would have housed offices and service rooms. Now they too had been taken over by plants, seeds from the skylung dropping through the cracked roof and springing up a forest amid the metal and plastiglass. Slivers of silver worked their way through the foliage.

'I was thinking,' started Akhezo cautiously as they crossed the hall. 'In an information transfer, what sorta things can the Council really tell us? I mean, why would they give anything at all? Couldn't they just take the information by force? Just asking out of curiosity, of course,' he added quickly. 'And since *you're* the person who's in the know around here . . .'

Domino slowed his pace and Akhezo grinned. Flattery; it worked every time.

The old man scratched his backside. 'Well, it won't harm for you to understand the theory. Here, boy, help me with this.'

They had reached a small workers' room at the far side of the hall, beneath which was the entrance to the tunnel that led from the skylung to a quiet part of the Limpets. It was the only route the Pigeons used to leave the skylung. They pulled at the rusty metal hatch in the middle of the floor and it swung open with a loud metallic screech. Domino lowered himself down into the darkness. Akhezo followed, stepping onto the ladder rung and shutting the hatch above him. At the bottom of the ladder, he jumped onto the staircase leading to the tunnel.

'See, the Council can't go round threatening its entire people,' explained Domino as they started down the staircase. His voice was so wheezy from exertion that he had to stop for breath after every few words. 'Well, it could, but it wouldn't last very long, and the Council wouldn't want to upset everyone and end up being thrown out into the wastelands now, would it? No. The Council has to be *careful*. Rule by force for too long, and that force would be turned against them. Therefore, they prey on the ones that can't fight back and no one cares enough to fight on their behalf – Limpets rats like you.'

Akhezo bristled at this but bit his tongue. The shifting shadows in the stairwell seemed to seep into his mind, darkening his thoughts. *You useless old man*, he thought, staring at Domino's back. *Just one push and you'd fall down these stairs and crack your rotting old head.*

'If the Council can't get everything they want by force,' continued Domino, 'they have to use other tactics. Spying's one, but that'll only get them so far. Neo's a big place, and its people are clever. They won't take kindly to such invasion of privacy. That's why it's illegal to track everyone's birthchips without an arrest warrant. It'd cause a riot if they did. So some things they do under the guise of better intentions. You've heard of their Elites, boy?'

Akhezo scowled. 'Of *course* I've –'

'Then maybe you've figured out that birthchip streaming conveniently gives the Council permission to take control of the strongest, most intelligent people. Prevent them from fighting for the other side. That's what the Elites are really – the Council's lapdogs.' Domino paused to take a deep breath, clutching the railing lining the staircase. 'There's other things the Council can do too to get things without force. For example, maintaining relationships with other powerful individuals and groups in Neo. That's one of their most important tactics. And the key to it is give and take, see? Neither side of the relationship should think the other more powerful. There has to be respect.'

Respect; it was a strange word. Akhezo didn't quite understand it. He understood admiration, awe. He felt that way about Cambridge. Sometimes, when the light hit her right, he felt that way about Neve. But he didn't understand respect. Everyone was born into this world the same. Surely anyone had a right to take what they wanted?

They descended the rest of the staircase in silence. The stairwell at the bottom was cluttered. Piles of boxes and crates were set against the wall, and bikes and a small rickshaw leant beside the tunnel to the Limpets.

Domino climbed onto the rickshaw's passenger bench. 'Well, what are you waiting for?' he croaked. 'Get on the bike, you lazy boy!'

Cycle it yourself, you stupid old man, Akhezo wanted to say, but he swallowed his retort, getting onto the bicycle seat with a sneer Domino couldn't see. As he cycled down the long tunnel, the rickshaw sliding in and out of the puddles of light from neon strips on the walls, Akhezo thought greedily about how it wouldn't be long before *he* was the one in the passenger seat, being driven around by the kind of people he'd never let himself become.

Akhezo stood beside Domino on a docking platform jutting from an inner-city curve of the river. Just two hours' rickshaw ride away through busy night-time traffic and they were in a whole other world. Akhezo had never been to the inner city before. Most of his running assignments were in and around the Limpets, or in the streets of the residential condominiums that crowded the inner edge of the river's Outer Circle. He'd never even left the Limpets before joining the Pigeons. Now, standing here in the heart of the city, he understood why no one cared about the slums. Who'd waste their time thinking about that place when they had all of this to experience?

Lights illuminated everything in a rainbow glow; boats bobbing on the river, tall buildings interlaced with bridges, the quick flashes of air-trams speeding between them. Weaving through it all were hundreds of people, wearing fashions Akhezo had never seen in his life.

'The Temple of the Fat Wives,' said Domino, gesturing to the boat floating on the water in front of them. He snorted. 'Ridiculous name, but apt. The two women who run it are indeed huge.'

The Temple of the Fat Wives was one of Neo-Babel's most popular floating shisha cafes. A squat, two-tiered boat, half hidden by a sweet-smelling cloud, it looked like any other shisha boat. It would have been unremarkable were it not for the intricate carvings etched deeply into its smoke-stained plastiwood sides and the delicate minarets adorning its roof. Coloured lanterns were strung across the boat's outer surfaces, dappling puddles of multicoloured light in the water below.

Akhezo was about to ask more about its strange name when he spotted Cambridge approaching them along the street. He was hunched over like Domino, the hood of a cloak shadowing his face, but Akhezo would recognise those bright grey eyes anywhere.

'Hey! Cambri—'

Domino clapped a hand over his mouth. 'Imbecile! Cambridge is in his undercover identity as a Limpets gang-leader. You are not supposed to know him. Don't even look at him again tonight, you hear me, stupid boy?'

Akhezo nodded, averting his eyes. Cambridge walked

past them as though nothing had happened and disappeared into the boat.

Domino pressed his mouth to Akhezo's ear. His breath was hot and sour. 'You're to hide yourself near enough to see what's going on between Cambridge and the Council member, remember. Not to hear,' he added in a growl. 'Just close enough to see. The Council member might have a spy of his own, so don't draw any attention to yourself. If you think Cambridge is in danger, move closer to check, but *do not* act rashly unless it is absolutely necessary.' He let go of Akhezo's mouth. 'Got all that?'

'Yes, Domino.'

'Right. Well, I'll be waiting at the Nasir. It's a cafe in that little arcade down there.' Domino rubbed his hands together and licked his cracked lips. 'They have a rum baklava I'm more than partial to. If all goes well on the boat, maybe we can get you one, ey?'

Akhezo raised his eyebrows. 'Bakla-what?'

'Ah, never mind, boy.'

After a quick scowl at Domino's retreating back, Akhezo crossed the walkway that led from the dock to the boat. Giddy shisha scents filled the air. He made his way further into the boat, searching for Cambridge. The place was packed. Every inch of the blackened floors occupied by smokers. Some stood round tall shisha poles with multiple smoking funnels, while others sat on cushions next to bulbous pipes secured to the floor with metal, leaf-shaped cases. The pots of water at the base of each shisha bubbled noisily. Ornately carved lanterns hung from the walls, their coloured windows giving the whole place a gaudy, under-water feel, and the light glancing and shimmering off the mosaic-tiled walls and ceiling was mesmerising.

Akhezo went up to the boat's top deck. A breeze brushed through the smoke-clouds hanging over it, cool and refreshing. He spotted Cambridge immediately at the back of the boat, sitting on a cushion in front of one of the flower-shaped shisha pots. Cambridge's hood was low over his face. Opposite him sat – Akhezo presumed – the Council member Cambridge was meeting with. He was a thin young man with a shaved head that gleamed in the moonlight.

Akhezo took place at a shisha stand a few metres away. He tried to do as he'd been told, watching Cambridge and the Council member out of the corner of his eyes, but he'd never had a lot of patience. After just a few minutes, he found himself getting restless. He wondered what they were saying. *Why not go listen?* he thought. *After all, I'm Cambridge's personal assistant now. He's gonna tell me what happened anyway.*

Akhezo stepped off his stool. Edging round a group of chatting smokers, he crept towards an unused shisha pot behind Cambridge and crouched in the shadow of one of its large metal leaves.

Cambridge's voice was just audible over the noisy bubbling of the shisha pot. 'You can check on your birthchip trackers – their names are Silver and Butterfly. All their ID information is there.'

A pause, then a soft voice belonging to the shaven-headed young man from the Council. 'We thought as much. I will have to confirm it for myself before we can finalise your payment, however.'

A group of smokers nearby burst into laughter and Akhezo missed the next part of the conversation. When they settled down he heard the Council member speaking again.

'You don't want money for this exchange?' There was a tone of surprise in his voice.

'No,' replied Cambridge. 'It's, ah, slightly unusual, I understand. But this sort of information, if it got out to others . . . I thought you'd appreciate my secrecy in coming straight to you.'

'Of course. What is it then that you want?'

'Materials,' said Cambridge simply.

Akhezo felt disappointed by this answer. He'd expected something exciting, something important. But Cambridge just wanted a bunch of dumb materials? For what, patching up holes in the skykungs or building new walkways? Those sorts of things were usually stolen or bought by the Pigeons' salvage teams.

'I would've thought a Limpets gang-leader has access to any materials he wants,' the Council member said.

'Yes,' replied Cambridge. 'But, not in the quantity we need.'

'I see. What is this material, then?'

His heart thudding, Akhezo leant forward, eager to hear Cambridge's answer –

A hand grasped the back of his T-shirt.

'Hey!' he cried as he was lifted into the air, forgetting he was meant to be undercover.

Cambridge and the Council member looked round at his shout. Akhezo caught the hard-edged look in the shaven-headed Council member's eyes before he was spun in mid-air and found himself face to face with an enormous woman. Her dark skin was adorned with gold tattoos. Her bulbous lips, painted a gaudy purple, stretched into a smile.

'Calpol!' The woman held Akhezo out for another woman wobbling towards them. She looked almost identical to the one holding him, but instead of purple her lips were painted orange. 'Look what I've found!'

'Oh, Lemsip, my dear,' simpered the woman in a shrilly voice, fluttering her eyelashes. 'A street urchin, by the looks of it.'

These must be the fat wives Domino told me 'bout, Akhezo thought, glaring at them. *He's right – they* are *fat. They look like they've eaten their own husbands.*

'A street urchin on the finest shisha boat in all Neo?' said the one with purple lips. 'We simply cannot have that!'

The women bristled, their chins wobbling in agreement.

'You know what we do with street urchins, don't you, my dear Calpol?'

'Of course, dear Lemsip!' The orange-lipped one lunged towards Akhezo, her fat lips stretched in a nasty smile. 'We throw them *overboard*!' She trilled the last word, grabbing the boy from the other woman and wobbling to the side of the boat.

Akhezo squirmed in her arms, but her fingers were

tight, pinchy things, and before he knew it he was being held over the side. The last thing he saw was the glassy black water of the river below before he was thrown into it, splashing and screaming and cursing, and wishing he'd learnt how to swim.

16

Butterfly's Ghosts

Midnight, the Outside. Voices scratched in the still and darkness of the night.

'Careful. Stay low.'

'Do you think they're asleep? Looks like it. That boy's snoring.'

'Yes, it seems so. Keep your voice down, we don't want to wake them. Search the ground for anything they've got with them. Take away any weapons.'

Butterfly stirred, waking from a dreamless sleep. He knew instantly there were people around him. He felt rather than saw their shapes in the darkness, and he heard a man with the lilting accent of Eastern Mainlanders say, 'If she has a knife, he might have one too.'

Butterfly's hand went straight to the knife he'd slid into the belt of his jumpsuit before going to sleep. He glanced over to where Silver lay beside him. It looked like she was asleep, but then she opened her eyes. In the moonlight, the whites shone bright and glassy. Her eyes flicked to the side, towards where the voices were coming from, and Butterfly gave a tiny nod. He knew exactly what she meant.

The next moment, the two of them sprang to their

feet. Butterfly brandished his knife as Silver grabbed one of the people, closing her arm around their neck, a knife also clutched in her other hand. There was scuffling as the other person backed to the opposite side of the pit, then a click. Light speared the darkness.

'Wait. Please!' shouted the man across from them in the Eastern Mainland accent Butterfly had heard earlier. He was tall, a curly beard covering half his face, and had dark, deep-set, intelligent eyes. He levelled the torch as Butterfly rounded on him. 'We are not here to harm you.'

'Then why are you taking our weapons?' growled Butterfly, squinting against the torchlight.

The girl Silver had locked under one arm spoke. 'Let me go. We can explain.' She was young, just ten or eleven, but there was a hardness in her voice that made her seem mature beyond her years. Long red hair curled round a soft, pretty face.

Butterfly knew he wouldn't be able to hurt her. 'Let her go,' he said to Silver.

As soon as she was free, the girl scampered over to the man on the other side of the pit. He bent down, curling an arm round her.

'Thank you,' he said, looking up at them. He hesitated. 'I have to ask – are you from Neo?'

'Yes,' said Butterfly.

'Then are you here to kill us?'

Silver's sharp intake of breath was loud in the quiet of the night. Butterfly felt his own heart clench.

'No,' he answered quietly.

The girl edged forward, tugging on the man's hand. 'I think they're telling the truth, Yasir. They don't have the face-mask things and they only have knives. No guns or anything.'

The man nodded. 'But we can never be too sure.' He gestured towards Butterfly and Silver. 'Your clothes remind us of them.'

'We're not here to kill you,' said Silver, stepping up. 'Or anything like that. We just want to find my parents. They were taken from Neo about a week ago. Neo-Babel, I mean. The city. Have you heard anything about them, or seen anyone come through here?'

'A few new villagers have arrived in the last week,' said the man. 'But they are Mainlanders. I wouldn't have thought –'

'No,' she said quickly, shaking her head. 'It's not them.'

'Well, perhaps they know something,' the man suggested.

Silver turned to Butterfly, her eyes bright with hope. 'It's worth asking,' she whispered. She turned back to the man. 'Could you take us to them?'

He seemed to think about it for a moment before nodding. 'Of course.' He bowed curtly. 'My name is Yasir. This is Emeli.'

Silver and Butterfly gave them their names, returning Yasir's bow.

'Wait,' said Emeli. 'Did you say *Butterfly*?'

Butterfly nodded. 'It's a little unusual.'

'It's not that,' she said. 'It's just . . . my big brother was called Butterfly. But we left him in Neo when I was a baby.'

Coldness like a fist of ice clenched Butterfly's stomach. He stepped back, his eyes fixed on the girl. Red hair, ten or eleven years old, and a name, a name he had forced himself to forget.

It can't be.

When Yasir had said the girl was called Emeli, he hadn't given it a second thought. It was a fairly common Mainland name. But as he took in her appearance, the baby in his dreams, in his memory, shifted and grew, turning into the beautiful little girl in front of him.

'Emeli,' Butterfly whispered. 'Emeli.'

The girl turned to Yasir. 'He's acting weird.'

'Emeli,' Butterfly said again.

Silver, who had been watching the exchange with a confused look on her face, suddenly clapped a hand to her mouth. 'Oh my gods,' she breathed. 'No, it can't be. She's . . . she's got to be a ghost.'

The girl put her hands on her hips, looking indignant. 'I'm definitely *not* a ghost!'

'Emeli,' said Butterfly, taking a tentative step towards her. 'What are your parents' names? Can you tell me?'

The girl looked back at him, her eyes widening. She twisted her hands together, shifting uncomfortably. Her voice was quiet when she finally answered, but Butterfly still heard what she said as though she had whispered it right into his ear. 'My father, he . . . he died a few months ago. But my mother's name is Eleanor. We call her Leanor.'

It was as though everything else in the world had fallen away. Butterfly stared at her, unable to process what was happening, and felt a dropping sensation in his stomach. 'Leanor,' he whispered. 'Mum.'

And then he fell backwards, spinning into black.

When he came to, Butterfly felt the warmth of blankets and the softness of a mattress beneath him. The air was sweet with a strangely familiar floral fragrance. A patch of coolness ran across his forehead, and he lifted a hand to feel a wet towel someone had placed there.

'You're awake, then.'

He opened his eyes.

The ghost of his mother sat beside the bed. She looked just as he remembered; milky skin, a bob of red hair curling down into large, clever blue eyes. A round chin that curved like the underside of the moon.

'You're dead,' he said.

The ghost smiled, and her eyes filled with tears. They trembled in the tender yellow light of the lantern hanging from the ceiling. 'No,' she whispered. 'No, sweetheart, I'm not.'

It took Butterfly a long time to process what his mother told him. He had spent ten years believing his family were dead. He'd been to their funeral, seen the blast of the explosion bursting from the condominium, felt its heat on his face. He couldn't help thinking of his mother and sister as ghosts, even though they were here in this village, alive.

By the time he'd got over the initial shock of it all, the day was full and bright, honeyed light streaming in through the window above him where he sat on the bed. His mother sat beside him. She had spidery lines around her eyes now and had lost weight, but otherwise she was exactly as he remembered.

'So someone came to warn you about the bomb?' Butterfly asked.

He was looking down at his mother's hand lying atop his. The gold wedding band round her wrist was cold on his skin. It made him think of his father, and he was sad that he'd not had the chance to meet him again, that he'd just missed him by a few months. But he'd spent so many years believing his father was dead that it didn't hurt too much now to keep thinking of him that way.

'Yes,' Leanor replied. 'Just after you left. A young boy, no more than thirteen. Walked straight into the flat as though it was his own and told us we had to leave immediately.'

'And you believed him?'

She nodded. 'Your father knew who he was, though he didn't say at the time. He just looked at me with Emeli sleeping in my arms and said we should follow the boy.'

'But where did you go?' Butterfly shook his head. 'I saw the explosion. I *felt* it.'

Leanor squeezed his hand. 'Not far. We'd only reached the first floor when it happened. The boy led us out a backdoor and down a staircase to the ground. We escaped across the gardens. After that, he gave us some money and told us to find someone called Little Mae in the Limpets. He said she'd help us leave Neo.'

'And that's it?' asked Butterfly, his voice rising as he felt a twist of anger. 'You just left? You didn't want to take me with you? You didn't want to say *goodbye*? I've spent the last ten years thinking my whole family was burnt to ashes.'

'Oh, my caterpillar boy,' Leanor whispered.

Butterfly's stomach tightened. Caterpillar boy was the nickname his parents had given him when they'd been informed of the Council's plan to give Butterfly wings. No one had called him that in ten years. Even Silver, who'd used the nickname when she was younger, had stopped after the explosion.

'You have every right to be angry with me, sweetheart,' said his mother, taking his hands in hers. 'I was angry for *years*. I kept thinking there must have been a way we could've taken you with us, or at least told you we were alive.' She brushed his cheek. 'But we couldn't have endangered you. We thought that if we tried to come back for you, the Council would kill you. As long as we knew you were alive –'

'But how? *How* could you know?'

Leanor smiled. She reached into the pocket of her dress and brought out a thin object with a red dot glowing in its centre. Butterfly recognised it at once as a birthchip charm. They were rudimentary trackers, showing only whether the birthchip linked to the charm was still activated; that the person whose birthchip it tracked was still alive. Young couples in the city often wore each other's tracker on chains around their necks.

'Where did you get it?' he asked.

132

Birthchip charms weren't easy items to obtain. You had to apply directly to the Council with a request, or look to shady street sellers for cheap imitations that the majority of the time were just ordinary lights. But this one had lasted ten years. It had to be a Council-supplied one.

'The boy who saved us from the explosion gave it to us.'

Butterfly looked up. 'You said Dad knew who he was?'

Leanor nodded, reaching out and squeezing Butterfly's hands. 'It was your Elite senior, sweetheart. It was –'

'Cobe,' breathed Silver. '*Cobe.*'

Butterfly and Silver were walking away from the village, towards the dark line of trees that ringed the clearing. Butterfly was sweating in his Elite uniform under the midday sun, but he had needed to get away from the village quickly. He couldn't spend one more second there. He felt terrible that he couldn't simply accept his mother and sister's existence with the happiness the occasion deserved, but it felt too strange talking to them, their white skin unblemished by fire-stains, their bodies unbroken and healthy. And finding out about Cobe's involvement in their escape had just made him feel worse.

'That night on the rooftop, he said that he knew Little Mae had helped someone escape before,' said Silver. 'I can't believe it was your family.'

'He never told me,' Butterfly said coldly.

She looked at him. 'You're *angry* with him?'

133

Butterfly avoided her eyes, walking on in silence. When they passed into the shade of the forest, he stopped abruptly. He felt that if he took just one more step he'd explode. He pressed his head against the cool bark of a nearby tree, breathing deeply.

'Cobe saved your family's lives!' Silver said behind him. 'He –'

Butterfly spun round. 'He *knew*, Silver! He knew that my parents were alive, and he didn't tell me. All those years thinking my family was dead, and he could've stopped it. Stopped the pain.'

'Butterfly, he –'

'He *what*?' Butterfly let out a frustrated growl. 'Cobe could've told me at any point. And he knew about the Council!'

Silver blinked. 'What about them?'

'They set up the explosion,' explained Butterfly dully. 'Mum told me. Apparently my dad had been told some top-secret information about the Council, and he'd warned them about it. He'd thought the person had been lying about the things they'd told him. Can you believe it? He'd wanted to *warn* the Council. But turns out it was all true, and they couldn't have Dad knowing about it and risk him telling other people.'

'Oh,' breathed Silver, her eyes widening. After a long pause, she asked hesitantly, 'But how does your mum know that was what actually happened?'

Butterfly laughed gruffly. 'Cobe told them. And that's another thing!' He threw his arms wide in an exasperated gesture. 'Cobe knew the Council had tried to kill my parents. He knew what they were really like, and *still* he didn't tell me! I've spent my whole life working for them, Silver!'

He turned, slumping his forehead back against the tree. A moment later he felt Silver's arm around his shoulders. She tucked her head into his neck and Butterfly breathed her in, her familiar scent calming him. They stood like that for a few minutes before he turned to face her.

'Can you put all this aside for now?' she said gently. 'Try and concentrate instead on the fact that your mother and sister are here, alive?'

'Yeah, we are.'

They spun round at the sound of Emeli's voice. She was striding towards them, her hands on her hips. She looked surprisingly intimidating for an eleven-year-old. Her pose reminded Butterfly forcibly of his mother when she used to get angry at him for breaking something when he flew inside their apartment.

'Your mother and sister *are* here alive,' Emeli said. 'But I can't promise you we're going to be alive much longer. It's been days since we've caught any fish and Yasir's mad for one. There's no telling what he might do without some. So.' She glared at him. 'Are you gonna help us catch some?'

The sight of his little sister standing there, all grown up with her hair curling down her shoulders like a fiery waterfall and her bright, intelligent blue eyes, dimmed his rage. He felt something else stirring inside him as he looked at Emeli. He couldn't believe this was the same person as the tiny baby he'd held in his arms all those years ago.

Butterfly managed a half-smile. 'All right, then, I'll help,' he said, and he reached out a hand to take hers.

17

Akhezo Dreaming at the Top of the World

Hundreds of miles away, Akhezo was having lunch. He sat on one of the vine-wreathed platforms skirting the highest pod of the skylung, chewing noisily on a piece of dried sausage he'd pinched from the kitchen earlier. It was one of his favourite spots to sit and look out at Neo-Babel. The city was particularly impressive today. It yawned open before him in a giddying swoop, its buildings and rickshaws – tiny as ants far below – and the great curve of the river's Outer Circle glittering in the sun. Usually it would have put him in a good mood to sit here looking out at the city, imagining it one day as his own. Today, however, nothing was brightening his mood.

'Still sulking, are we?'

Akhezo whipped round to see Neve's grinning face peeking out from behind the door, her silver and pink hair bright in the sunlight. He scowled and turned his back on her.

'Thought so,' she said. She settled beside him, dangling her legs between the railing lining the balcony edge. She pointed at the river. 'Hey, why don't you jump in? The water looks nice and cool, and I heard you like a swim –'

'Get lost!' he snarled.

Neve laughed. 'Oh, relax. I'm just playing. So. Cambridge has shut you out now? Even after saying you were a . . . what was it . . . an *invaluable* part of this final flight thing?'

Akhezo blushed. 'I didn't say that.'

'Yeah, you did. What *was* so invaluable then, that now you're back where you started? Didn't shine Cambridge's shoes as bright as he wanted? Wipe his bum a bit too roughly –'

Akhezo swung a punch at her, and she shrieked, bubbling with giggles as she ducked his fist and shimmied along the balcony out of reach.

'Just joking!' she sang. She tilted her head back, letting out a long sigh. 'Anyway, I dunno how you can stay grumpy when the weather's so nice.'

Akhezo felt another blush heat his cheeks as he looked at her. His eyes travelled down the length of her body, all bones and sharp edges under the baggy canvas overalls she wore. One of the straps had fallen off her shoulder, pulling down the white top underneath. Her exposed shoulder was a smooth-skinned curve, sharp and small and perfect. He had an overwhelming urge to reach out and curl his hand round it.

Neve raised an eyebrow. 'What?'

'Nothing.'

To distract himself from thoughts of Neve, Akhezo focused on the distant high-rises of the inner city, their tall shapes no more than dark silhouettes against the sky. *I'll be living in one of 'em one day*, he thought. *I'll have my own air-tram that stops right outside my door and all the trainers I could ever want, even though I'd never have to run ever again.* An image came to his mind; Neve, laughing, standing there above it all with him, her bare shoulders white and round like perfect moons in his sky.

I'll have it all, he thought.

Neve scooted back beside him, startling him out of his daydream. 'So, you gonna tell me what happened? Or am I gonna have to live the rest of my life thinking you can't even wipe a bum properly?'

'Nothing happened.' Akhezo scowled. 'Just tried to listen in on the exchange, that's all. As if *you* wouldn't do the same.'

She grinned. 'Of course I would've. Though *I* wouldn't have got caught.' She dodged the punch he threw at her. 'Sorry, sorry! Come on, tell me what happened.'

'Just did.'

'I mean, what did you *hear*, what were they *saying*? It must've been important for Cambridge to do the exchange himself.'

Akhezo shrugged. He thought of how everything had changed after the information exchange. Instead of a thrill of pride when Domino's voice called out of the speaker in his room, calling him to Cambridge's office, he felt his gut clench at the memory of plunging into the river. The foul water had been all around him and inside him too, as he'd swallowed it when his lungs screamed for air. He'd thought he'd die like that, with the disgusting taste of the river and the coldness of it pressing against him, squeezing him until he could barely move, but a passing junk-boat had spotted him, the Reds on board pulling him out.

Cambridge didn't save me. That was the first thing Akhezo had thought as he lay on his side, coughing up water. *He didn't save me.* It surprised him how much that hurt.

'Hey, what's wrong with you today?' Neve grumbled, poking Akhezo. She stood up. 'Fine, then. Don't tell me. *I* won't bother telling *you* the news I was coming to share.'

Akhezo rolled his eyes. 'All right, I'll tell you. But don't get excited – it was only materials. Nothing interesting. That's all Cambridge wanted.'

Her eyes narrowed. 'Materials? What sort?'

'Dunno. That's when those stupid women . . . Anyway, Cambridge said something 'bout not being able to get as much as he needed from the Limpets.'

'But the Limpets have everything!'

He nodded.

'Wait.' Neve chewed her bottom lip thoughtfully. 'I think this might be to do with what I was coming to tell you.' She started pacing back and forth. 'Yeah, I think it is!'

'How?' asked Akhezo excitedly, getting to his feet.

She turned to him, her face alight with a feverish glow. 'You said Cambridge wants a load of materials he can't get in the Limpets?'

'Yeah. And?'

'Well, I was coming to tell you that I'd overheard Domino and Cambridge talking about some delivery they were expecting tomorrow night. All pretty normal. But then Cambridge said he wanted Domino to make sure no one in the skylungs was around when the delivery arrived.'

'That's weird,' said Akhezo. 'They usually want us all there to help bring the stuff up.'

'There's more,' continued Neve, nodding. 'See, Cambridge told Domino to be *really* careful with the delivery, as though it was something dangerous. Whatever materials he wanted from the Council . . . this must be it!'

Akhezo grinned. 'We've got to find out what it is!'

He thought about how Cambridge had left him drowning in the river, even how his mother had abandoned him when he was just a baby. He was tired of adults failing him. It was time for him to stop putting his hope in them and start making his own instead.

'There's only one way the delivery'll be getting in,' he said. 'The tunnel to the Limpets. We can wait for it there.'

'What about Domino?' Neve asked, a shiver of unease in her voice. 'He'll be there.'

Akhezo smirked. 'He's just a useless old man. We can take care of him.'

18

Caterpillar Boy

In the shallows of the river a few miles from the village, Emeli was teaching Butterfly and Silver to fish. She showed them how to brace their legs against the rush of the water, to keep as still and quiet as possible, and then lunge forward in one quick movement to pierce the fish with the spear. Emeli, however, was having difficulty with the keeping quiet part. She hadn't stopped talking about her life in the Outside since they'd left the village. Butterfly was listening patiently, seeming to warm to his little sister. At first, he'd been tentative around her, but Silver had noticed that he'd started opening up more, laughing more easily.

Silver stood on her own a little way downriver, watching them. She had changed back into the plain clothes she'd been wearing when they left Neo-Babel yesterday; the grey jumper that hung off one shoulder and dark green trousers. Her skin was slick with sweat under the heat of the sun, but she barely noticed, wiping her brow with the back of her hand absentmindedly.

Since arriving at the village, she had felt like Butterfly had slipped out of reach. As though their worlds – which had always orbited each other's with a steady, even gravity – had somehow broken apart; his swinging off to trace a new orbit the moment the word *Mum* had left his lips. They'd only been at the village for just over half a day, but already Silver felt anxious to move on. The flush of hope that had filled her when she'd found out about the village had quickly disappeared after it became clear that no one had seen her parents passing through, or knew anything about their whereabouts. To see Butterfly now with his mother and sister only reminded her of her own parents' absence.

She shook her head. *Stop being so selfish*, she told herself angrily. *Butterfly has spent years without his parents. If anyone deserves this, it's him, and no friend would ask to take it away from him so soon.*

Laughter erupted upstream as Butterfly speared a fish. He held his spear aloft in a triumphant stance, the fish's metallic scales flashing in the sun as it squirmed. 'I got one!' he called, catching Silver's gaze. A huge grin lit his face. It was dazzling, like looking straight at the sun.

She forced herself to return his smile.

'Yasir will be so pleased!' Emeli beamed. '*Five* fish! That's loads more than we caught last time.'

It had taken forty minutes to return to the forest where the village was hidden at its centre, walking slowly through sun-blushed meadows and sloping hills. The village was a large space, filled with one-storey buildings all made from an assortment of wooden planks, metal sheets and other flat pieces of material that had been hammered together haphazardly. Green sheets of tarpaulin stretched over every roof.

'How did this all start, Emeli?' Silver asked as they walked through the village.

Emeli shrugged. 'Oh, I don't really know. You should ask Yasir – he set it up.'

She led them to the cooking house, a rectangular building on the far western side of the settlement. Unfurling clouds of steam rose from the chimneys that peppered its roof. Inside was a long corridor. Off to both sides were a series of rooms, all equipped with cooking equipment. Silver and Butterfly followed Emeli to a room at the back with a stove and wooden table, a selection of pots and crockery piled on its worn surface.

'These are some of the only machines we have in the village,' Emeli said, gesturing at the stove. She pushed aside a stack of plates on the table for Butterfly to set down the container with their fish. 'Yasir doesn't let us use anything that'll interfere with the natural world too much.'

'But what powers it all?' asked Butterfly.

'A solar generator Yasir built,' she explained. 'We've got just enough electricity to power everything – that's how we recharged your torches. But when we're outside the village, Yasir only lets us use natural methods to do things. Dad wanted to divert some of the river straight into the village, but Yasir wouldn't have it. Said it was . . .' She stopped and fell silent. Her voice had broken slightly at the mention of her father.

Silver understood immediately how Emeli was feeling. She couldn't think of her parents without remembering that awful night walking through their apartment, not knowing whether she'd ever see their faces again. Emeli must still be grieving over her father's death.

Perhaps sensing the mood darkening, Butterfly reached forward and touched his sister's shoulder tentatively. 'Did Dad ever tell you that when you were a baby he sung to you?' he asked.

She looked up at him with big eyes and shook her head, blinking back tears.

'He sang to you all the time,' Butterfly went on. He sat on one of the chairs round the table. 'I only saw you once, but when Dad sang to you then, you gurgled back, like you were trying to sing along.'

Emeli giggled. She stepped closer to him, holding on to the edge of the table. 'Dad told me *loads* of stories about you,' she said, launching into a story about an unfortunate incident concerning baby Butterfly and a vacuum cleaner, her voice shrill and full of delight.

After Emeli's story, the three of them cooked the fish on the stove in oil the villagers made from nuts, and when the food was ready, they carried the plates outside. There was a bench under the shade of the cooking house's roof. Leanor and Yasir were there already. Emeli and Butterfly placed the plates on the table and slid onto the bench. Silver set down a jug of water and sat down opposite Yasir.

'Looks great.' Leanor smiled.

'Butterfly caught *three* fish, Mum!' said Emeli as they began helping themselves to the food. 'He was really good for his first time.'

Butterfly nudged his sister. 'I had a good teacher,' he

145

said, and a smile as bright as sunshine beamed across her face.

As the three of them started chatting, Silver leant towards Yasir. 'Emeli said you created the village. Could you tell me more about it?'

'Of course,' Yasir said. 'You must be very curious. Neo citizens always are when they first arrive.'

Silver looked puzzled. Then she gasped. 'Did *everyone* here leave Neo?'

He nodded. 'We have had a few people from nearby settlements visit, and once even a nomad ice tribe from the New Arctic passed through with their magic men. But none of them stay for long. Being so close to the city troubles them.'

'You mean you've met people from *outside* Neo?' Silver was still reeling from the fact that all these people had left Neo. The thought of people who had actually been born and raised in the Outside made her feel giddy.

Yasir smiled, his dark eyes twinkling. 'What did you think? That the people in Neo were the only ones in the world?'

'No! I just . . .' She looked down at her food, pushing it with her fork. 'It's so difficult to imagine the outside world when you've only ever known Neo.'

'I understand,' he said kindly. 'I myself was once like that. But I left Neo over ten years ago and I've felt free ever since. It was like a blindfold being lifted when you never knew you wore one.'

Silver nodded. 'So you set up this village when you left the city?'

'Not straight away,' Yasir explained. 'I spent a few years at a settlement far upriver, but most of the people there had strong anti-birthchip beliefs. I did not want to get caught up in those issues, so I left and joined with a couple who had recently left Neo. We searched for a good spot to build a settlement that would function in tune with nature, and . . . well, here we are.'

'And you've been here since?'

He nodded. 'My friends left after a few years. They felt vulnerable, so close to the city. But I wanted to make sure that any who left Neo could find us easily, and that the village would become a place where anyone could stay as long as they liked.'

'But when you found us in the trap,' Silver pressed, 'you asked us whether we'd come to kill you.'

Yasir leant in closer, lowering his voice. 'I did. You see, there are not many settlements this close to Neo. People are superstitious of the lands here – they say that ghosts walk the hills. In my twelve years of living here, I have never seen anything. But I have heard rumours.'

'Rumours?'

He nodded. 'Rumours of masked men with guns and bombs and other unspeakable weapons. They say they come from Neo under the cover of darkness and burn whole settlements to the ground. Kill all that live there.'

A shiver ran down Silver's spine. She stared back into Yasir's dark, serious eyes. 'I don't understand,' she said. 'Why would the Council do that? Me and Butterfly – we work for them. They've never mentioned anything like that. Why would they destroy the settlements? Surely they'd be *happy* that people were contacting us from the Outside after all these years of isolation?'

Yasir let out a long sigh. 'Do you know why the Council ordered Butterfly's family to be killed?'

'Yes. Butterfly told me.'

'And you think a government that could do that to its *own* people would not do it to others?'

Silver shook her head. 'They've got no reason to.'

'No reason?' Yasir raised his eyebrow. 'Silver, Neo is a miracle city. In an entire world where civilisations hundreds of centuries old have fallen, still it stands. It survived the riots and wars, the sea-level rises, the slow demise of the modern world. It survived the Great Fall. Can you imagine how great it must have been *itself* to do so? It is not the only settlement that did, no, but the one that has been least changed, because of the delicate balance the Council have skilfully kept. Neo's very existence is a promise. A promise to the remaining Mainland and Red Nation and Afrika peoples that here is a *start*. Here is a new beginning for them, a place where the world they once knew has survived. Not unchanged, not undamaged. But is has survived none the less. Now, do you see?'

Silver did not see. If their city meant so much to those left in the ruins of the outside world, how could the Council *not* open it up to them? Not let the ones that had lived through the horror of the Great Fall have a chance at enjoying the life she and all the others had led whose home *hadn't* been destroyed?

She shook her head. 'Surely that gives Neo even more responsibility to help those people?'

Yasir gave her an almost pitying look. 'Only a young person as selfless as yourself would think like that. Just think about it for me. Think why the Council would want these hills and valleys kept as ghost-lands in a magic man's tale.'

'I'll think about it,' Silver agreed, but she didn't say what she added in her mind: *Though I doubt I'll ever believe it.*

Yasir leant back, a wry smile creeping across his face. It crossed her mind that he might know more than he was letting on. She wondered for the first time who exactly this man was. Who he'd been back in Neo-Babel before he'd exchanged its world of grey streets and metal walls for this quiet green place where only trees and rivers stood in anyone's way.

19

Red

Silver slept badly that night. She wasn't used to the openness of lying in a bed, and the conversation with Yasir kept replaying in her mind.

Considering what had happened to Butterfly's family, it did make sense, but she was sure there had to be another explanation. An explanation in which the Council were not murderers, razing whole settlements to the ground just because they . . . because they *what*? They were afraid that the arrival of outsiders would disturb the balance of the city? That they'd not have enough resources for everyone? Slaughtering people just to protect resources seemed horribly ruthless. Silver couldn't image how the people she had grown up admiring – the people who'd taken her in and taught her to be exceptional, to be an *Elite* – could at the same time deal out death so coldly to people who had done nothing to deserve it except exist.

Then she remembered Senior Surrey's threat of tracking her birthchip. She remembered the feel of Ember's blade on her neck, the misery of the Limpets, and thought that maybe it wasn't so unrealistic after all.

The hours crawled on, moonlight filtering in through

the window above the bed. Emeli had given Silver her bedroom in her and Leanor's house, while Butterfly, Leanor and Emeli were in Leanor's bedroom. The three of them had not stopped talking since lunch. Silver could hear their voices coming from the neighbouring room. It made her think of her parents, and how happy they would all be when reunited.

She couldn't bear to think of the alternative.

Finally too restless to try to sleep any longer, Silver pushed back the blankets and got out of bed. A long walk might help clear her mind. Taking care not to make any noise so she wouldn't be called in to join Butterfly, Leanor and Emeli, she pulled on her jumper and trousers and opened the door.

Light seeped across the wooden floorboards from under the door to Leanor's bedroom. A peal of female laughter sounded from behind it, and Silver recognised Butterfly's low, slightly husky voice. She was just turning to leave when the sound of him speaking her name stopped her.

She took a few tentative steps closer to Leanor's bedroom. The wood creaked under her weight, but no one seemed to hear it.

'I remember Silver when she was young,' Leanor was saying. 'Always following you everywhere you went, like a little shadow.'

'I can't believe we've been friends for so long,' said Butterfly, a smile in his voice.

'Yes.' There was a pause, and when Leanor spoke again her voice was quieter. 'Now Emeli's asleep, there's something I've been wanting to ask you. Silver – is she . . . is she your girlfriend?'

Butterfly laughed, a little too quickly. 'No! She's just a friend. My best friend.'

'I know you, sweetheart,' Leanor said. 'Even if it has been ten years. You care more for her than just as a friend.'

There was a tense pause. Silver crouched behind the door, her heart racing, waiting for Butterfly's answer.

'You love her, don't you?' prompted Leanor gently.

Another pause. Then, so softly Silver almost didn't hear it, Butterfly said, 'Yes. I love her. I have done for years. For as long as I can remember.'

At his words, a thousand feelings rushed through Silver at once; excitement, fear, something new she couldn't identify. Hope? Something brilliant, something terrifying. But what Butterfly's mother said next swept all those feelings away.

'I was afraid you'd say that.'

Butterfly gave a strangled laugh. 'What?'

There was a long pause.

'What, Mum?' he repeated, his voice hard now. 'Why were you afraid –'

'Sweetheart, isn't it obvious? She's a Red.'

The words dropped like bullets in the thin night air. Silver shrank away from the door. *Of course*, she thought. It should have been obvious. No Mainlander would want their son to be in love with a Red. She was angry with herself. After a lifetime of insults and dirty looks, it shouldn't have been a surprise. It shouldn't hurt this much. Still, she didn't want to hear any more. Her eyes filled with tears. As she turned to go back to her room, Butterfly's voice stopped her for a second time.

'What's that supposed to mean? Silver is a Red?'

'You know what I mean, sweetheart. I thought you'd know better than to fall in love with one of them –'

'One of *them?*'

'Well, yes –'

'What does Silver being a Red have to do with *anything?*'

'We know what Reds are capable of, dear,' said Leanor. There was a pleading tone in her voice now. 'We've heard stories from the travellers that have come through the village. The tales of the magic men. And remember the planes all those years ago –'

'She's nothing like that!' Butterfly interrupted, so loudly Silver flinched. 'You can't judge her that way, shoving on her what other people have done. She gets that every day from people in the city. I would've thought at least she wouldn't get it from you.'

The silence was tense. When she next spoke, Leanor's voice was surprisingly cold. 'Well, don't say I didn't warn you,' she said. 'I can't control what you feel or think, even though you are my son and I would have thought you'd have better sense than this. Love her if you must. Just don't forget her blood runs Red.'

It was an old saying, one Silver hadn't heard in a while. To hear it now was like a punch to the gut. She felt tears sliding from her cheeks as she crept back silently to

Emeli's room. Still fully clothed, she climbed under the blankets on the bed and curled into a ball.

Just don't forget her blood runs Red.

Silver saw now that in leaving Neo-Babel, she *herself* had forgotten. Away from the taunts and whispers and looks of other citizens, away from the Stacks and the Limpets and the very fabric of the city itself, where the word Red and what it meant was stitched into the geography of the city, she had forgotten what she was. But she promised herself that night, as she lay crying, her tears riding the waves of Leanor's words, that she would not let herself forget ever again.

The next morning, Silver slipped out of Leanor and Emeli's house just after sunrise. Birdsong filled the air. A wispy fog clung to the bottom of the buildings as she made her way to Yasir's house on the north-western edge of the village. His house was set apart from the others, facing out over neat patchwork land where the villagers grew vegetables and fruits. She was surprised to see him sitting on the steps of his porch, a glass of steaming liquid cupped between his hands.

Yasir smiled as she approached. 'An early riser too, I see.' He touched the space on the decking beside him. His smile disappeared. 'Or perhaps just a restless night. Has our talk yesterday been troubling you?'

'That's not it,' Silver replied, sitting down. She picked at a loose thread curling from the bottom of her trousers, gritty with dirt. 'It's just . . . well, I've decided to leave the village today.' She saw the look on his face and continued quickly before he could speak. 'Seeing Butterfly with his family reminds me too much of my own parents. I have to keep looking for them. I was just coming to ask if you had any ideas of places I could try.'

'To find them?' Yasir stretched his legs down the steps. 'I am not in contact with the other settlements nearby, but I do know where a few are. I can give you directions.'

Silver nodded. 'Thank you. You're not going to try and stop me?' she added jokingly, trying to lighten the mood.

He barely smiled. 'Your reasons are your own. I should not try to stand in the way of them.'

'I don't suppose you're going to tell me what *your* reasons were for leaving Neo?' She'd asked him this question many times yesterday, but he'd not yet given her an answer.

Yasir laughed gently. 'I do not suppose you will stop *asking* me?' He met her eyes and smiled, before looking back out at the forest, his face solemn. 'You are a sweet girl, Silver. You obviously care for Neo very much, and respect the Council. After all, they raised you into this fine girl that sits beside me. I do not wish to upset you.'

'I know the Council aren't perfect,' she said, feeling a prickle of annoyance at his patronising tone. 'I've seen the Limpets and the anti-birthchip demonstrations, and gods know I've had my own share of bad experiences with them. I don't *expect* them to be perfect. But they've done a lot for me.'

If it weren't for the Council and DNA streaming, Silver

knew she'd have been nothing but another Red, struggling to make an existence in the worst-paid jobs in Neo, or maybe even running away to the Limpets to make a career as a criminal. *I owe my life to the Council*, she thought. *I'm not about to turn my back on them just yet.*

Yasir sighed deeply. 'I suppose you should know the truth,' he said. 'See, back in Neo, I too worked for the Council.' He set his cup down and folded his hands in his lap, looking out at the forest beyond. 'I was a senior member of the Department of Engineering and Resources, managing a team handling the production and distribution of Neo's sustainable energy. I take it you understand how the city's energy supply works?'

Silver nodded. 'The majority of energy comes from sustainable sources like the geothermal processor and solar panels. Then it's transmitted across the city wirelessly.'

'Exactly,' he said. 'And people are given energy permits based on their jobs, their household data, and so forth. Well, have you ever heard the term energy leeches?'

She shook her head.

'It is a term the Council use for people who take energy from the wireless transmitter without permits, or who take more than their permits allow. It is very difficult to accomplish, and requires a lot of resources that are not freely available in Neo. But it does happen.'

'Isn't it easy to trace where the stolen energy is going?' Silver asked.

'Most of the time,' agreed Yasir. 'But sometimes it is more difficult. The energy has taken a by-route, meaning it has been leeched from one place but is consumed elsewhere. In those instances it is more difficult to uncover the leeches. We would shut one source, just for another to spring up. And there was a further problem. We started to notice that more and more energy was being leeched, but despite leeching sources being uncovered, thousands of watts of energy were unaccounted for. I checked the numbers again and again, but they remained the same. When I brought it up with the Head of Energy at the time, he was sure I was mistaken. He said we must be missing some of the leeching sources.'

'So what did you do?'

'I did as he instructed – checked for leeching sources we might have missed. But I could not find any. I became convinced there must be more to it. With Lee, one of my most trusted colleagues, I began a secret investigation into the missing energy. We went again over the numbers and kept exacting records on all energy transactions in the city. We managed to get help from an analystician called Nico, who built a model for us to test energy trajectories. And we modified our machines to expand the boundary for energy detection from that of the city walls to five miles beyond.'

Silver's frown deepened. '*Beyond* the city? But why?'

'One night,' continued Yasir, ignoring her question, 'we finally found what we had been searching for – an energy transmission that went over the wall.'

She gasped. 'You mean energy was being leeched from the *Outside*?'

He nodded. 'The numbers correlated with the

unaccounted leeched energy, so we knew for certain that someone was leeching energy from beyond Neo.'

Silver shook her head, amazed. 'Do you know who it was?'

'We never found out,' said Yasir. 'But I have my suspicions. Having lived here in the village for six years now, I have seen many people from Neo pass through. Some have no idea where they want to go. They only know that they had to get away from Neo. But others head straight for a settlement just a couple days' walk from here. I have never been myself to check, but I am fairly certain there is an anti-birthchip resistance there.'

Silver bristled. She was about to ask why there'd be an anti-birthchip group outside the city and why they were leeching energy when Yasir continued his story.

'But just to find that energy was indeed being leeched from outside Neo was an incredible discovery. The three of us celebrated that night. After hours of drinking, Nico said he wanted to go back to the lab to run some tests. Lee went with him. I had too much to drink, so could not go with them. I dragged myself home, and the next day headed off to work as normal.' He let out a deep, heavy sigh.

'What happened?' she asked quietly, fearing the answer.

Yasir looked at her. There was a hardness in his eyes that scared her. 'There had been a terrorist attack by one of the anti-birthchip groups in the Council District,' he said. 'A bomb. When I arrived, there were policemen everywhere, and most of the Council District was cordoned off. The bomb had taken out half the

Department of Engineering and Resources. My office and labs were completely destroyed. They had found the bodies of three employees who'd been working late that night. One was a policeman, and the other two . . .'

'Nico and Lee,' breathed Silver.

'A little more than convenient, do you not think? All that work destroyed, and two of the people who had known about it gone with it. I have no doubt they wanted me dead too.'

She nodded. 'That's why you left. Otherwise they'd have done to you what they did to Nico and Lee.'

'No,' said Yasir, surprising Silver. 'No, I was not afraid of dying. I left Neo because now I *knew* there were people outside. That people were leaving, and surviving, and learning about a life without walls. It had nothing to do with fear, or even rebellion. I just was not able to continue living in Neo after knowing what I now knew.'

They sat in silence for a while, looking out over the farmland, the dark line of the forest beyond. Silver thought about whether she could have stayed in Neo-Babel knowing what Yasir knew. What he'd told her yesterday and today changed everything. Everything she knew about her city, about the Council. Even her own place in it all had been tarnished and twisted and spoilt.

Yasir broke the silence. 'The instructions to the nearest settlement. When would you like them?'

Silver had almost forgotten the reason she'd came to see him. 'Can you give them to me now?'

'Now? You mean to leave right away?'

159

She nodded.

He touched her shoulder. 'Then we will miss you and Butterfly.'

'Actually, I'm going on my own,' said Silver, avoiding his eyes. 'I want Butterfly to stay. He's only just found his mother and sister again. I can't take him away from that so soon.'

Yasir watched her carefully. 'If you are sure. One moment.' He went into his house, returning a minute later with a sheet of paper.

'Thank you,' Silver said as he gave it to her. She looked down at the hand-drawn map and remembered something he had said earlier. 'Yasir, you said something about a settlement two days' walk away that people from Neo have been going to. The anti-birthchip one.' She held up the map. 'Is this it?'

'Yes,' he said, his expression growing dark. 'And if my suspicions are correct, they are a very extreme anti-birthchip resistance.'

She smiled wryly. 'I've been dealing with those all my life.' She thought of the most extreme anti-birthchip group in Neo-Babel. 'They can't be as bad as the Pigeons.'

Yasir shook his head. 'If what I've seen over the years is true, they might in fact be *working* with the Pigeons. That is why I thought you should know. You should not expect them to welcome you warmly, Silver, especially not once they discover who you are, and who you work for.'

160

20

A Chance

'You're sure they said tonight?'

'Yeah.'

'As in, Thursday? Thursday night?'

'*Yes.*'

'Tonight?'

'Akhezo,' growled Neve, 'if you ask me again I'll cut your tongue in half. I know what I heard. It's tonight.'

Akhezo scowled. It felt as though they'd been hiding behind the stack of crates in the stairwell at the Limpets' tunnel entrance for so many hours the night had come and gone, and he was growing increasingly restless. The only positive of spending the whole night in the stairwell was being so close to Neve. She'd brought along a book she'd stolen from Cambridge's collection and was teaching herself to read. The book was propped against her thighs, and she leant back against the wall behind the crates, her fingers tracing lines of text. Akhezo kept stealing sideways glances at her. He liked watching her eyes moving as they followed the letters across each page. It made him think of her eyes roaming over him.

'Maybe something's happened,' he said. 'We should've

waited at the Limpets' entrance instead, the delivery might've been held up –'

Neve groaned. 'Oh, *will* you just –'

A sudden noise stopped her; low rumbling accompanied by a high-pitched squeaking. It was the rickshaw.

They scrambled to their feet and edged to the side of crates, crouched to stay hidden. Akhezo drew out a knife from his pocket.

Neve's eyes widened. 'What –'

He raised a finger to his lips. He peered round the side of the crates. The sound of the rickshaw was growing louder, and maybe he was imagining it, but he thought even from this distance he could hear Domino's asthmatic wheeze.

'What is *that* for!' hissed Neve. It was more of an accusation than a question. He knew she meant the knife. 'I thought we just wanted to find out what the delivery was. I thought we'd try and work round Domino being here.'

Akhezo whipped round, making her flinch. 'Shut it!' he snarled. 'Just follow my lead.' As he turned away, he felt a thrill of excitement. *This is what being a man feels like*, he thought. *I don't need Cambridge. I don't need Domino. I can take what I want – including the life I want to have. No more waiting round for others to give it to me.*

The rumbling of the bike was loud now. It couldn't be more than a few metres from the tunnel entrance.

'Maybe we shouldn't do this,' said Neve. 'I mean, why do *we* care what's in the delivery? Domino told us to never ask questions.'

'Yeah?' snapped Akhezo, not bothering to look round at her. 'Well, I'm fed up of doing what Domino says. Look where that got me – drowning in the river like a dying fish. I'm sick of it, always getting told what to do.'

She touched his shoulder. 'Please, I don't wanna have to leave the Pigeons and the skylung. I can't go back to before –'

'Don't you get it?' he said, twisting round and grabbing her hand. 'We can have anything we want, Neve! We don't need the Pigeons, Domino, Cambridge. None of that. We can have anything in the whole city. I'll get it for us.'

But she just blinked and pulled out of his grasp. There was a screech and clatter as the rickshaw pulled into the stairwell, the driver breaking too late and crashing into something.

'Imbecile!' wheezed Domino.

'Sorry, sir.'

'Just get on and unload the boxes.'

'Yes, sir.'

In the shadow of the crate-stack, Neve was staring at Akhezo with wide, pleading eyes. He hated her then. The feeling welled inside him like a cloud swelling across the sky, until he felt like reaching out a hand and slapping her to get that look off her face. *Why can't she understand that kids like us can't* afford *to be nice?* he thought angrily.

He turned his back on her and slinked into the slip of darkness to the side of the crates. He peered around the stairwell. Its sickly yellow light made it hard to see, and the crates obstructed his view, but he could tell Domino and the rickshaw driver stood just a metre or so away. Their elongated shadows slid across the floor like spilt water. There was the sound of thuds as things were lifted out of the rickshaw and placed on the ground.

'Gently!'

'Sorry, sir.'

There was the metallic *clink* of coins as Domino paid the driver, then squeaking tyres as the rickshaw returned down the tunnel.

'Stupid Red,' Domino grumbled. 'The way he was going, he'd have got us all blown up, manhandling these explosives like a bunch of rotten vegetables.'

Akhezo's whole body tensed. *Did Domino just say* explosives? He felt a chill run through this body, half fear, half excitement. *Explosives*. Even the word sounded dangerous; the kind of word you had to whisper or it would burst apart in your mouth and burn your tongue. He shrank back from the edge of the crates.

'Did he say . . .?' Neve whispered.

Akhezo nodded.

'Oh,' she breathed.

They could hear what sounded like Domino moving the boxes of explosives along the floor of the stairwell. Akhezo listened, unsure of what to do. He'd not banked on the delivery being something like this. Not that he'd really thought about what it might be. He'd just wanted to get one up on Cambridge and Domino. Now he was here he felt a little embarrassed. He slipped the knife back in his pocket.

The dragging sounds stopped. Shuffling footsteps, then the creak and dull ringing as the old man started up the metal staircase. They waited until the hatch at the top of the stairs slammed loudly shut before moving out from behind the stack of crates.

There were six boxes at the foot of the stairs. There were no markings on them, but Akhezo could almost feel the power of the explosives inside radiating out of them.

'What I don't get,' he said, 'is why the Council would just hand these out. I mean, Cambridge was going under his fake identity as a Limpets' gang-leader and all, but there's still no way the Council would just *hand* him a bunch of explosives.'

'You're right about that.'

They both jumped as a young man stepped out of the shadows of the Limpets' tunnel entrance. He wore slim black trousers, a long-sleeved grey top and black boots. As he walked, his head was dipped low. Light from the neon strips glanced across his shaven head.

Akhezo recognised him immediately. 'You're that Council member from the shisha boat!'

The man nodded. His dark eyes darted around, skittering across Akhezo and Neve as though they were painful to look at. He craned his head upwards to follow the arc of the staircase. 'This is underneath one of the skylungs, isn't it?' he said. 'Incredible. We never knew.'

While the man wasn't looking, Akhezo slipped the knife out of his shorts and tucked his arm behind his back.

'Who *is* this?' Neve asked him in a whisper.

'The Council member who did the information exchange with Cambridge on the shisha boat,' replied Akhezo, not bothering to keep his voice down.

'Scum,' she hissed.

'I can hear you, you know,' said the Council member, turning to them.

Neve spat at his feet. 'I don't care.'

Akhezo almost laughed. There was the strong, fearless girl he knew. He stepped forward, all of a sudden filled with confidence. 'Why are you here?' he asked.

The Council member ran a hand over his shaved head. 'I need you to do something for me.'

'And why would we do anything for *you*, Council snob?'

'Because otherwise, I'll tell the Council where your hideout is.'

Akhezo shrugged. 'You're gonna do that anyway, aren't you? We don't owe you anything.'

'I mean it,' said the man. He opened his palms out in a sincere gesture. 'I won't tell them if you do me this one favour. I just thought, after seeing how you snuck up on us in the Temple of the Fat Wives, that you'd be perfect for the job. But if you're not *up* to it –'

Akhezo made a scoffing noise. 'Oh, I am,' he said quickly. He shrugged. 'Go on, then. What d'you want done?'

The man took a step closer. 'What did you overhear on the boat?'

'This and that.'

'Well, your friend on board the boat –'

'He's *not* my friend.'

A smile flickered across the man's face. 'Well, *he* told me you're tracking two Council members. I need you to block their tracking for me.'

Akhezo stared at him. 'Why?' he asked.

'That's none of your business.'

'Well, they've already left.'

The man nodded. 'I know. They have birthchip blockers with them. I need you to turn them on.'

Akhezo blinked. 'You want me to turn their birth-chip blockers *on*? What, so they can't be tracked any more?'

'That *is* what they are for,' said the Council member. 'If you do that for me, I won't tell my seniors about your group's hideout.'

Akhezo sensed something shifting in the air, the power balance tilting in his direction. *This is it*, he thought. *This is the moment it all starts. This is my chance.*

'Will you do it?' asked the man.

After a pause, Akhezo nodded.

The man smiled, relief dancing behind his teeth. 'Good. I'll meet you here again this time tomorrow. Have it done by then. Come alone, and don't tell anyone about our deal.' He nodded towards Akhezo's right hand. 'And don't even *think* about using that, or I'll have to use this.' He pulled up his shirt, revealing a gun tucked into the waistband of this trousers.

Akhezo felt his throat go dry, but he tried to look calm.

'Tomorrow, then,' said the man. 'And what's your name?

Just in case you go back on our deal and do tell the Council about what I said, I'll have to know who to punish –'

'It's Akhezo,' he scowled. 'And you are?'

The Council member turned to leave. 'Don't push it.'

The moment he was gone, Neve started towards the staircase. 'Come on! We've gotta tell Domino and Cambridge.'

'What?' Akhezo lunged forward and grabbed her arm. 'We don't have to tell 'em anything.'

Neve stared at him. 'Yeah, we do. A Council member knows our location. He's obviously lying – he's gonna tell the Council. And then . . .' She struggled out of his grip. 'We've *got* to tell them.'

'Yeah?' Akhezo sneered, his top lip curling. 'And tell 'em what? Oh, Domino, Cambridge, while we were hiding down here to find out what your top-secret delivery was – which, by the way, is explosives, wanna tell us what *that's* for . . .'

'I don't care. This is bigger than that.'

'Fine,' he snapped, pushing her away. 'Do what you want. But don't come crying to me when they kick you out for spying on them.'

Neve ignored him. After one last angry look, she started up the stairs. When she was halfway up, Akhezo turned and broke into a run, heading in the opposite direction down the tunnel to the Limpets. He spotted the Council member up ahead. A dark, slinking figure slipping along the shadows, yellowy light glancing off his head.

'Hey!'

The man stopped, turning. 'Changed your mind already?'

Akhezo jogged to meet him. 'Nah, I'll still do it. But I want something else in exchange.'

'Something else?' The man's eyes narrowed. He tucked his hands into the pockets of his trousers, watching Akhezo carefully. 'You *don't* want me to keep the location of your group's hideout from the Council?'

Akhezo shook his head. 'You can tell 'em,' he said. 'I don't care. I want . . . I want money instead.'

He hadn't planned on saying it; hadn't known *what* he would say. But now it was out of his mouth, it seemed right. After all, that was where everything started, wasn't it? And where everything went? Money, and violence. From what he'd seen, those were the two laws of the world. He couldn't turn down the chance at having one of them. He thought of lying on the deck of the junk-boat, soaked and choked half to death in river-water, thinking over and over how Cambridge didn't save him. *No one'll save you*, Akhezo had realised. *You've just gotta save yourself.*

'How much do you want?' the Council member asked.

'Ten thousand.'

'Forget it,' the man laughed, and he turned to go.

'Wait!' Akhezo cried. He cast around for a more realistic number. He'd never had any money of his own to be sure of its scale. Eventually, he ventured, 'A thousand.'

The Council member stared at him for a moment before nodding. 'One thousand, then. You're sure about this?'

'Definitely.' Akhezo grinned.

The truth was, he'd never been surer about anything

in his life. He wasn't an idiot. He knew the man would tell the Council about the Pigeons living in the skylung. He knew it was all over for them. But now he had a way to make it *without* them. When it all came crashing down, he'd still be standing.

No more Domino, no more Cambridge, no more Pigeons, Akhezo thought as he walked back to the stairwell. With that amount of money, he'd be set. An image of Neve flashed into his mind, sunlight half obscuring her face, glinting off her silver and pink hair. *They* would be set, he corrected himself. He saw the smile that'd break across her face when he told her of his fortune. *No more useless adults*, he thought. *Just me and Neve at the top of the world*.

21

The Kiss Before the Storm

After saying goodbye to Yasir, Silver went back to Leanor and Emeli's house to pack her things. The sun was rising. Despite the clear skies, there was the soft smell before rain in the air, and beyond the clearing a bank of clouds gathered. She packed quietly; the last thing she wanted was to wake the others in Leanor's room. But, just as she stepped out of the front door onto the porch, a voice behind her made her stomach drop.

'Silver?'

Butterfly emerged from the house, wearing his white top, now grey with dirt, and blue trousers. His birthchip blocker hung from his neck. Silver looked at it with fresh eyes, seeing it for the first time for the thing it was; their rejection of the Council. Everything Yasir had told her might have made her believe that the Council had done – *was* doing – awful things, but somehow she had already known that when she and Butterfly had chosen to use the birthchip blockers to stop their own people from finding them.

Butterfly froze, his eyes hardening as he noticed the backpack slung across her shoulders. 'What are you doing?' he asked.

Silver didn't answer.

He stared at her. 'You're leaving.'

'I have to,' she said, avoiding his eyes. 'I need to find my parents. Please, just let me go.'

Before he could reply, she spun round, half tripped down the porch steps, and ran across the clearing towards the forest beyond, her long ponytail whipping behind her.

'Silver!' she heard Butterfly call at her back.

She ran on, ignoring him. She knew that if she stopped, he'd offer to go with her, and she couldn't let that happen. Soon she was in the cool shadows of the forest. Sunlight trickled through the dense canopy above like golden snow filtering down into narrow streets. She darted between the trees, concentrating on running; the crush of leaves beneath her feet, her quick, shallow breaths. Her heartbeat thudding in time with her footsteps.

They were deep into the forest when Butterfly finally caught up with Silver, grabbing her arm and yanking her round so hard she stumbled. They rolled, crashing to the floor. Twigs snapped under their bodies. She pushed him off her and got to her feet, but he caught her leg and pulled her back down, pinning her to the floor.

'You were just going to leave?' Butterfly said, a hurt expression on his face. 'Without telling anyone? Without telling *me*?'

Silver stopped struggling. She sighed. 'I told Yasir. He said he'd tell you for me. I knew if I told you, you'd come with me. I couldn't let you do that.'

Butterfly stared at her for a few more seconds before rolling off her. He sat up, one hand holding his head, his fingers tangled in his messy sweep of hair. Silver wanted to go to him, but the words his mother spoke the night before ran again through her mind.

Just don't forget her blood runs Red.

She felt as though her very touch was contagious now. As though her Red body was a diseased one, all the things people hated about them hidden under her skin like ink, waiting to stain anyone she touched. She sat up beside Butterfly, their bodies just an inch apart. It was hard to ignore the electric pull between them that made her finger-tips twitch in his direction. Silver couldn't believe she'd spent her life touching him without even thinking about it. Curling up beside his body at night. Hands clasping together. The sides of their legs pressing together under a table. Touches as frequent and as natural as breathing. Touches that she'd thought had always meant nothing more than friendship, but now she knew how wrong she'd been. A light rain began to fall, filling the air with a soft pattering. She imagined it washing her clean, running away all her dirty Red blood from her skin like mud.

'Of course I wanted to tell you,' Silver said eventually. 'But I couldn't take you away from Leanor and Emeli so soon after finding them.'

Butterfly shook his head. 'That was my decision to make.' He reached out to take her hand.

'Don't,' she said, standing up quickly and turning away.

'Silver –'

'I heard what Leanor said last night.'

There was a pause. 'I wish you hadn't.'

Leaves crinkled beneath Butterfly's weight as he pushed himself up. A second later Silver felt his hand on her shoulder. She flinched, but didn't shrug him off. The rain was falling faster now, thicker, drumming a beat like a thousand tiny hearts suddenly coming to life. She barely noticed it. His hand on her shoulder was hot, his touch seeming to swallow her.

'She's right,' Silver whispered, turning round. 'I *am* a Red. And you deserve more than that.'

'No,' said Butterfly. His voice was surprisingly hard. Rain ran down his face but he barely blinked, his eyes glaring fiercely into hers.

'But –'

'No,' he repeated. 'I'm not going to let you be like this.'

'Like what?'

'Like *this*!' He gestured angrily at her. 'Sorry for yourself.'

Silver flinched. '*Sorry* for myself?' she whispered. Tears sprang to her eyes. 'That's not fair.'

Butterfly shook his head. 'I don't care. Come on, Silver. You know I don't care that you're a Red. That word means *nothing* to me. You're my best friend, you always have been, and you should respect me well enough not to act like this.'

The rain was roaring now, filling the forest with an ocean sound.

Silver glared at him. 'Why shouldn't I feel this way?' she said, her voice rising. She rubbed a hand across her eyes, wiping away the tears and the rain that were falling down her face. 'It's the way I've been made to feel since I was born. Red this, Red that, *all* the time. Even your own mother doesn't want you loving a Red. Why should I expect you to feel any different?'

Butterfly half growled, half laughed. She felt as though she hated him right then – *How can he laugh? How* dare *he?* – and she went to turn away, but then he said, 'Because of this!' and grabbed her face and kissed her.

For a second, Silver stared at his face all of a sudden so close to hers. Shock locked her body rigid. Then a warm, relaxed feeling flushed through her, and she closed her eyes and kissed him back.

It felt so natural, so normal, it seemed ridiculous they hadn't done it sooner. That they were doing it for the first time now, here in the forest under the rushing rain that wetted their faces and filled their mouths with a pure, clean taste. As they kissed, Silver could feel a new world blossoming between their lips. She sighed into Butterfly, holding him in her arms as if he were the whole world. In that moment, he was.

Butterfly's kiss, its pressure, its heat, felt like a promise being burned into her skin. A promise of the word he had whispered last night. A word Silver never knew she had been yearning for before now –

Love.

They drew apart. They were both smiling.

Butterfly blinked away the raindrops running down his face. He lowered his hands, trailing them down Silver's shoulders and arms, and taking her hands in his.

The world shivered. There was a flash of light behind

Butterfly's head. Silver jumped, pulling apart from him. Just a heartbeat moment of nothingness. Then –

The sky in front of them exploded in a terrible burst of noise and colour. They dropped to the ground, shielding their faces as they felt the whip-crack of an angry wind rush at them, and the smell of smoke riding the air. There was a long, drawn-out moment of silence. Then the sounds of screaming and crying, piercing and horrible in the shattered air.

Silver couldn't make sense of the noises. She felt mud beneath her hands and wondered dimly why she was on the ground. She could still taste Butterfly on her lips, fresh rainwater filling her mouth. The last thing she knew she'd been looking into his fierce blue eyes, his face so close to hers she could feel the electricity shivering in the drenched air between them. Then she'd seen a flash, felt a deep shudder through the ground. Now here she was, on the forest floor, her body tensed and her heart thumping.

Something glowed in the forest beyond, lighting the sky from underneath. Thoughts and images – scarred, broken – fell through Silver's mind like shattered glass. *Oh*, she thought, realising with a sudden rush of clarity what had happened. *There's been an explosion.*

It took a moment for it to hit her.

An explosion!

She jumped up. Butterfly was already sprinting towards the burning in the distance where a roiling, red-black cloud hung low in the sky. For a second, Silver hesitated. A thought flickered across her mind: *The village*. And then she was running, running after Butterfly, running towards the bruised, rain-churned sky, running towards the village, towards Yasir and Emeli and Leanor, towards the screams and cries that shivered in the air like a nightmare refusing to break.

22

The Exploded World

Water and fire; the world seemed to have dissolved into those two elements. As Silver stumbled into the clearing, the village opening up before her, she saw that fire had claimed everything, latching onto the buildings, the trees. The people. And still the rain poured, as though the gods above were trying to put out the flames that had licked suddenly across the world, eating it alive.

She stood at the lip of the clearing, dragging breath into her lungs, unable to make sense of what she was seeing. Bits of burning things floated down through the air, blurring the clearing into a smear of grey and green and orange and black. They brought with them the acrid stench of ash and melted metal, and when Silver licked her lips she found them sour on her tongue. The taste was strong, like a punch to the gut, and she knew then with absolute certainty that this was what Yasir had been talking about.

This was the masked men with guns and bombs and other unspeakable weapons. *This* was the soldiers from Neo burning whole settlements to the ground. *This* was the killing of all who lived there. *This* was the Council –

Her Council.

Silver couldn't see any soldiers in the village yet. She was about to go look for them when she spotted Butterfly, running straight for Leanor and Emeli's house. Half of it had collapsed.

No, she thought. *Not Leanor and Emeli. Not again.*

In an instant she forgot about looking for the soldiers and ran after Butterfly. Things snatched at her attention as she went. Screams like fingernails dragging across metal. Shadows blossoming across the burnt ground. She tried to close her ears, and she wanted to close her eyes too, but it was just too horrible, there were too many terrible things. Though her brain tried to block them out her eyes demanded to see them, the images crowding and blotting out everything else, and she was so full of death but still it kept creeping, crawling into her skin and clogging up her veins until her entire being was filled with the horror of it all.

Outside Leanor and Emeli's house, Silver slowed to a walk. Ahead, Butterfly picked his way through the churned-up wood and broken, jagged slashes of metal, sticking up into the air like animal teeth. She followed him, an uncontrollable shaking rattling through her body now. All around her, the air was filled with sounds. Screams, shouts, cries, and, underneath it all, the rain, still pouring down, making the fires rear up and hiss at it. But above the noise rose an animal cry, so close she felt a shiver dance across her skin.

Leanor or Emeli, she thought. *It has to be.*

Butterfly had already disappeared into the half of the house that was still standing. As Silver followed, darkness closed round her. Smoke clung to the air, biting her eyes, but she could make out shapes in the grey, and as she moved, objects started to materialise. There was a bedframe. A table lying on its side.

A body.

Silver stepped closer. The white of Butterfly's shirt came into focus. He was kneeling on the floor, cradling something. She saw the scene in pieces; a tumble of red hair, the delicate curve of a wrist hanging limp.

The wailing grew louder.

Who? she wanted to ask. *Emeli? Leanor?* But she couldn't speak. She stood there, staring at Butterfly's back, her mouth hanging open.

After what seemed like hours, Butterfly looked round. His face was expressionless. His lips moved.

Silver didn't understand what he'd said.

He said it again, slowly. 'Shut the *hell up.*'

And all of a sudden, she realised the horrible wailing sound was coming from her. Silver slammed a hand across her mouth. Staggered back, crashed into the upturned table. Pulled herself to her feet. Butterfly had turned back round to the body in his arms and she suddenly felt like this was all wrong, her being here in this horrible, private moment, in this burnt-out broken house with its broken bodies and broken hearts and broken lives that had only just been put together again. The white of the back of Butterfly's shirt seemed to hiss at her, *Go.*

So she went. Scrambling and stumbling out into the village, into rain that still fell in driving sheets. Dazed and deadened by what she'd just seen – *It happened again to Butterfly, gods it happened* again – Silver moved through the fiery cloudscape that was the village. She passed more houses, more fire, more bodies. Bits of bodies too. They looked ridiculous, like scraps of a toy that had been ripped apart by a petulant child. Luckily, the horror of it washed over her. She couldn't feel it properly. Not yet.

After a few minutes, Silver's Elite instincts took over. She knew she had to find Yasir to make sure he was safe. She began to run in the direction of his house. When she passed villagers stumbling out of their houses or crawling along the floor, she stopped quickly to help where she could. Too often it was too late to help.

Yasir's house was at the other end of the village, but Silver felt like she'd only been running a few seconds before it came into view, a burning husk on the horizon.

'Yasir!' she shouted. She knew he wouldn't be able to hear her but it made her feel better. Hearing his name leave her mouth made him real.

Made him alive.

The house was ablaze. Heat rolled off it, flames licking across its walls and roof, reaching flickering red fingers into the sky. Silver ran round the house once. There was no sign of him. She glanced about, not looking for anything in particular, then nodded to herself.

I'm going in.

She ran up the porch and into the house, dancing between flames. She ducked into the first room on the left, looking around for anything man-shaped. Nothing. There was no sign of Yasir in the next room either. All the time, the flames licked closer. Silver was coughing now, her lungs filling with smoke, and she knew the fumes would overcome her. She had to get out. She stumbled back into the house's main corridor. All she could see were flames. Behind her, something crashed down and a rush of heat and ash charged forward. She backed away, staggering blindly, feeling for a way out, and just as she thought she'd be trapped in these burning walls forever –

A voice out of the fire and shadows.

'Help!'

It was Yasir.

Silver darted towards his voice and found another room wreathed in flames. A beam had fallen from the ceiling, pinning Yasir to the floor, but she almost laughed with joy at the sight of him. She ran over, grabbing his head and wiping the grit out of his eyes.

His eyes widened. Recognition, relief flashed in them. He coughed, struggling to speak. 'What . . .'

'Shhh.'

Silver laid his head back down. She grabbed the beam and pushed. It didn't move at first, but then she felt its weight start to roll away, and she kept pushing until it fell to the floor and Yasir's body was free. Her hands rushed across it, searching for broken bones. Everything felt intact. Carefully, she helped him to his feet, curling an arm round his waist, and then they were stumbling out of the burning room, out of the burning house.

Air had never tasted so good to Silver, even if it was still filled with smoke and ash. They half fell, half ran down the porch, not stopping until the heat of the flames was behind them. Yasir was holding onto her. He stood completely still, staring at the village, shaking his head slowly.

Silver peeled apart from him. 'Will you be all right on your own for a while?' she asked.

'I . . . I have to help.' Yasir blinked, and seemed to regain his composure. 'I have to help my friends,' he said, more firmly this time.

She nodded. 'I'll come back and help too, but right now there's something I need to do.'

Without waiting for a reply, she turned and ran back into the village. As she ran through it this time her mind was clearer. She was in control. She felt years of Elites' training rushing through her blood, and moved with accuracy, purpose, and with a clear, hard objective, just as Senior Surrey had taught her that time in the shooting range. Then, her objective had been to find her parents.

This time, it was revenge.

You're going to pay for this, Silver thought, anger surging through her veins

She hadn't believed Yasir at first. She'd not wanted it to be true. But seeing the village destroyed like this confirmed everything. Whatever she'd thought about the Council had been wrong. They weren't her family. They weren't her friends. They were *murderers*. And she was going to stop them.

Her hatred for the Council flared in her chest again. *You're going to pay for this.*

She was almost at Leanor and Emeli's house when

the group of masked men emerged from the woods. They held guns in their hands. Neo-Babel's flag was emblazoned across their uniforms.

Silver hissed.

You're going to pay for this.

The swarm broke as they entered the village. The soldiers ran in different directions, some heading into the burning buildings, others moving towards wounded villagers where they stood or lay on the wet ground. For a moment nothing happened, and a horrible thought flashed through Silver's mind; that she had got it wrong, that they were actually here to *help*.

Then sharp studs of gunfire cracked the air. The soldiers that had approached the villagers moved away from them, leaving the bodies lying on the floor where they'd been shot.

Something snapped inside Silver. Hard and painful, it broke, and she was suddenly so angry, so full of a red, blinding rage, that without thinking she ran straight for the nearest soldier, hurling a cry from her lips.

23

The Birthchip Charm

Cobe lay on the chaise lounge in his bedroom in the Stacks, staring out through the glass wall at the city. He'd just got back from an assignment. He hadn't undressed yet from his Elite uniform, and as the late morning sun shone through the window, the amber light glittered on the waxy material of his jumpsuit, warming the skin underneath. Yet still he felt cold, unable to shake the feeling of slow dread that had crept under his skin over the last two days.

From the moment he'd said goodbye to Butterfly at the door of their bedroom the morning of Tanaka's funeral, time had stretched out. Every minute since he'd felt Butterfly's absence like a pulse. Especially here, in the bedroom they'd shared for ten years. Butterfly had moved in with his Elite senior earlier than was usual after his family's death in the explosion, and it felt wrong to Cobe to be lying on the chaise lounge without Butterfly sprawled in the chair next to it, or to walk past the empty bedpod beside his own.

Even outside their bedroom, he couldn't rid himself of the feeling that some part of him had been carved out, lost forever. Cobe had carried a charm that tracked

Butterfly's birthchip for so many years he barely noticed it, but now it weighed him down, the light nestled inside it constantly reminding him that Butterfly was gone.

He could see the birthchip on the table in front of him now, its steady red light an unbeating heart. *Hurry up, Akhezo*, he thought, scowling at it. *Hurry up, you little Limpets rat.*

As Butterfly's senior, Cobe had been held accountable for his and Silver's disappearance. Somehow, Ember had got off lightly, but Cobe had spent hours with Senior Surrey answering question after question; what had happened in the days leading up to their disappearance, what possible reasons they could have had for being in the Limpets that time when the scouting party had found them. Then, when Senior Surrey had grown frustrated with his unhelpful suggestions, he'd given Cobe so many assignments Cobe barely had time to sleep.

Unfortunately, this had included the assignment on the shisha boat. Cobe had no choice but to tell Senior Surrey that Silver and Butterfly had left the city. He couldn't risk lying about it any more, not now others in the city knew about their whereabouts. If word got back somehow to the Council that Cobe had known and hadn't told them . . . He shuddered to think what would happen. Still, he hadn't minded being busy. It had taken his mind off the vacant bedpod in his room, the feeling of emptiness his life now had without his Elite junior in it.

But two days ago, everything changed.

When Cobe had been called to the Head of the Elites' office, he'd been expecting another interrogation surrounding Butterfly and Silver's disappearance. So when Senior Surrey began the meeting by discussing his opinions on birthchip laws, Cobe sat up straighter in his chair, surprised.

'To tell you the truth,' said Senior Surrey, 'I sometimes find the whole system ridiculous.'

Senior Surrey was sat behind his desk in his usual seat. He wore a grey silk tunic with dyed red sleeves that looked to Cobe like blood running down his arms. An amused expression played on his face. He leant back in his chair, gazing at the small tree in the corner of his room.

'I've never understood why we have laws preventing us from freely tracking our citizens' birthchips,' he said. 'After all, we have the technology, and the records are just *waiting* to be looked at. It seems a waste, to not use them freely.' He leant forward and placed his hands on the desk. 'It's not that I disapprove of the current legalities surrounding birthchip tracking. But I do think in certain circumstances it is a hindrance. After all, we wasted hours speculating about Silver and Butterfly's whereabouts before we had to find out from an anti-birthchip activist they had left Neo-Babel. It seems absurd that someone like that can use birthchip trackers freely, whereas we are bound by laws.'

Cobe nodded. Though the hooded man on board the Temple of the Fat Wives claimed to be a Limpets' gang-leader, the Council had long suspected him of being involved with the powerful anti-birthchip group the Pigeons. The Council had only approved the reward of explosives to the informant because it would allow them to track the delivery and discover where the Pigeons were based.

'Well,' said Senior Surrey, his dark eyes smooth and hard like stones. 'I thought that since we now know Butterfly and Silver are out of the city, what harm could it do to break one little law and use their birthchip trackers to find out exactly *where* they are in the Outside. Do not worry. The Council approved my infringement in light of the circumstances.'

Cobe flinched as though he'd been punched. *He's tracking them!* He felt sick at the thought. He reached a hand to brush over his head, then forced himself to lower it as soon as he realised what he was doing.

Senior Surrey cocked his head. 'Is something the matter?'

'No, sir,' Cobe lied.

The polite smile on Senior Surrey's face had vanished. 'I thought finding out where Silver and Butterfly are would be your utmost concern. Butterfly is your junior, after all, and I understand you and Silver are friends.'

'Yes, sir.'

Senior Surrey smiled, but his expression was still cold. 'Good. I'm glad we are of similar minds.' He stood up suddenly and walked to the glass door at the back of the room. He slid it open. A warm wind brushed into the room, bringing with it a trill of birdsong, distant city noises. 'Do you know why Butterfly and Silver might have left the city?' he asked, turning back to Cobe.

'No, sir.' Cobe felt sweat beading across his forehead, but he resisted the urge to wipe it away. 'Unless . . .'

'Unless?'

'Perhaps it has something to do with Silver's parents?' Cobe didn't think he was giving anything away by telling the truth about that part. After all, the Council must have realised that was the triggering factor in her and Butterfly's disappearance.

Senior Surrey stared at him as if deep in thought. When he next spoke, his voice was low and dangerous. 'They won't be coming back.'

Cobe felt fear like a knife-twist in the heart. 'What . . . what do you mean, sir?' he asked, trying to keep his voice steady.

'They can't leave and expect to come back,' said Senior Surrey coldly. He walked back to the desk and sat on its edge, looking down at Cobe. His smile didn't reach his eyes.

'But, sir –'

Senior Surrey raised a hand to quieten Cobe. 'I have a theory. See, we have been experiencing energy leeching from somewhere beyond the city walls for some time now. No need to act so surprised. I am telling you this, Cobe, as you are an Elite, and you have proved yourself worthy of the information. Alongside this, there have been concerning developments as anti-birthchip groups grow stronger, gaining more information. My thought is the two are related, and that there is an anti-birthchip movement *outside* Neo as well as within it, and that this is who is leeching our energy.'

Cobe felt his heart thudding. He'd never heard

anyone talk so confidently about the Outside, especially someone within the Council. He clenched his hands under the desk to stop them shaking. Something bad was coming, he could tell.

'I believe that Silver and Butterfly may have found the anti-birthchip group's settlement,' continued Senior Surrey. 'Maybe that was the reason they left, and they have been working for the anti-birthchip cause for a while. I do not know. But what I *do* know is if that is where they are, then we must take advantage of this opportunity.'

Cobe swallowed. 'What do you mean, sir?' he said, barely able to get the words out.

Senior Surrey smiled. His handsome face was friendly, and he looked as though he was considering something very pleasant, but there was a biting edge to his voice as he answered. 'I mean to follow Butterfly and Silver to the anti-birthchip resistance outside the city, and destroy them all.'

It had taken everything Cobe had in him not to run out of Senior Surrey's office right then. He'd forced himself to walk calmly away after being dismissed, then up through the Stacks back to his bedroom. But all the while, it'd felt as though his chest was exploding.

Now, two days later, as he glared at the red light of the birthchip charm on the table in front of him, Cobe felt that same chaotic surge of despair and unease rising inside him. How could he have objected to Senior Surrey's plan? His hatred of anti-birthchip groups was as strong as any Council member's. But his feelings for his Elite junior were stronger. He'd known the second the words had left Senior Surrey's mouth he wouldn't let Butterfly and Silver get killed. To ensure their safety he had to find a way to turn their birthchip blockers on.

The opportunity had arisen yesterday evening, when Senior Surrey sent him on assignment to oversee the delivery of explosives to the Pigeons and follow it to where the group were based. Cobe's luck had been in. Not only did he find that Limpets rat Akhezo skulking in the stairwell and managed to negotiate for him to turn Butterfly and Silver's birthchip blockers on, but he'd also had the location of the Pigeons' hideout to bring back to Senior Surrey. He hoped that would take Senior Surrey's attention away from Butterfly and Silver for a little while.

Still, he couldn't rely on that. Senior Surrey was a man who saw his decisions through with a steady, fierce determination, so ever since the previous evening, Cobe had been waiting anxiously for Akhezo to turn on Butterfly and Silver's blockers. As long as the red light was still lit in the birthchip charm, it meant they were still not safe.

'Come on, Akhezo!' he growled, slamming his hand on the table. He got up and paced in front of the glass wall, trying to ignore the glowing red dot. Then, on the sixth or seventh lap of the window –

The light was off.

Cobe didn't dare believe it. He ran over to the

birthchip charm, picking it up. No red eye nestled at its heart. The light was really *gone*. He fell to his knees, clutching the birthchip charm with shaking hands. He couldn't believe it. He'd done it. His Elite junior was safe.

'Butterfly,' he whispered. 'I –'

The sharp sound of knuckles on the bedroom door made him look up. He heard a voice murmuring behind it. Blinking back the tears that had come to his eyes, Cobe brushed down his clothes, stuffed the birthchip charm in his pocket, and went to open the door.

'Cobe!' Taiyo exclaimed as he opened it. She was standing next to Allum, the top of her head only reaching his waist. She swayed her hips, swinging her hoop-hemmed dress, and smiled tentatively. 'We were wondering whether you wanted to get lunch with us. We haven't spent much time together since . . . since, you know, because *someone* thought you might want space.' She shot a dark look upwards at Allum, who rolled his eyes. 'But I think it's about time we start hanging out together. Otherwise, when Butterfly and Silver come home, they'll be angry with us for not staying friends!'

'Great idea!' Cobe said, with so much enthusiasm Taiyo raised one eyebrow. 'Let me just change and then I'll come along.'

'Really? I thought you were going to turn us away and carry on sulki—'

Allum laughed quickly, ruffling her hair. 'Come now, baby girl. He said yes, didn't you hear? Now, what do

192

you fancy, Cobe? We were thinking the Dumpling Bar in Chinatown.'

'Sounds perfect.' Cobe grinned, and he truly meant it.

It was bright outside. Cobe felt giddy under the heat of the sun as they walked down Noda Parkway, flushed with relief at the thought that he might just have saved Butterfly and Silver. Of course, he couldn't be sure, but he'd given them a way to evade Senior Surrey's plans now, and he had this strange sense that it would work. Perhaps it was the warmth of the springtime day, or perhaps it was just the buoyancy of being in his friends' company, but something told Cobe that Butterfly and Silver would be safe now.

'I'm going to get those giant dumplings,' said Taiyo. 'You know the ones – pork and honey. They're so big even *you* couldn't fit one in your mouth whole, Allum!'

Allum glanced over at Cobe and winked. 'Oh, is that so, baby girl? Well, I think *that* sounds like a bet.'

Cobe laughed, but was cut short as he stumbled into someone.

'Watch it!' a voice hissed.

It was Ember. She looked striking, her hair a flaming red under the sun. She was dressed in a colourful scaled cape, her eyebrows decorated with the thick brushstroke pattern popular among Neo-Babel's fashionable women.

'Sorry, Ember,' he muttered.

Taiyo danced forward. 'We're just off to the Dumpling Bar. Do you want to come?'

Ember brushed the girl aside, grabbing Cobe's hand

and pulling him away. 'I was just coming to find you,' she said. 'I have good news about our juniors.'

He nodded. *So she knows about Butterfly and Silver's birthchip blockers activating too*, he thought.

'I've just come back from Central Police Command,' she continued. 'Surrey let me oversee the dispatch of the special team of police soldiers he sent to the location outside Neo where our idiot juniors are. They've been scoping the place out for the past half-hour. Apparently, there is a village. A *village*! Probably full of anti-birthchip sympathisers and escaped criminals. So Surrey ordered the soldiers to kill the lot of them. They're doing it right now.' She laughed coldly. 'How incredible is that?'

Cobe stared at her. The ground beneath his feet seemed to have dropped away.

'I came here because I wanted to thank you,' said Ember.

He made a choking sound. '*Thank* me?'

'Indeed. You conducted the information exchange with that anti-birthchip scum. Without his information, we wouldn't have known Butterfly and Silver were outside, and Surrey might not have decided to track their birth-chips. It's all thanks to you. I assumed you were as weak as the rest of them, but maybe not. Well done.'

With that, Ember shot one scathing look at Taiyo and Allum behind them before stalking off, her scaled cape flashing in the sun.

Taiyo reached out to grab his hand. 'What's wrong, Cobe?' she asked, but he staggered away from her.

It can't be, he thought. *It just can't*. Blindly, he spun round and began to run. Allum's voice boomed at his back but Cobe ignored him, running faster, down the broad sweep of Noda Parkway, clipping past people who jumped out of his way. As he ran, he bit back the tears that were filling his eyes.

He'd never considered that the birthchip charm might have turned off because Butterfly was dead.

24

Fire and Ice

Back in the broken house. The smell of burnt things, and heavy smoke thickening the air. Rain drumming the roof.

Butterfly wasn't dead, but his mother and sister were. Kneeling on the floor, he cradled Emeli in his arms. He'd not moved since he'd first found her and picked her up. Like Emeli, Leanor had been flung from the bed where she had been sleeping. She lay face down on the floor. She could have just been sleeping, but her body was shaped wrong. She was too still.

Minutes had stretched by after Silver left. Though half the house had been blown apart, there were no flames feeding on the part that still stood, and so Butterfly hadn't needed to move. A small miracle, or perhaps an apology. The smoke that filled the room kept him and his mother and sister hidden from the rest of the world. Huddled in its cloudy arms, he'd almost forgotten that there *was* a rest of the world when the gunfire began.

Unlike Silver, there was no rage. No anger accompanied the realisation of what was happening, no hard, hot fire. Instead, a coldness spread through him. He hadn't heard Yasir's story, but he'd had his own suspicions about the Council's actions in the Outside from what his mother and sister had told him. After all, the Council had tried to kill his family. They clearly had no reservations or loyalties, even for their own.

Butterfly placed Emeli gently on the floor beside Leanor. 'I'll be back soon,' he whispered.

As he turned to leave, he stepped on his backpack lying in the doorway. Silver had been wearing hers that morning, but he'd followed her without his. *Of all the things not to have been damaged*, he thought, and he almost broke down again right there in the doorway. But instead he forced himself to remain calm. He opened the bag and pulled out his stungun.

From the corridor came the sound of hurried footsteps. Butterfly looked up see a masked soldier scrambling into the house. For a split second, they stared at each other. Then –

Butterfly dived forward as bullets flicked over his head. He collided with the soldier and they fell onto the floor in a tumble of thuds, bodies crashing. Butterfly scrambled up. The soldier still had his gun, and was starting to raise it, but Butterfly was quicker. He lunged forward with his stungun. Immediately, the soldier's body turned rigid. Then he slumped down, unconscious, the gun falling from his hand.

Butterfly stared at it. An N70 pistol, just like the ones they practised with at the shooting range. He tucked the stungun into the waistband of his trousers and bent down to pick up the real gun.

Outside, in the world of fire and rain. Crushed primroses underfoot. Birds screaming high overhead. Huge, engorged clouds emptying and emptying on the pitiful landscape as though trying to wash the world away.

Silver ran towards the soldier. He hadn't spotted her, and she slammed into him from behind, sending his gun flying. They smashed into the ground. Digging her fingers into the mud-slicked earth, she brought her knee up to meet with the soldier's stomach. Then she scrambled past him, reaching for his gun.

She had forgotten about the bag on her back. The stungun inside it.

Silver grabbed the soldier's gun, feeling the familiar shape of the N70 in her hands. She spun round. Aimed it at the soldier. He was back on his feet and turning to look at her. Her hand trembled slightly but she held it still enough, and when his masked face lifted –

You're going to pay for this.

She pulled the trigger.

The bullet hit the soldier in the forehead. He spun. Fell to the ground. Lay still.

Silver stared at his body. It was the first time she had killed someone. She was surprised at how natural it felt, as if the bullet was just all the anger inside her hardened into a tiny shell and expelled from her fingertips. Expelled from her heart. She felt nothing at all for the soldier. Turning away, she scanned the village for more soldiers. The red fire still burned inside her. In her mind bullets clustered, clamouring to be let free.

Holding the soldier's gun tight in one hand, Butterfly stepped out of Leanor and Emeli's house. Rain rushed to meet him, but he barely noticed it as he picked his way across the rubble, his ears pricking at every gunshot. He followed the sounds further into the village. Immediately he spotted soldiers darting from house to house. A spattering of gunfire rose and fell as they found survivors then moved on. It was quick. Clinical. Still Butterfly felt only coldness, and an itch in his trigger finger.

The soldiers hadn't seen him yet. They were busy with their work, and the rain cloaked him, blurring him into the landscape so he was nothing more than a shadow against the smoke and fire. He approached the building where one soldier had disappeared inside, flattened himself against the wall, and waited. When the soldier ran back out less than a minute later, he darted out.

Butterfly aimed low. The bullet glanced off the soldier's leg and the man turned, his masked face swinging towards him, an arm raising his gun –

A clean, crisp gunshot ripped through the air.

The soldier jerked forward. His gun went off – the bullet went wide of Butterfly – then he fell to the ground, still. Behind him stood Silver. Her face was so cold and hard that Butterfly didn't recognise her at first. She lowered her gun, running over and dragging him round the corner of the building. They slammed back against the wall, panting.

'You shot . . .' he breathed.

Silver didn't seem to hear him. 'Emeli? Leanor?'

Butterfly shook his head.

'Oh,' she whispered. Her face softened for a moment

before hardening again. She nodded to his gun. 'Let's go.' She made to move out onto the street but Butterfly grabbed her.

'What are you doing?'

'They're killing everyone,' said Silver, her voice breaking. 'We need to stop them.'

'Where's your stungun?' Butterfly demanded.

She shook her head. 'There's no time for this.' She tried to twist out of his grip but he held onto her, fingers digging into her skin.

'You'll get killed running around like this, Silver. We need to get away. We need to move . . . move my mother and sister.' His voice caught on the last few words.

But Silver wrenched herself free from him, and after a final look – her eyes burned like the buildings around them – she ran back out into the street.

Butterfly cursed, kicking his heels into the ground to run after her. There were a group of soldiers up ahead. He knew that if Silver charged straight at them she wouldn't stand a chance. She might take a few down, but they were outnumbered, and they weren't using the measured efficiency the Council had taught them to on assignments. Her reckless anger was going to get her killed. He had to stop her.

Moving the gun to his left hand, Butterfly pulled out his stungun and gave one final burst of speed, pulling the trigger. A shock of blue-white leapt ahead. It caught Silver in the back. She straightened suddenly, falling to the ground. Before the soldiers could notice them, he scooped her up and, clutching her in his arms, ran back towards the other end of the village. The sporadic stutter of gunfire laughed at his retreating back.

'Sorry,' Butterfly whispered, holding Silver tightly to his chest. 'I'm sorry.'

He didn't know who he was apologising to.

25

Down the River and Away

First there was grief. Acceptance, and the full, hard blow of it, crippling Butterfly to his knees. The questions, the anger, came later.

Four hours since the explosion. Butterfly stood in the shallows of the river, a few metres away from where he'd left Silver under a willow near the bank. He'd rolled up the bottoms of his trousers and taken his boots off, letting the water rush around his legs, cleaning the ash-grime and mud from his skin and carrying it downriver in dirty brown rivulets. There was some blood too; red curls, fragile and quickly disappearing into the blue.

Butterfly held his mother and sister in his arms. Their bodies were inside a small funeral boat he'd made from tree branches tied together by the ropey leaves of the willow. In Neo-Babel, the custom for many Western Mainland cultures was to float the bodies of the deceased down the river on a wicker-reed boat, handmade by their living relatives, with the funeral procession following behind in a black wind-boat. Out here, he wouldn't be able to follow Leanor and Emeli, but he could at least send their bodies down the river and away.

The first time Butterfly had been to his family's funeral,

he'd thought they'd been killed in a different explosion. Two boxes, his mother and baby sister in one, his father the other. Now he knew that all they'd contained was air and dust. But this funeral was real. He had to get it right.

He'd found the perfect place for it. A quiet, secret part of the river, sheltered on either side by gorse bushes and small trees. A large willow clung to the bank, brushing the tips of its long arms across the water's surface. When Butterfly had first found it, the afternoon had still been wreathed in grey light, a drizzle falling that rustled the grass and pattered off the leaves of bushes and trees. But as he waded into the river, the heavy bulks of the clouds rolled away. They left behind the startled face of the sun amid a gleaming, spotless sky. Sunlight swept across the land, a kiss upon his forehead.

He tipped his head back, letting the light warm his skin. As the sky cleared, the eerie hush of the valley gave way to gentle afternoon sounds; birdsong, the bubbling of the river. Butterfly thought how his mother and sister had died in a dark, smoke-choked place. It was not fair. They belonged here, in the light, in the warm golden rush with the promise of life carried on the air.

It slammed into him again then; grief so hard it was like the sky had fallen and was crushing him to the ground. He let the tears be squeezed out of him, but he refused to give in to it. He'd not give the Council the satisfaction.

Butterfly glanced over at Silver, where she lay beside the tree. She was still sleeping, curled on one side, her knees tucked into her chin. It reminded him of how they lay together in his bedpod back in the Stacks. That life seemed a whole world away now.

He waded further into the river, the small boat balanced on his arms. The water was a solid coldness around him. He moved deeper in until the water was up to his chest and, standing there, he finally felt the full force of what had happened.

An agony rushed through him, dragging tears from his eyes like fingers were scrabbling, scraping them out. Butterfly tried to imagine Leanor and Emeli's blackened skin turning back to untouched white as the water washed over them. He knew he needed to let go now, but he didn't want to. He wanted to hold the boat with his mother and sister's bodies forever. He wanted to stay standing like this in the river with the water rushing round him until it rose up and took him into its cool arms too.

There was a trill of birdsong in a nearby tree, and it was that that finally gave Butterfly the strength to let go, remembering how Emeli had told him she loved birds. He dropped his arms down, taking his support away from the base of the boat. The momentum of the water took the boat a couple of metres downriver before its weight grew too much and it dipped under the surface, just a dark, blurry shadow lowering to the riverbed.

'Goodbye,' he whispered. He felt he should say something more, but he had no words.

Butterfly climbed out of the river, dark patches blos-soming on the bank where he walked, the water dripping from his clothes. All of a sudden, a red-hot rage consumed him. He'd held it back till then. The grief had held it back. But now the river had taken all he had, leaving a hard, burning core. He didn't think he'd ever been angry before. Not properly, not really. Not until he'd felt what it was like to have his whole world exposed as a lie and to know that he'd talked to – he'd *worked* for – the very people that had stolen years of happiness with his family away from him.

They had told him his family were dead. They had made him put on a suit with arms too long for his six-year-old's body, had made him go to a fake funeral to watch the boats drift out towards the gate over the waterfall. Small boats like two broken wings that the water tugged away from him. And now Butterfly was at their funeral again, knowing he would never have one more second with his family.

It felt as though a hand was tightening around his throat. He needed air. He needed to be *in* air. Above, the empty blue sky glittered like a promise. Butterfly tore off his shirt and spread his wings. He was so blinded by rage that when Silver stepped out from the willow, the anger exploded out of him and, thinking her a Neo-Babel soldier come back to finish the job, he swung round at her, roaring, his wings flaring like sharp white flames behind him. Silver shrunk back. Her face and clothes were streaked with ash and dirt and blood. A cut split her bottom lip almost in two. 'What . . . what happened?' she asked. 'Did you shock me to stop me going after the –'

'Yes, I shocked you!' Butterfly roared. 'What were you

thinking, running around like that while soldiers from Neo were taking every living thing down? You thought you could take them? You thought just because you're a precious Elite, killing them would be *easy* for you? That it would mean nothing? Or what?' His voice lowered to a hiss. 'Maybe you hoped they'd realise you're an Elite and throw their guns away. Maybe even ask you to join them? Is *that* what you wanted?'

Silver narrowed her eyes. She said nothing, but her mouth was tight, and she didn't flinch as Butterfly made a sudden movement backwards.

'It's because of you my mum and sister are dead. Your parents are probably fine. They must've left like mine to get away from the Council, and who can blame them after what we've seen? We should have *let* them leave. Instead, you had to follow them, and we led the Council straight to the village. Straight to . . .' His voice broke. 'To my family. Those birthchip blockers must have been fake. They were fake, and we just walked straight into the village, not caring or worrying that Senior Surrey might track our birthchips after finding out we'd disappeared. We may as well have shot them all ourselves. We as good as killed them.'

Silver shook her head. 'You shouldn't have stunned me,' she said in a cool voice. 'You should have let me kill the soldiers.' Then she turned and walked away.

'Where are you going?' Butterfly asked.

'To check the village,' she answered, not looking round. 'There might be survivors.'

He followed her through a gap in the gorse bushes and out into the open countryside.

Silver glanced back at him. 'Are you coming, then? If not, I'll meet you back here when I'm done.'

Butterfly stopped and stared after her. She looked so small, so vulnerable against the rolling green valleys and hills, the distant line of the forest where Yasir's village was buried at its core, smoke still rising from the dying fires. He knew he should go. It was the right thing to do. But the thought of returning to the place where his mother and sister had died was too much.

Without saying anything to Silver, he turned, launching himself into the air. Butterfly didn't care where he was going. He just had to move. He flew for so long his body began to hurt with the effort, but he didn't stop. The pain felt good. He *needed* it. As he flew, the pain dug into his back where his wings sprouted, achy and hard. It replaced the agony he felt inside with an agony he felt in his bones and muscles. Replaced an unbearable agony with a bearable one.

At the same time, it did nothing to help at all.

26

Cambridge's Weakness

Akhezo scrambled through the metal hatch into the room at the base of the skylung. He was panting and red-faced, having been up and down the staircase that led to the tunnel to the Limpets what felt like a hundred times that day. As he pulled himself over the edge of the hatch for what he hoped would be the last time, someone grabbed his ankle.

'Hey!' he shouted, as the hand dragged him down and he fell forward onto the floor.

'Thanks, Akhezo!' Neve trilled. She crawled over him and out of the hatch.

He jumped to his feet. 'You complete –'

'What about me?' she gasped, batting her eyelashes and flapping a hand at her face. 'Why, dear Akhezo – were you about to say that I'm wonderful? That I'm the most *beautiful* girl you've ever seen? That I'm –'

'A useless little rat that needs to shut her trap.'

They jumped, turning to see Domino shuffling into the workroom. He was dragging an armchair behind him. 'Well, don't just gape at me. Come and take this chair down to the rickshaw.'

'What d'you need *that* for?' Akhezo grumbled. 'Cambridge told us to only bring the essentials.'

'This *is* essential!' snapped Domino. 'When you're old and have a back like mine, you'll understand the beauty of the perfect chair. Now, hurry and get it down. We should've been out of here by now.' Not waiting for an answer, he lowered himself down the hatch, wheezing heavily.

'That's it – save yourself, old man,' hissed Akhezo when Domino was out of earshot. 'Don't worry that *we* might be blown up with the skylung while we're trying to drag your stupid chair out of here.' But he took hold of the armchair anyway. He nodded at Neve. 'Get the other end. We'll bring it down together.'

'Of course, my dear! I long for anything we can do *together*.'

'Oh, if you're gonna start this again –'

'Fine, fine, I'll stop!' She grinned, holding up her hands and hurrying to help him with the chair.

Neve had been teasing Akhezo for the past few days about something she'd apparently overheard him say about her while he was asleep. He'd denied it, of course, but it was true. Neve had been in his dreams lately.

They carried Domino's armchair down the staircase, Akhezo supporting its weight from underneath, while Neve held onto it at the top.

'So,' Akhezo said, keeping his eyes on the steps before him. 'You gonna miss this place?'

It was the sort of question Neve might have scoffed at before now, but their experience in the stairwell the night of the Council member's appearance had changed something between them.

'Yeah, I'll miss it,' she said quietly. 'It was our home.'

'It sure beat the Limpets, anyway.'

'Yeah. It did.'

The ringing of their clunking footsteps was the only sound in the narrow stairwell. All of the Pigeons had already left the skylung with essential supplies and equipment over the course of the afternoon.

'Hey, Akhezo?'

'Yeah?'

'What did you do before?' Neve asked. 'I mean, back in the Limpets. Before coming here.'

'I worked for this Red who ran a forge,' he answered.

'What about your parents?'

Akhezo hesitated. 'My mum abandoned me when I was born.' He forced a laugh, though inside he felt a stab of anger. 'Mr Kwan was always saying he got a good deal, getting me free like that.'

'I wish my parents had left *me* when I was born.'

'What d'you mean?'

'My dad liked malt beer,' said Neve, her voice trembling. 'He liked it more than he liked me and Mum. He used to . . . Anyway, that's probably why he sold me, when Domino came looking. Beer money.'

They made their way down the last few steps in silence. When they reached the bottom of the stairwell, they dropped the armchair, and Neve sat on it, drawing her knees up to her chest.

'Is that what that was?' Akhezo asked, remembering the day she arrived at the Limpets. There had been bruises on her face; blue-black shadows in the hollows of her eyes and cheeks.

She nodded.

He jabbed her with a finger. 'So that's why you threw a punch at me, huh? Wanted to even things out?'

It wasn't funny, but Neve laughed anyway. 'Yeah.' She smiled, fiddling with one of her ear piercings. She glanced down. When she looked back up her eyes glinted. 'That and I could tell you were easy bait.'

Akhezo grinned. He was about to reply when a voice rang down from the square of light at the top of the stairwell.

'Hello? Is anyone down there?'

'Cambridge!' said Akhezo excitedly. He raised his voice and shouted back, 'Here!'

'Ah, good,' Cambridge called, descending the stairs so quickly it looked as though he was skipping. 'I was afraid you'd all gone. I see our chariot has arrived!'

There was the unmistakable squeaking of bicycle wheels coming down the tunnel. By the time Cambridge reached the bottom of the stairs, a rickshaw had pulled into the stairwell.

'Let us board, my dear friends,' he said, throwing an arm around Akhezo and Neve.

Since Neve had told him about their encounter with the Council member, they had been back in Cambridge's favour. Akhezo was glad for that. Here was another shot to prove his worth to the leader of the Pigeons. All his feelings about wanting to leave the Limpets and hating

Cambridge had vanished when, instead of reacting angrily to their spying and tossing them out of the skylung as Akhezo had thought he would do, Cambridge had thanked them instead.

The rickshaw moved down the tunnel to the Limpets, the neon strips of light lining the tunnel blurred behind the material that was draped across the front of the passenger bench.

Akhezo was squeezed in the middle of the bench between Neve and Cambridge. 'Sir –'

'Cambridge, please.'

'Er . . . well, I've been thinking 'bout something.'

'What something?' Cambridge asked, smiling.

'I wanted to know why you seem so sure about the skylung getting destroyed,' said Akhezo hesitantly. 'I mean, of course it was bad for the Council to know where we are, but that Council member did say he wouldn't tell . . .'

Cambridge raised an eyebrow. 'And you believed him? I've been around long enough to know that Council members aren't afraid of lying to get what they want, my dear boy.'

Just as I am, thought Akhezo, glancing away. He'd not told anyone about turning off the Elites' birthchips. He still wanted the money the Council member had promised, but now he wanted it to give to Cambridge as a sign of his loyalty.

'But I do admit,' continued Cambridge, 'there's more to it than that. You see, I *wanted* the Council to track the delivery.'

Akhezo's eyes widened. 'You wanted . . .?'

Cambridge nodded. 'I needed explosives, and we didn't have access to nearly enough materials to make the amount I needed. I also knew that asking the Council for explosives would enable them to track the delivery. *That's* what they've been waiting for all these years – their chance to find our hideout once and for all.'

'So we didn't really save everyone.' Akhezo scowled.

'No, no!' Cambridge said quickly, squeezing Akhezo's shoulder. 'That's not true at all. Without you two, I wouldn't have known for definite that they did track the delivery, and then we'd have moved out of our beloved home for nothing. Your input was essential.'

'But, sir,' said Neve. 'Why would you *want* the Council to know where we were?'

'Good question, my dear girl. You see, I know what the Council are like. They're rash and trigger-happy. They prefer quick revenge over a more thought-out approach. I knew that if they discovered where we were operating from, they'd want to destroy all evidence of us. Quickly.'

Akhezo shook his head. 'But why would you want *that*?'

'Because we're ready,' answered Cambridge.

'For what?'

'For the Pigeons' final flight!' Cambridge grinned, and his face was alight with the same feverish glow Akhezo had seen that day when he'd first reported the news about those two Council snobs. 'My dear friends – it's finally time for us to take down the Council once and for all.'

*　　*　　*

213

The Pigeons' temporary hideout was in a large hall on the bottom floor of the Limpets. It felt strange to Akhezo to be so deep within the earth. It was difficult to tell what time of day it was without any windows or balconies to watch the sun rise or set, to look out at the night-time city full of multicoloured lights. The only light came from the lamps set into the walls, filling the hall with a flickering yellow.

Most of the Pigeons were busy sorting things out from their move. Akhezo watched from where he was sat against the wall beside Neve. She was sleeping with her head resting on his lap, her arms curled round his crossed legs, and he forced himself to focus on the activity in the hall to block out thoughts of Neve so close to him, the feel of her body against his.

'Akhezo? May I, ah, have a moment?'

Cambridge had crouched down beside him so quietly Akhezo hadn't even noticed.

Akhezo nodded. Cambridge sat, leaning back against the wall. His green eyes were softer than usual. He reached out to touch Akhezo's hand where it lay on the ground.

'I wanted to apologise,' he said. 'On the shisha boat . . . I let those two women throw you overboard. I didn't save you.'

Akhezo remembered how betrayed he had felt, lying on the deck of the junk-boat, soaked through and shivering. He nodded curtly.

'I wanted to help you,' Cambridge went on. 'But I couldn't have. It would have shown the Council my weakness, and would have put you in terrible danger.'

Akhezo raised his eyebrows. 'Your weakness?'

Cambridge squeezed Akhezo's hand. He let out a long sigh. 'Do you know how I became leader of the Pigeons?' he asked.

Akhezo shook his head.

'I had a daughter,' explained Cambridge. His voice was quiet. He looked down at the floor as he spoke, his eyes glazed. 'I *have* a daughter,' he corrected. 'But she doesn't want anything to do with me. Her mother and I separated when our children were young. At birth, my daughter had been streamed into the Council for their Elite training programme, you see. I didn't agree with it, but her mother . . . ah, she always did care too much about her social status. She revelled in the newfound glory our daughter had brought us, and in time, our differences on the matter were too much to overcome.'

'Sorry, sir,' muttered Akhezo.

Cambridge nodded absentmindedly. 'I don't know what the Council did to her, but as the years passed, my daughter grew more and more distant from me. Eventually, she refused to see me. She told me I would ruin her reputation at the Council with my anti-birthchip talk. That she was . . .' He took a deep breath, stroking Akhezo's hand tenderly. 'That she was ashamed of me. Her mother felt the same. She wouldn't even let me visit our son, and it has been so long since I've seen my children, I am terrified I would not recognise them any more.' Cambridge looked up at Akhezo. His green eyes flashed with their usual bright-ness. 'Ah, do you see, Akhezo? *Children* are my weakness. I may have lost my own, but I have found comfort in saving children such as yourself and Neve from pitiful futures in the Limpets, and exposing you to the ways in which birthchips tear us apart.'

'I had no idea,' breathed Akhezo. He thought he would have felt angry at Cambridge calling him a child, but right now, with Cambridge's hand stroking his, talking to him as though a father, Akhezo didn't care. In that moment, he felt like a child –

Cambridge's child.

'If I'd stopped those women from throwing you overboard,' explained Cambridge, 'the Council would have seen how deeply I care for you, and it could have made you a target. I couldn't do that to you. Can you forgive me?'

Just as Akhezo opened his mouth to reply, screams and shouts erupted from the central cavern, and Pigeon members jumped to their feet, rushing towards the doorway.

'This is it!' shouted Cambridge, leaping up. 'The explosion! The skylung! Come on, my young friend!' He started across the hall and was soon swallowed by the crowd.

Neve was sitting up blearily, startled out of her sleep. Akhezo grabbed her hand and pulled her to her feet.

'It's happening, Neve!' he cried.

It took them twenty minutes to find an opening in the face of the Limpets where they could actually see out, as many of the slum-dwellers had gathered to watch the skylung burn. Akhezo caught flashes of yellow out of the corners of his eyes as they ran. Each flash sent his heart racing faster. After climbing to the Limpets' top tier, they finally found an unoccupied stretch of ledge and clambered out onto it, staring at the view that had opened in front of them with wide eyes.

A huge circle of fire glowed against the dark, light-spotted backdrop of the inner city. The factories of the Industrial District blocked the lower parts of the skylung from view, but Akhezo still felt as though he could see the whole circle, a fiery ring burning in the deepening evening light.

'What are we going to do now?' Neve whispered, taking one of his hands. She was trembling.

'I'm gonna find that Council member. There's something he owes me.'

'What do you mean, there's something he *owes* you?'

Akhezo grinned, turning to her. 'After you left, I went after him. I didn't tell you 'cause I wanted it to be a surprise, but I got money from him. We're gonna be rich.'

She just blinked. The light of the flames danced in her eyes.

'*Money*, Neve,' he repeated. 'For tuning off the birthchips. I thought we could give the money to Cambridge, as a present. With the skylung gone, I think he'll really appreciate it. And I was gonna set aside a little for you, too,' he added, his voice softening. 'Thought you could get something nice for yourself . . .'

Neve leaned forward suddenly and kissed Akhezo's cheek. 'Thank you.'

'So we'll go?' He grinned, squeezing her hand.

'Tomorrow? I was meant to meet him tonight but the skylung's destroyed now. We'll have to find him in the Council District.'

She bit her lip. 'That place has always scared me.'

'You should get used to it,' Akhezo said, his smile widening. 'After all, once the Pigeons' final flight is over, it's gonna be ours.'

27

Shadows in the Forest

Night had fallen by the time Silver arrived back at the river. The moon – full, gorged, gloating – sat high in the sky, and a fog stirred, curling across the ground like smoke. Butterfly saw the beam of her torch slicing through the darkness as she came, reflecting off the gleaming skin of the river she was following up to the place where he sat beneath the willow.

It had been hours since she'd left. The anger had fallen away from Butterfly, somewhere up there in the air as he'd moved over the green fields and forests. His whole body had burned with pain, each new beat of his wings sending a fresh burst of fire through him, and he'd flown until his body was screaming in agony. Maybe that had been what had saved him from the anger. As the pain had filled him, it had pushed away the rage. After all, there was only so much feeling one body could hold.

He watched Silver approach, feeling ashamed at the things he'd said to her. The truth was he didn't blame her for his mother and sister's death; he blamed *himself*. For being one of the Council's puppets for so long, for not thinking of the danger they could bring by staying in Yasir's village. And, although he had little space in his heart for anger now that the grief was back, like a tight fist in his chest, there was a part of him that blamed Cobe, too.

Cobe was not only Butterfly's Elite senior; he was his friend. How could Cobe have known about his family being alive for so many years and not tell him? Yes, Butterfly had only been six then. But he'd still have wanted to know. Maybe he wouldn't have been able to leave Neo-Babel, but he'd at least have known better than to continue to serve the very people who'd tried to kill his family.

'Did you find anything?' Butterfly asked when Silver was closer.

She shook her head. Her eyes were clouded with darkness, and he could see the weight of searching through the dead village dragging her body down. When she reached where he sat in the curve of the willow's roots, she collapsed to the ground, her teeth chattering.

'Are you cold?' he asked.

'Yes. Did you not want to make a fire or something?'

Butterfly stiffened at the word *fire*. Images flashed through his mind; his mother and sister's house, wreathed in smoke, Silver's ponytail swinging as she ran towards the soldiers through flickering, fiery shadows. He could almost taste the burnt air on his lips.

She pushed herself up quickly. 'I'm sorry, I didn't think.'

'It's fine,' he said, shaking his head. 'I can make one if you want?'

'No, I'm all right.' Silver was watching him carefully,

as though he might lash out at her again at any second. She gestured at the space next to him. 'Can I?'

Butterfly nodded, moving over so there was more space in the nest of roots beside him. Silver slipped off her backpack and sat down. At first, her body was stiff, careful not to touch his, but after a few minutes she leant into him, resting her head on his shoulder.

It killed Butterfly to feel her against him. Her heat, her smell, her small, female frame; it killed him that she was here, and his mother and sister weren't. He wanted to scream. He wanted to push her off him. To get as far away from her as possible. Instead, he took a deep breath and lifted an arm to lie across Silver's shoulders.

'I found Yasir,' Silver ventured after a few minutes of silence. The tone of her voice made it clear that she hadn't found him alive. 'I . . . I didn't see Leanor and Emeli, though.'

'I sent them away,' said Butterfly.

But he hadn't really. They were right here with him, curled in his heart, where he'd never let go of them.

The next morning, Silver jerked awake, startled and delirious, gripped by the fever of a nightmare. Pulling herself up from where she had slumped down the willow's trunk, she looked round for Butterfly.

He was sitting on the riverbank with his back to her. Soft morning light lit the curve of his shoulders, his messy brown hair. She watched him, the echo of her nightmare still shivering in the air before her. But it wasn't a nightmare; it was a memory. And she knew that unlike a nightmare, it would never leave her, no matter how many times she woke and opened her eyes, praying to the gods it was gone. Silver couldn't imagine how much worse it was for Butterfly, who'd lost his family a second time. It made her think of her own parents. Were they alive still, or had something awful happened to them, too?

She shook her head. It was too painful to think about. Brushing down her clothes, she got up and walked over to Butterfly.

He turned as he heard her approach. 'I need a wash,' he said, his voice flat. 'Change out of these clothes.'

Silver gestured at the willow tree. Its leaves hung across the river, blocking the view upstream. 'We could wash on either side in the river?' she suggested.

Butterfly nodded. 'I'll go on the other side.'

'All right. See you in ten minutes.'

Once he was gone, Silver took off her filthy clothes and waded into the river. The cold water clenched around her body, making her gasp, but she pushed on, moving deeper. It was so peaceful here in the private little strip of river; birds singing as their tiny shadows flitted across the sky, the smell of grass and fresh water and sunshine warming the ground. Blossom and midges dancing like dust in the slating sunlight. As she cleaned herself, Silver tried to focus on these things. They helped her hold back the memories of yesterday, the fire and burning and gunshots and bodies, blackened and broken.

Don't think about it, she told herself, chanting it almost like a prayer as she washed the dirt off her skin and out of her hair. *Don't think about it. Just don't think about it.*

When she was clean, she left the river and dried herself with the blanket from her backpack, then dressed in her Elite uniform. 'Are you done?' she called round the willow.

Butterfly didn't reply.

After calling once more and still not getting a reply, Silver edged round the tree. The upstream part of the river came into view. She could see the wide silver path of the river as it reached up into distant forested hills, and there, waist-deep in the water just beyond the willow's rustling curtain –

A completely naked Butterfly.

Silver felt herself blush furiously. All at once, the memory of their kiss in the forest yesterday came back to her so strongly she could feel the heat of Butterfly's hands cupping her face. The soft pressure of his lips on hers. The hunger she'd felt stirring deep inside her, both for Butterfly and the word he'd whispered the night before behind a closed door; *love*. A small, beautiful world that had come into her life so unexpectedly. She wondered how it was possible to be around someone all your life, and then wake up one day and see them with completely new eyes. Or had the feelings always been there, buried away inside their hearts until they'd been ready to face them?

Silver's eyes were tethered to Butterfly's body. He was facing away from her. Water-slicked skin stretched gently over tight muscles, broad across his shoulders and back before sloping down to narrow, perfect hips. His wings were folded against his back as they always were when he wasn't using them. They too glistened with droplets of water. As her eyes trailed slowly down his body they caught on the curve of his buttocks, half hidden by the water that lapped against him. For some reason, the sight made Silver feel like crying.

She shook her head. Forcing herself to pull her eyes away from Butterfly's body, she strode along the bank to where his backpack lay in a pile with his clothes. 'I'm not looking,' she announced loudly. She pulled out the blanket from his backpack and held it out in his direction. 'Here.'

When he didn't answer, Silver looked round. Butterfly hadn't moved, and now she could see his face, she saw that his eyes were glassy and hollow. They stared straight ahead at nothing. The emptiness in them made her heart ache.

She walked to the edge of the water. 'You've been in long enough.'

Butterfly turned, finally registering her. He looked down quickly at his body.

'Yes, you're naked,' she said matter-of-factly. She held out the blanket and waved it. 'That's what *this* is for.'

Cupping a hand between his legs, Butterfly climbed out of the water.

Silver handed him the blanket. 'Dry yourself, then put your clean clothes on. I'll wash the other ones for you.'

They spent the rest of the morning like this; Silver giving Butterfly directions to look after himself and him obeying silently. She hated this wordless, blank-faced grief. Her own grief and terror at what had happened

224

yesterday – and what she *herself* had done – was waiting to take her in its grip. But as long as Butterfly was like this, she couldn't let her own feelings take over. She owed him more than that.

An hour later, they were ready to leave. Silver wasn't sure how to broach the question. Did Butterfly want to go back to Neo-Babel perhaps, or did he want to stay by the willow forever? Going to find her parents was probably the last thing he wanted to do, but she had to ask. Yesterday's events had made her all the more desperate to find her parents, and she felt an anxious twist in the pit of her stomach every time she thought of them.

'Shall we go now?' She asked hesitantly. 'I have the directions to a settlement. Yasir thought my . . . he thought it might be good for us to look there, though he warned me it might be an anti-birthchip resistance. If we follow the river we should go straight to it.'

To her surprise, Butterfly nodded. His piercing blue eyes met hers, and for a brief second she thought he was going to smile or laugh or cry or scream or *something*. But then they slid away, as blank as ever.

'All right, then,' whispered Silver, pushing back the tears that had sprung to her eyes.

They walked in silence for hours. They kept moving, putting as much distance as possible between them and the destroyed village, but Silver could still feel the darkness at her back, threatening to swallow her whole. After a while, the open countryside turned into dense forest, the riverbank steepening into cliff edge pocketed with boulders and straggling tree roots. Sharp lines of sunlight cut through the trees. Silver had been able to ignore the dark thoughts that tugged at her while they had been walking out in the open, but here in the eerie forest-world, it was harder for her to ignore them.

They haunted her, those faceless ghosts of the Neo-Babel soldiers she had killed. In the shadows of the forest, she could feel them walking beside her. Soundless creatures, silent echoes of the men they had been. Between the columns of tree trunks they moved, but when she turned her head to look there was nothing there; just a ripple in the air, a sigh in the darkness. Her eyes focusing again and again on nothing.

Thin trickles of light were filtering through the twists and knots of leaves above, dappling the forest into a sun-speckled landscape. When Silver had woken from the nightmare that morning, she'd thought the day would be better. She'd thought the sunlight would chase away the ghosts of the night, push the darkness away. But daylight played tricks of its own. Skitters of sunshine glanced off the metallic skins of the soldiers. Sparkling beads of dew nestled in the curved palms of leaves flashed out of the shadows like hungry eyes.

While Silver was haunted by those she had killed, Butterfly was haunted by those he had lost.

For the most part, his mind was empty. A desolate space where grief coiled like a snake in the night. Thinking rustled it, made it stir and hiss expectantly, so

226

he tried not to think at all. But as he walked, his mother and sister danced out of reach in the forest's shadows. They called to him from behind the twisted web of vegetation, their faces flickering like static each time he moved his eyes.

'*Butterfly*,' they whispered. '*We're here, come join us! We escaped the fire and the soldiers. Come see!*'

When the grief was strong he followed their voices, drifting from the path by the river Silver was following ahead, but then the grief would spring back and slam into him so hard he knew he was delirious and he remembered how cold their bodies were and he understood that they were dead, dead.

'Take this.'

It was the first thing Butterfly had said to Silver since leaving the river that morning. They'd been walking through the forest for over two hours. She was so used to walking in silence that she almost didn't realise he had spoken.

She turned. Butterfly was holding out his backpack, his wings spread behind him.

'Take it?' she asked, walking back down the slope. 'Why?'

He didn't meet her eyes. 'I need to fly,' he said, handing her the backpack.

Panic gripped Silver then. She was terrified of being alone, in this forest with its ghosts and shadows. But she swallowed, reminding herself that it was the least she could do to let Butterfly go.

'Do you want me to wait here for you?' she asked, swinging his backpack over one shoulder.

'No. I'll be able to find you. Just follow the river, right? Anyway, I might be able to see the settlement from the air. What should I be looking out for?'

'Yasir said it's in the ruins of a city abandoned after the Great Fall.'

Butterfly nodded. 'I'll keep an eye out,' he said, and before Silver could reply, he flew up into the forest canopy, sending down a shower of leaves as he broke out into the sunlit world above.

She continued alone along the cliff-side path. As the hours slipped by, she told herself Butterfly would be back soon. When she stopped for lunch, she was so sure he'd arrive any minute that she even brought out some food for him. But he didn't come. Left alone with her thoughts, Silver finally felt the full force of what she'd done at the village yesterday. All day she'd been afraid of thinking about it. Now, her feelings burst inside her, rushing through her like the river far down to her right. What surprised her was that it wasn't how she'd expected to feel.

Ember had killed once. Some birthchip hacker smuggler had escaped after a raid on their hideout, and he'd been too far for her to scan his birthchip or use a stungun. Ember had probably wanted to kill him anyway. She didn't have to aim for his head. Silver still remembered how eager Ember had been as she'd recounted the story. It was that same glow in her eyes she'd seen that day in the storage room as Ember pressed a knife to her neck.

That's why Silver had thought she'd be different. She didn't think she was anything like Ember. She had always thought killing someone would be a huge, awful weight you could never throw off. That it would knot your insides with guilt until you couldn't feel anything else. But as she walked alone through the forest, remembering searching the village yesterday for survivors, she was filled with the same rage that had caused her to pick up the gun and shoot the Neo-Babel soldiers in the first place.

Silver had found Yasir's body laid over two other bodies, as though he had been trying to save them from the bullets. The thought of it made her want to scream. Anger; that's all she felt. There was no guilt, no shame. *No*, she thought. *The problem is I didn't kill* enough *of them*. And as she walked, her rage rolling off her in waves into the forest, the ghosts of the soldiers crept away into the shadows, giving up on haunting this wild-eyed girl who clutched her hands into fists at her sides.

28

The Ghost City

Silver had got so used to walking through the forest on her own that when Butterfly landed in front of her, she felt strangely angry at him. The forest had become *her* place.

'Good fly?' she said casually, glancing once at him before striding past.

He jogged to catch up with her. 'Are you angry with me?'

She ignored him.

He grabbed her arm. 'Will you talk to me –'

'*Now* you want to talk?' Silver hissed, wrenching herself out of his grip. 'Well, I don't want to. Go back to the air, fly boy.'

It sounded so ridiculous they both laughed, but that only made Silver angrier. She stomped away from Butterfly, pushing on through the forest. The light was starting to fade, filling the tree-columned landscape with washed-out pink. It would almost be time to make camp before nightfall, but she felt too restless to stop.

Butterfly caught up with her again. 'Silver, come on.'

She veered away. Down below, the river roared past. He dashed after her and tried to take her hand, but she jerked away from him, swerving to the right, and misjudged her step. There was little room up on the rocky lip of the gorge. Silver only had time to feel her mouth drop open in surprise when the muddy ground beneath her slid away and she fell down into the river below.

She dropped hard into the water. She went to scream from the shock of it and the cold water filled her mouth and nose, making her choke. The river raged around her. It tossed her so hard she couldn't tell which way was up. She scrabbled at the water, trying to follow the patches of light that glowed in places along the river. *I'm not going to die like this!* she thought, thinking how much she wanted – *needed* – to kill one more Neo-Babel soldier. Just one more to make right what they had done to Butterfly. To Yasir. And as though some river god had heard her plea, her face suddenly broke the water's surface.

Silver gulped in air. She tried to tread water to stay afloat, but the river was too strong. It swerved round a corner, swinging her near the side of the channel, and she spotted a large flat rock sticking out from the cliff-face. She reached out to grab it, her hand just inches away, and she realised at the last moment she wasn't going to make it –

Something slammed into Silver from behind, propelling her forward, and her fingers clasped the rock. Gasping with relief, she pulled herself up. The rock was just big enough to hold her. She hugged the muddy cliff-face. Above, the side of the gorge rose in a vertical ascent. She couldn't climb it; she'd fall.

'Here, Silver! Look!'

Butterfly stood at the top of the gorge, pointing to where the cliff-face rose less steeply. Rocks and tree roots jutted out at different angles, promising hand- and footholds. Silver dug a foot into the mud. She pushed herself up and started making her slow ascent. It was hard work. Now she was out of immediate danger, her body seemed to have realised how cold it was, and she shivered so badly her hands slipped. Finally, she made it to the top of the gorge.

Butterfly was at her side immediately, touching a hand to her back. His wings were spread wide behind him. 'I'm sorry,' he said. 'I didn't mean for you to fall. And then after pushing you, the tip of one of my wings got pulled under and I had to get away from the water before –'

Silver scrambled to her feet. 'You helped me?'

He looked confused. 'Yes. You were drowning –'

'You think I'm useless!' she shouted, slamming her hand into his chest and pushing him back. 'Poor little Silver, can't do anything right. Can't even stop an assassin when he's right there in front of her. Can't even be trusted to find her parents on her own. You're right – this *was* all my fault. None of this would've happened if it weren't for me.'

Butterfly stared at her, saying nothing.

Silver felt tears sliding down her face now. This realisation made her angrier. 'How dare you stop me?' she cried, beating her fists against his chest. 'How dare you stun me so I couldn't kill the soldiers? I wasn't afraid! I wasn't scared of getting killed!'

'No,' said Butterfly. His voice was quiet but strong,

and he took her fists in his hands, holding them away from him. 'I didn't think any of that. *I* was the one that was afraid – of *you* getting killed.'

His words angered Silver even more. She swung her backpack off – throwing Butterfly's at him – and reached into it, pulling out a gun. It was the pistol Butterfly had taken from the soldier. She had found it when checking for something in his backpack earlier.

'Go on, fly away,' she said, jerking the gun at him, her hands shaking. 'That's what you always want to do. So do it. I don't need you. I don't need you to protect me. I can find my parents by myself just fine. Go on. Go.'

'You're not going to shoot me,' Butterfly said quietly.

'Oh, I'm not?'

Silver flicked the gun to the side and pulled the trigger, the shot ringing loud in the forest.

He didn't even flinch. 'Silver, put it down –'

'Your mother and sister died!' she shouted, swinging the gun back to him. 'The Council killed them, and Yasir, and every other person in that village. Just for surviving. Just for living! How can you *not* want to kill them? How can you be so calm? Don't just stand there. Come on, do something, *do* something, show me that it hurts –'

Butterfly flew forward, letting out a cry. He grabbed the gun out of her hand so quickly she didn't have time to react. He raised it, aiming at her heart. 'You think it doesn't kill me?' he said hoarsely. 'It kills me, Silver. They were my family. I wanted to kill every last one of those soldiers. *Every last one*. But if I kill them, then why shouldn't I kill you? We're all the same. We've all been trapped inside Neo, trapped by what the Council choose to tell us. Do you think those soldiers knew what they were doing? Why they were doing it? What about all the things we've done as Elites. Did we ever question our orders? Did we ever take the time to find out why we were doing those things, what the other side of it all might be? I wanted to hurt those soldiers so badly. Trust me, I did. But we had no right, because up until now we've both been one of them.' His voice lowered to a whisper. 'So tell me to shoot. Tell me to shoot the soldiers, Silver. And I'll start with you.'

Silver dropped her head, tears falling fast down her face.

'Thought so,' said Butterfly, though not unkindly. A moment later, he wrapped his arms round her.

'I'm sorry,' she choked through her tears, her face pressed against his chest. 'I thought I could make it right. I wanted to get them back for what they'd done.'

Butterfly kissed the top of her head. 'I know,' he said gently, stroking her back. 'But they're not the ones to blame. You were only hurting yourself more.'

Silver closed her eyes. He was right. She pulled back and Butterfly cupped a hand round her chin, pulling her face up. His thumb brushed her lips. They kissed gently then, slowly, deeply, losing themselves in each other's embrace. For a few moments, they were able to put aside everything that had happened. Not forget; Silver knew they'd never be able to forget yesterday's events. But just hide for a little while from the truth of it all.

They found a cluster of large trees in which to make

234

camp for the night. It felt safe and quiet here, amid the thick-leafed canopy and gnarled trunks, the distant rush of the river like a lullaby. Silver made a fire while Butterfly strung their hammocks between two of the trees. After eating the curried flatbreads Yasir had given Silver before she left – one of her favourite foods usually, but tonight she could barely taste it – they settled themselves in the hammocks. It was completely black in the forest without the flickering light of the fire, but Silver felt strangely safe. She curled up in the blanket and looked over at Butterfly.

'About today,' she said. 'I wasn't angry at you.'

'I know,' he said after a moment's silence. 'I know it had nothing to do with me. You just needed to get it out of your system.'

Silver clenched her hands into fists. 'It's *my* fault this happened. If we hadn't left Neo to find my parents, we wouldn't have gone to Yasir's village, and the Council wouldn't have come and –'

'You don't know that.'

'No,' she agreed. 'But I feel that way. Yasir told me about the rumours of the Council destroying other settlements outside Neo, but I can't help but think it was our birthchips that led them there. You know, I didn't really worry about them tracking us before.'

Butterfly's eyes were glassy in the moonlight. 'It's because we didn't know what they were capable of, then,' he said quietly, and they fell silent, Silver thinking just how true that statement was.

* * *

Early the next day, they cleared the campsite and set off, following Yasir's directions to the settlement nearby. The forest was quiet that morning, the air dull with a clinging fog. They progressed faster than yesterday as the forest had thinned, the ground was not as uneven or steep, and by late afternoon, the trees were so sparse Silver and Butterfly could see open land beyond. It stretched out before them under a low sky heavy with clouds.

As the fog shifted, Silver saw that across the plain was a blocky cluster of grey buildings. It stood out amid all the green like an ugly forest. Even from this distance, she could see that the city was dilapidated. The concrete exteriors of the buildings were crumbling and worn. There were piles of rubble where houses had been demolished. Though this city was nowhere near the size of Neo-Babel, it still looked fairly large.

'The settlement,' she breathed, feeling a thrill of anticipation.

Butterfly nudged her shoulder with his. 'You sure about this? Your parents might not even be there.'

'I know,' she said. 'But you know what? I've got this strange feeling they *are*.'

It took them half an hour to reach the outskirts of the city. By this time, a light drizzle had begun to fall. It pattered quietly on the metallic skins of the vehicles that sat in the street and the low buildings on either side, their insides hollowed out and empty. Unlike Neo-Babel, the streets of this city were wide. The buildings were much lower too, most just a few storeys high. And whereas

Neo-Babel's streets and buildings were awash with colour – city flags hanging from balconies, lights and advertisements strung across streets – this city was colourless, the whole place wreathed in a dull grey. The only colour came from flashes of green, where weeds and straggly plants pushed their way up between cracks in the pavement.

Silver and Butterfly walked in the shallow path the street carved, their feet half hidden by the low fog. The city was eerily quiet. The only sounds were debris crunching underfoot as they moved, wind moaning through the desolate streets.

'I don't like this,' whispered Silver. Even though the place was clearly deserted, she still felt like she had to keep her voice soft. Now she understood why the magic men called these places ghost cities. The air shivered with their whispers.

'Yasir said there might be an anti-birthchip resistance here?' Butterfly asked.

She nodded. 'He thinks . . .' She caught herself and stopped, swallowing. 'He *thought* they were linked somehow with the Pigeons back in Neo.'

'Then where are they? This place is pretty large. They could be anywhere.'

'He said they'd be somewhere in the centre.' Silver nodded at the cluster of tall buildings in the distance that stood a few storeys higher than the structures around them. 'They'd have a good viewpoint from there. Maybe that's what's helped them stay out of trouble with the Council for so long.'

They continued towards the city centre. Silver's entire

body felt on edge, and she kept thinking she saw movement out of the corner of her eyes. But when she turned, there was nothing. Only the silent, empty husks of the buildings and broken things scattered across the ground. After walking for half an hour, they reached a cross-junction. A wide building blocked their way.

'Left or right?' asked Butterfly.

Silver shrugged. 'I don't think it really –'

'STOP WHERE YOU ARE.'

A voice, magnified as though it was speaking through a megaphone, boomed out of the eerie silence.

Silver and Butterfly dropped to their knees, pulling out their stunguns. Silver swung round, trying to pinpoint the location of the speaker, but the fog had shifted again, and it wreathed the buildings and ground in a hazy grey cloud.

'LOWER YOUR WEAPONS.'

'We're from Neo-Babel!' Silver called as she threw her stungun to the floor, still looking round for the speaker. 'We're searching for my parents who left last week. We don't mean any harm.'

There was a barking laugh, so loud it made her flinch. 'THAT'S WHAT THEY ALL SAY. OUR GUARDS ARE COMING TO GET YOU NOW. IF YOU HURT THEM, THEY WILL USE THEIR WEAPONS AGAINST YOU. UNDERSTAND?'

Without waiting for Silver and Butterfly's reply, four people dressed in clothes very similar to Elite uniforms ran out suddenly from the building in front of them, guns in their hands. One grabbed Silver. He yanked her upright and ran his hands roughly over her body while another stood by, his gun levelled at her head. After the guard searching her seemed satisfied she was not carrying anything dangerous, he locked Silver's arms behind her back. She saw that one of the other guards had done the same to Butterfly. The other two still held guns at their heads.

There was a sudden rushing sound as a man sailed down the face of the building in front of them. A rope tautened behind him and the next instant he landed on the floor with a thud, lifted a megaphone to his mouth and said –

'BOO.'

Silver's eyes widened as she saw who it was. The man was a Red, like her. He had a weather-beaten face, skin darkened by the sun and etched with lines and scars. There was a shadow of stubble on the lower half of his face, and more shadows under his small eyes, as though he hadn't slept in days. Though she'd only seen it once before, she would have recognised that face anywhere –

The assassin.

Here he is, she thought savagely, hatred bursting through her. *The man who had started it all.* Her world had turned upside down in just a few weeks. Her parents abducted. Her life as an Elite over, Butterfly's mother and sister dead. And this man was where it had all began.

With a growl, Silver threw herself forward, managing to wrench her arms out from the guard's grip. She ran straight for the assassin, her fingers curled into claws –

Crack!

Something struck the back of her head. She fell to the floor, darkness clenching round her like a fist.

29

An Unfortunate Encounter

Getting to the Council District was more difficult than Akhezo had anticipated. Not only was it hard to sneak away under Domino's beady gaze – 'Where are you going now, lazy boy? Come here and rub my back. You may as well be of *some* use while we're stuck here' – but without any money, he and Neve had to travel through the inner city on foot.

After a failed first attempt the morning before, they finally managed to slip away from the Limpets unseen the next day. They set off just before dawn. That was the best time to evade Domino, since he liked to sleep in late.

'Who's the lazy one now, eh?' muttered Akhezo as he passed Domino's sleeping body.

The old man was lying atop one of the few mattresses the Pigeons had brought to their temporary Limpets home. Akhezo resisted the urge to draw on his face. Pigeon members were already busying themselves with the day's tasks, and he didn't want to be reprimanded by them. He did, however, manage to flick something he'd picked from his nose in Domino's direction.

'Akhezo!' Neve giggled as the ball of snot landed in Domino's tangled white hair.

At first, their journey was easy. They left the Limpets, crossed the Industrial District on foot, and followed a bridge over the river's Outer Circle. Once they got deeper into Neo-Babel however, Akehzo was lost. The city felt much bigger down here on the ground, and the only time he'd been this far in was for the information exchange on the floating shisha boat, and he and Domino had taken a rickshaw there from the Limpets. Akhezo and Neve didn't have any money for one.

'So, which way now?' asked Neve.

They stood by a river-junction where a small waterway busy with wind-boats led off the wider channel of Circle Twelve into a pretty residential area of Chinatown. Akhezo's eyes travelled over the latticed window covers and lanterns strung across the streets.

'It's definitely not that way.' He turned and leant against the railing, looking out over the busy waters of Circle Twelve. An idea struck him. 'Hey, Neve. Fancy a boat ride?'

'Huh?'

Akhezo grinned. 'Follow me.'

He darted down the riverside street, squeezing between the morning crowds. He'd spotted a large commuter ferry up ahead. From what little he knew about Neo-Babel's boat services, these ferries usually led into the heart of the city.

As they drew closer, Neve grabbed his arm. 'The sign says it's going to the Council District!' she said excitedly. 'But we don't have any money . . .'

'We don't need any. Come on.'

They snaked through the riverside crowd until they neared the platform the ferry was waiting beside. A couple of crew members stood at the end of a short bridge leading onto the boat, checking tickets as people boarded.

Akhezo pointed to a place along the ferry's open deck where its natural curvature brought it close to the street. 'We can jump into the boat there.' The drizzle that clung to the air meant the deck was empty. As long as the crew didn't see them, they'd be able to slip inside once on the deck.

'That's a big jump,' said Neve.

'Scared?' he taunted.

'No way.'

A horn sounded, blasting through the morning noise of the busy streets, and the ferry began pulling away from the dock. They pushed through the crowd, running towards it. The boat moved surprisingly fast for its size. When they had caught up with it, the gap between its side and the street was wider than before.

Akhezo hesitated. 'I don't think –'

'Chicken,' sneered Neve.

Without another word, she climbed over the railing and jumped. She landed on the ledge that ringed the deck, clinging to its railing, then pulled herself up and over it. She turned, waving to Akhezo.

'You annoying little . . .' He scrambled over the railing. Just as he was about to jump, a sudden memory flashed into his mind; cold water swallowing him, flooding his lungs. Gritting his teeth, he pushed the memory away and jumped. There was a moment of

243

rushing air before his body slammed into the side of the ferry. Pain jolted through him at the impact. He dropped for a second before his fingers – arms raised above his head – caught the ledge. Hands clasped his, steadying him.

'Thanks,' Akhezo said gruffly once he'd climbed over the railing onto the deck.

Neve winked. 'No problem. Though *I* think you did it on purpose just to feel my hands on you again. Joking!' she added quickly, dancing out of reach of his fist, her laughter tinkling in the air.

The ferry took an hour to reach its stop outside the Council District. As they disembarked, Akhezo was sniggering at something Neve had said, but he quickly fell silent as he took in the view.

They were on the outer side of the river's Inner Circle, looking across at a geometric landscape; wide, straight boulevards set down in troughs between sparse gardens of rocks and stern-looking trees, and glassy black buildings that looked wet in the misty light. The whole place screamed of expense and luxury. Akhezo's stomach tightened excitedly. *Soon,* he thought, *that's gonna be* ours.

He began walking along the riverside, scanning the edge of the Council District for a way in where they could avoid the guards standing at the end of each bridge. He was so distracted watching them that he walked straight into a figure coming the other way.

'Watch it!' hissed the woman he'd bumped into, pushing him off her roughly.

Akhezo's jaw fell open. The woman was the most beautiful person he'd ever seen in his life. Her green irises were so bright they didn't look as though they could be real, and her lips were coated in a slick of red that matched her hair. A feathery cape fluttered around her in the wind.

The woman's lip curled. She grabbed the collar of his top and yanked him towards her. 'What business could a boy like you possibly have in the Council District?'

Akhezo felt his cheeks colour. Her sweet perfume was making him giddy. 'I'm here to look for someone who works here, miss,' he mumbled. 'Maybe you know him? He's got this shaved head, like an egg –'

'A shaved-head?' the woman said sharply, her eyes narrowed. 'Was he skinny? Dark-eyed?'

Akhezo nodded. 'Shifty, too. Eyes always looking round.'

The woman smiled. White teeth flashed between red lips. 'It turns out I *do* know who you mean,' she said, brushing down Akhezo's top and pinching his cheek. 'Why don't you and I go for a nice sweet treat? We can discuss your friend there. On me, of course.'

'Yes, miss,' he said breathlessly. He looked round at Neve. 'My friend's here too. Can she come?'

'Of course!' Still smiling, she motioned to Neve to join them, then took one of their hands each in hers and started forward, walking towards a nearby rickshaw stand. 'Now, enough of this "miss" nonsense. You are both to call me Ember, understood?'

'Yes, Ember,' they sang in unison.

'Good.' She gripped their hands tightly in hers, her

245

long black fingernails digging into their skin. 'We are all friends now. I wouldn't want you to feel like you couldn't tell me *everything*.'

30

Iarassi

The assassin stood in front of Silver, grinning, blood on the tips of his teeth.

She was back in Neo-Babel, on the balcony in Pantheon Square. Her hair had come free of her ponytail and it whipped round her face, stinging where it flicked against her skin. The wind moaned, rushing through the buildings that stood nearby, their windows broken and their insides emptied, like those of the ghost city where the assassin and his guards had captured Silver and Butterfly.

'I'm not afraid to shoot you this time!' shouted Silver.

The assassin didn't say anything. His grin was wide, his mouth black and deep, like a knife slashed through the night sky.

'I will shoot you!' She tried to raise her gun but her body wouldn't move.

The wind moaned louder. Without taking his eyes off her, the assassin lifted up his arm, pointing it towards the stage across the square, and pulled the trigger.

Silver screamed.

There was the sound and smell of a gunshot, Tanaka's head bursting open, both impossibly close and far away at the same time, and the assassin's grin widening, his eyes

turning into dark pools of blood, his gaping black mouth
forming the word –
   'BOO.'

Silver jerked awake. She winced instantly at the movement, rubbing a hand over the back of her head, which
was heavy with a dull ache. The pain threaded itself
beneath her eyelids, making it hurt when she looked
round, taking in her new surroundings.

   She was in a small room, just large enough for the
narrow bed she was lying on and the wardrobe against
the opposite wall. Butterfly slumped against the bed by
her head. He was fast asleep. From outside the room
came loud noises; shouts and yells, running footsteps,
metallic screeches and crashes and thuds. *This can't be
the ghost city*, Silver thought. *Ghosts are not nearly this
noisy.*

   She reached down and squeezed Butterfly's shoulder.
He woke with a start, a cry strangled in his throat.

   'Hey,' she said. 'It's just me.'

   He relaxed. 'Silver, you're not going to believe –'

   'Where's the assassin?' she interrupted. She pushed
herself up and threw off the blanket that covered her. 'I'm
going to do what I should've done the day of the parade.'

   Butterfly stood up quickly and pushed her back down
on the bed. He brushed the hair from her face. 'You're
not going to want to do that.'

   'He started it all,' Silver hissed. 'If he hadn't killed
Tanaka, *none* of this would have happened!'

   Butterfly shook his head. 'There's something you need

248

to know, Silver. The assassin – there was a reason he seemed familiar to you.'

She stared at Butterfly, breathing hard. 'What do you mean?'

But just as he opened his mouth to explain, the door to the room swung open.

'Hello.' The assassin stepped into the room, grinning.

Without a second's hesitation, Silver launched herself at him, but Butterfly grabbed her round the waist, holding her back.

'Get off me!' she snarled, struggling against his grip.

Butterfly held her tighter. 'Just let him explain –'

'Let me go!'

'He's your *brother*, Silver!'

At Butterfly's words, she fell still. She felt rigid with shock. The whole room seemed to shrink, spinning closer and tighter until it was just her and the assassin – her and her *brother* – staring at each other with questions in their eyes, just as they had done that day on the balcony above Pantheon Square.

'Joza,' Silver whispered.

His grin widened. 'You remember.'

She *did* remember her brother, but she wished she didn't. She breathed in deeply, unable to stop the furious red that was charging through her. She felt as though she was back at the balcony of Hemmingway House, watching in horror as Tanaka's head burst open. Joza looked almost identical to how he'd looked that day; brown factory-worker clothes, stubble across his chin.

Bright brown eyes that stirred half-forgotten memories deep inside her. She felt sick at the sight of him.

'I'll wait outside,' Butterfly said, touching her shoulder. He leant in closer and added quietly, 'Please listen to what he has to say.'

'I'll try,' Silver replied through gritted teeth.

When Butterfly had gone, Joza sauntered over to the bed, but after a sharp glance from Silver seemed to think better of it and backed away, leaning against the wardrobe. He fiddled with his fingers. 'Well,' he said. 'Not quite the sibling reunion I was expecting, I've got to admit.'

She narrowed her eyes. 'What *were* you expecting? You left us when I was three years old. You never got in touch with Mum or Dad again. Oh – and then you shot the president right in front of me.'

The grin fell off Joza's face. 'If you want an apology for that, you're not getting one. But I had reasons for the other things. Leaving you all.'

'Let's hear them, then.'

Doing a quick mental calculation, Silver realised that Joza must be thirty now. What excuse could he possibly have for abandoning his family for so many years? She'd promised herself never to think of him again. As she was so young when he'd left, she'd managed to convince herself that her faint memories of an older boy hugging her and playing with her in her parents' apartment were just dreams. Echoes of a life she'd never had.

'Did our parents tell you much about me?' Joza asked.

She shook her head.

'Then how do you know –'

'Who you are? When I was young, I had memories about you, so I asked Mum and Dad what'd happened. They didn't want to lie, so they explained it all. I know that you left and never came back. But they never said why you left, or where you went.'

Joza nodded. 'They didn't know that themselves until the night I arrived at Zhangdong Street and forced them to leave Neo with me.'

'It was . . . it was *you*?' Silver gasped. 'Wait. Where are they now? Are they here?' Her heart was racing. This was what she'd been waiting for all this time; to see her parents again, to hold them in her arms. To know that they were safe.

'It *was* me,' Joza said. 'And they *were* here. But I'm afraid they went to a settlement to the east yesterday morning with a team of Ghosts to recruit some last-minute help. You won't be able to see them for a while.'

The relief that Silver had felt disappeared, leaving her cold. 'So instead I get you?' She laughed harshly. 'What a consolation prize.'

He glanced away, his shoulders stiff. 'Can we walk? It's easier to explain if you can see . . .'

'Fine.' She got off the bed and moved to the doorway. 'But this had better be good.'

'Oh, it is,' Joza said, grinning again.

Outside the room, Butterfly was leaning against a railing. He turned as he heard the door open. 'Did Joza explain it to you?' he asked Silver.

'Not yet,' answered Joza before she could reply. He

nodded towards the railing. 'I wanted her to see this first. Thought it'd make her a little less . . . resistant.'

Silver didn't say anything; she was too distracted by the view. As she joined Butterfly at the railing, she could see they were standing on a ledge lining the side of a huge hall four storeys high. Every inch of the hall's floor was hidden beneath people and machines. She was reminded instantly of the central cavern of the Limpets, or even the Stacks, with the balconies running along every level, looking out into the building's hollow centre. But unlike the Limpets, this place was well-built and organised, and unlike the Stacks, there were no walkways criss-crossing the space. The noise from the hall was tremendous. The whole place buzzed with activity.

Silver turned to her brother. 'Where are we?'

'One of the buildings at the centre of Iarassi.'

'Ia-*what*?'

'Iarassi – it's what this city used to be called. But I can call it the ghost city if you'd prefer. Anyway, come on,' Joza said, starting down the ledge. 'I'll show you around.'

31

The Truth

Joza led them down a flight of stairs to the main hall. He had to shout for Silver and Butterfly to hear him over all the noise as they followed close behind. 'We hollowed out this building five years ago,' he explained, gesturing round at the busy space. 'The windows are blacked out, so from the outside it looks just as dead as the rest of the city, and we're right in the centre of Iarassi, so it's easy to spot anyone coming. Anyway, the few times Neo soldiers have come into the city, they haven't even bothered venturing this deep. It's a pretty perfect base for us.'

They weaved through the crowded floor, squeezing past a couple of trucks whose large wheels were being pumped. Silver was feeling disorientated by all the activity, the strange machines and equipment people were working on. She wondered what it was they were preparing for.

'Who's us?' she asked.

'Our anti-birthchip group,' said Joza. 'The nickname Ghosts has grown on us – we're in the ghost city, after all. But really we should call ourselves the Pigeons. That's the name of the group back in Neo we're aligned with.

We've been working with them for the last two years. It was thanks to them I got into the Council District to assassinate Tanaka.'

Silver stiffened at his words. 'And what did you hope to gain from *that*?'

'We needed the Council to be vulnerable. In a state of transition. He had to go to make way for a new regime.'

'Which is?'

'We don't know yet,' admitted Joza. 'That's for the new Council to decide, or whatever governing system comes into power. But what we *do* know is that it will be one without birthchips. Without walls. Without the destruction of other settlements. A free society. A new Neo.'

They were in the middle of the hall now. The noise pressed around Silver like a physical force, jostling her like the crowds of people moving past. They passed the base of a crane, its driver waving to Joza as they went. Silver felt a surge of anger. Joza seemed popular around here, but where had he been all *her* life?

'So that's what you've been doing all these years?' she asked. 'Preparing to take down the Council?'

Joza nodded. 'Though really it started before I left. See, I worked for the Council too. But I discovered something. I was eighteen, and new to my role in the Department of Security. I overheard a senior Elite discussing something he referred to as a Purge, but when I enquired about it I was rebuffed by my colleagues. So, I cornered the senior Elite and asked him about it the next day. He didn't tell me anything, but it seems he warned the Council about my enquiries, for I was quickly transferred to a different department.'

'A similar thing happened to someone else,' said Silver, thinking of Yasir. 'And your father,' she added, turning to Butterfly.

'I'm not surprised,' said Joza. 'It's difficult to keep secrets in a closed city. Anyway, after that I tried to get on with my work, but I just couldn't forget about this Purge thing. So I started an investigation.'

'Did you find out what it was? The Purge?'

He slowed and glanced round at them. His face was serious. 'You and Butterfly experienced one for yourself.'

Silver's chest tightened. Images flashed through her mind; water and fire, smoke clogging the air. Screams and cries and her own, animal wailing. The heat of the flames as she searched Yasir's house. A body in Butterfly's arms.

'I left the city after finding out about them,' Joza continued, talking over his shoulder as they walked. 'It made me sick to think that settlements were outside, defenceless and unaware of what might happen to them. From inside Neo I'd not be able to do much for them, so I reckoned that *outside* the city I could form some sort of resistance to defend them.'

Silver felt guilty at her quick judgement of her brother. She was still angry at him for abandoning her family, but she heard the compassion in his voice as he spoke of helping the settlements in the Outside. If she was honest with herself, it sounded like something Butterfly would have done.

'How did you protect them?' she asked Joza, her voice a little softer now.

'We had many strategies. Evacuating settlements, monitoring techniques – that sort of thing. We'd only resort to force when it was completely necessary to avoid the Council getting too suspicious. That's how the Ghosts grew.' He spread his arms wide, turning in a circle, grinning widely. 'You know, I still remember when it was just me. Look at this. *Look* at this!'

They had reached the other end of the hall. There was a canteen on this side with an assortment of benches and tables, and smoke was unfurling from the cookers against the back wall. The smell of frying food made Silver's stomach rumble, but she ignored it.

'What you've said still doesn't explain why you left us,' she said. 'You could've told Mum and Dad what you were doing.'

'No, I couldn't have,' Joza sighed. 'I didn't want any of you to have to lie for me. And I didn't want you to feel as though you needed to come with me and help too. Of course, if I'd known that you'd become an Elite under the very person who told the Council about my enquiries . . .'

Silver gasped. '*That* was Senior Surrey?'

He nodded.

'But how does any of this relate to you taking Mum and Dad out of Neo just weeks ago?' she asked. 'This all happened years ago.'

'I'd like to know that too,' said Butterfly, who up until now had been silent. 'You didn't get round to telling me earlier.'

All of a sudden, Joza looked uncomfortable. He sat at an empty table at the edge of the canteen and motioned for them to join him. Silver took Butterfly's hand under the table as they sat down. The feel of his skin against hers was the one constant she had now in her life. Everything else seemed to be changing too fast for her to keep up with.

'Actually, Silver,' said Joza tentatively, 'I needed *you* to leave the city. I knew that you wouldn't do that for anything less than helping our parents.'

She frowned. 'You wanted *me* to leave Neo? Why?'

'I have a favour to ask of you. And you too, if you're willing,' he added, glancing up at Butterfly. 'See, I've been here in Iarassi with the Ghosts for the last five years, working towards this. Everything we did before – trying to stop the Purges, or minimise their damage. None of that was sustainable. This . . .' He motioned around at the hall. '*This* is our chance to stop the Council completely. And I need your help to do it. I wouldn't have dragged you out here and put you through all this unless it was absolutely necessary.'

Something about what he'd just said felt wrong to Silver. She felt her heart twist. 'Put us through all this?' Suddenly, she understood exactly what had happened. 'Our birthchips,' she whispered, her voice dull with supressed anger. 'You knew they'd follow us.'

Joza grimaced. 'Yes. We've got a relationship with Little Mae in the Limpets, and over the years we've cultivated her reputation. We knew you'd be going through her, and she had orders to inform the Pigeons when you left. But we wanted you to bring the Council *here*, Silver. To Iarassi. It wasn't our plan for you to stop at the village. What we wanted, you see, was –'

But he didn't finish his sentence, because Butterfly had stood up suddenly, leant across the table and punched Joza hard in the jaw.

Joza fell to the floor. A few people nearby ran over, crouching over him to check if he was all right, but Silver just peered round the table and looked down at her brother. He was kneeling up from where he'd fallen, clutching his jaw. He looked at her with a painful expression in his eyes.

She resisted the urge to throw an extra punch of her own. She turned to Butterfly, who was breathing heavily, his hands in fists by his sides. 'Nice one,' she said, and they walked away.

32

Cobe's Secret

The inner city was busy that night. New York Strip, one of Neo-Babel's most popular entertainment hubs, was especially crowded, its riverside streets writhing with people. People roaring with laughter on the bars lining the balconies, people picking their way from boat to boat in the floating arcade that bobbed on the river. A few Limpets beggars tried their luck with the drunks hanging outside club entrances, while the more enterprising poor wove their way along the riverside, selling theatre and club tickets and portable shishas. Groups of gossiping young Mainland and Japanean women sauntered along. They were dressed in the latest fashions; metallic capes and ridged hats, colourful bands of decorative paint striping their faces, the heads of decorative pet micro-pandas and blue foxes poking out the tops of their bags.

As Cobe pushed his way through the crowd, some of the young women glanced hopefully in his direction, but he didn't notice them. He moved quickly. Head down, eyes on the floor. He turned off the main strip onto a side street. Halfway down, he slipped inside a shadowy entrance.

All Elites had membership to the Manhattan Apartment,

one of Neo-Babel's most exclusive private clubs. Because of its limited membership, the club was never very busy, and that was exactly why Cobe was going there. For the last few nights after Ember had told him about the attack on the village where Butterfly and Silver had been staying, he'd wanted somewhere quiet to drink. *Drowning your sorrows*, he thought. *I think that's what they used to call it.*

At the club entrance, a bouncer scanned his birthchip. Usually, he was allowed straight through, but this time the bouncer laid a hand on his shoulder. 'Sir. Follow me, please.'

'Is something wrong?' asked Cobe. Perhaps the club's management were cautious of letting him in again after last night's visit, which had ended with him asleep on the floor at the foot of the bar, a pool of vomit by his mouth soaking into the varnished plastiwood floors.

The bouncer didn't reply. He steered Cobe into a small room he'd never been in before, with curving walls in a semi-circle shape. Heavy curtains hung across its entrance. A padded seat draped in the same material lined the rounded walls.

'Wait here,' the bouncer instructed before leaving.

Cobe had just enough time to wonder what he was waiting for when there was a rustle of movement behind him, and he felt a sharp bite in the back of his neck.

He was unconscious before he hit the floor.

A touch of laughter, a small man in a hat. Bright lights going by.

Cobe blinked. Stared blearily around. Blinked. He felt dazed, slow, as if tar had seeped in behind his eyeballs and clotted his brain. He bounced and knocked his head against a taut piece of semi-translucent fabric to his right, realising dimly he was in a moving rickshaw.

More laughter. The tinny click of a lighter flicking open and then a sweet, sickly smell.

The man beside him held out a pipe. 'Shisha?'

Cobe shook his head. He recognised the squat figure with its fat round head and bulbous eyes. A name bubbled to the top of the soup that was his brain; Finch. Pinchy Finchy, as he was better known in the Stacks; a senior Council member who worked in the Department of Security. Pinchy Finchy who had wandering hands.

The rickshaw swayed. Cobe almost fell unconscious again, his eyes turning in their sockets as he felt a tug of drowsiness. Laughter drifted in and out of his mind. Lights outside, whizzing past. He struggled to hold on, to stay awake, but everything felt fuzzy and out of reach. He turned to Finch and tried to speak but couldn't. The sickly sweet smell of the shisha had wrapped around his tongue, squeezing it still.

'You'd better rest up while you can,' said Finch in his thick voice. He exhaled slowly, filling the rickshaw carriage with the heady smell of sugared apples. His fat, chapped lips stretched into a smile. 'Senior Surrey is *not* best pleased with you. I imagine this is going to be a long night.'

Senior Surrey? Cobe's mind latched onto the name, and the Head of the Elites' cold, handsome face flickered into his mind. There was a jolt of something deep in his chest, but as soon as it came it was gone, and then the face was merging with Finch's, and, smiling, Cobe closed his eyes, mumbling softly, 'Pinchy Finchy, Pinchy Finchy,' until he drifted back to sleep.

When he next woke, Cobe felt a cold hard floor beneath him and goosebumps dotting his exposed skin. There was a sharp hospital smell in the air, and silence.

Unlike in the rickshaw, his mind was sharp and clear. He lay unmoving, his eyes squeezed shut. He remembered the bite of a needle in his neck. The sweet smell of apples. Pinchy Finchy's gurgling laughter. Whatever was happening to him, he realised, it was the Council's doing.

Cobe opened his eyes. A single bulb stared down at him out of a grey ceiling. He couldn't see anything else. He shivered, and realised suddenly he was completely naked. He sat bolt upright, clutching at himself, and the room swung into view. It was large, with the same grey walls and floor as the ceiling, empty except for a plastimetal table at one end on which lay a gun. He recognised the room as one of the interrogation cells in the basement levels of Central Police Command.

A burst of laughter from behind him made Cobe turn round. He tried to scrabble to his feet, but he was still dizzy and his legs were jelly. They crumpled beneath him and he smashed back to the floor.

Ember let out another laugh as he tried to shield his body from her view. She was leaning against the wall in front of him. She wore her Elite uniform, though her hair was wild and loose around her face, and there was an ugly smile on her painted lips.

'Sorry about your clothes,' she said, tossing a bundle of fabric to him.'You vomited on yourself in the rickshaw, so we threw them away. Must have been Finch's shisha. The smoke didn't agree with the drugs we gave you.'

'What do you want?' asked Cobe coldly, pulling on the underwear and plain top Ember had given him.

She pushed herself off the wall and sauntered over, sneering down at him as though he was a Limpets beggar on the street. 'What do *I* want? I don't think that's the right question to be asking. I think I should be asking you, Cobe, what *you* want.'

'What do you mean?'

'Since your mind seems to have been addled by the drugs,' Ember sighed, 'let me explain it to you.' She circled him slowly as she spoke. 'Yesterday, when I was leaving the Council District to do some shopping in the inner city, I ran into two little Limpets rats. One of them told me rather a strange story. See, this boy – Akhezo – seemed to think he had made some sort of *deal* with you.'

Cobe said nothing, but inside his heart thudded madly.

'Ridiculous, I thought at first,' she continued. 'Yet the boy's story was scarily accurate. He described you in perfect detail, even down to your pathetic little mannerisms and what you were wearing that night. And his story about meeting you beneath the Pigeons' skylung also rang true, since following the delivery was part of your assignment. However.' She paused in her circling. 'One thing about his story didn't make sense.'

Cobe knew what was coming, but he didn't see how he could avoid it. His eyes darted round the room. There was only one door, and Ember stood in his way. He doubted he could overpower her in his current state. What had the drugs done to him? Then he remembered –

The gun on the table.

Ember took a step towards him. 'Why would one of our own Elites want to stop us tracking Butterfly and Silver?' she asked, taking another step closer. 'To stop us destroying a settlement that could be home to an anti-birthchip group?' Another step. 'Care to tell me? Why would someone want to do that? Why would *you* –'

Cobe lunged forward, thrusting his knee up into her stomach. She doubled up for a second, just long enough for him to run over to the table, and he reached out, his hand inches away from the gun –

Smack!

Something crashed into his back. He fell hard onto his face. A moment later, his whole body went rigid as a stungun pressed into him. Pain screamed through his body at the electric shock. He struggled to remain conscious. Cobe struggled to his feet to run but Ember grabbed his neck, yanking him towards her. He choked, scrabbling at her hands tight around his throat.

'I should have known to expect nothing less from you,' she hissed. 'But what I want to know is why. *Why* did you do it?'

Cobe tried to lift his knee to kick her, but his body wouldn't cooperate. It felt weak, useless. 'Put . . . me . . . down,' he said. Each word was painful to get out, her hand was squeezing his throat so tightly.

'Not until you tell me! Why did you want us to stop tracking Butterfly and Silver?'

He swallowed. 'I . . . didn't want . . .'

'Didn't want *what?*'

'Didn't want . . . them killed.'

Ember dropped him instantly as though his words had burned her. He crashed to the floor, breathing hard. She gave him a cold look. 'You didn't want those traitors dead? Well, thanks to you, they're not.'

Cobe jerked his head up. 'They're not . . .?'

'No. But four of our soldiers are. The bullets that killed them were the same ones that our Elites and police and soldiers use, so we've a pretty good idea that they were shot by Butterfly and Silver.'

Relief flooded Cobe's body, but he had only a moment to relax before Ember darted forward, grabbing the collar of his top and jerking him towards her.

'Why?' she asked. 'Why do you care whether they died? Silver and Butterfly betrayed us. They're probably working for an anti-birthchip group. If you aren't on their side, then why not let them die for the sake of our city? Because they're your *friends?*' She dropped her voice to a whisper. 'I know who else are your friends. Would you betray us all just to save them, too?'

Cobe didn't answer.

Ember smiled. 'Shall we test that theory? Shall I kill Allum to see how far you'd go for them? Or perhaps Taiyo. She's so small, but I bet she bleeds like a pig –'

'No!' he burst.

She laughed. 'Well, unfortunately Allum and Taiyo are out of bounds. But I do know who we *can* spare.' She let go of him, lifting her wrist to her arm and touching the screen of her comms cuff. A few seconds later, Allum's voice issued from the microphone.

'What is it, Ember?'

'The boy and girl. Bring them here.'

Allum must have been nearby, for after just a few minutes, the door slid open and he entered the room. He held a gun to the head of an Afronese boy. The other hand clutched a girl's shoulder. Cobe recognised them immediately from that night under the skylung; Akhezo and his friend.

'Here,' said Allum, pushing them forward. He didn't even glance in Cobe's direction.

Ember nodded. 'Thank you. You may go.'

'Wait!' shouted Cobe as Allum turned to leave. 'It's not true what they're telling you, it's not –'

But Allum had already stepped out of the room, the door sliding shut behind him.

Ember laughed. 'What did I tell you? You're just as worthless to him now as these Limpets rats.'

She grabbed the girl and the boy by the back of their necks and dragged them over to Cobe, pushing them onto their knees. Then she stepped over to the table and picked up the gun that lay on its top.

266

'Please!' whispered the girl, her eyes fixed on Cobe. Her face was streaked with tears. 'Help us!'

Akhezo stretched out an arm to take one of her hands in his. There was fear on his face, but when he spoke, his voice was steady. 'Don't worry, Neve. I'm here. It's gonna be fine.'

Ember stood behind them and pressed the gun to the back of Neve's neck.

The girl shuddered, but she didn't cry out. 'Please, please, please,' she kept saying, her eyes never leaving Cobe's.

'We only need one of them to take us to the Pigeons' new hideout,' said Ember. 'So which one will it be, Cobe?'

He stared at her. He wouldn't dignify that question with an answer.

She shrugged. 'All right, then. Let's play a little game.' She began to recite a children's rhyme in a song-song voice, moving her gun from Akhezo to Neve with each beat. 'Eeny meeny miny moe, catch a Limpets rat by its toe. If it squeals don't let it go, but kill it quickly with one hard blow.'

On the last word, her gun fell on Neve.

Above the girl's head, Cobe saw Ember smile. He hesitated for a second, the entire world shrinking down to just the four of them in that room, Neve's teary eyes on his, her mouth moving almost silently now, 'Please, please, please, please, *please* –'

Bang!

He snapped his eyes shut. Blood – warm, wet – splattered

his face, and he heard Neve's body hit the ground. There was a scream. Scrabbling noises. Thuds.

'Get off me, stupid boy!'

A dull smack, and then silence.

Cobe opened his eyes. Akhezo was slumped unconscious in front of him; Ember seemed to have hit him with the hilt of the gun. Beside him, Neve lay face down on the blood-splattered floor. Cobe had seen death before, but it had never really affected him until now. It was something about how small the girl's body looked. How her fingers were stretched out, as though still reaching for Akhezo's hand. He swallowed down the bile that rose in his throat.

'If only I could kill the boy too,' Ember sighed. 'Unfortunately, we need him alive. Well?' Her eyes met Cobe's. 'Ready to tell me why you went to such lengths to save Butterfly and Silver?'

Suddenly, he was too exhausted to lie. The truth was easier. 'I love . . .' he began. But he couldn't finish the sentence. He realised he'd never said it out loud before. Not even to himself.

Ember stared at him. Then she laughed, her cold laughter ringing in the empty room. 'I always thought you had a thing for Silver, you filthy, Red-loving –'

'Not Silver.'

For a moment Ember looked confused. Then her eyes widened. 'Oh,' she breathed, a smile twisting across her lips. '*Butterfly*. This is even better. But in case you hadn't noticed, Cobe, he's always had a thing for Silver.'

'I know that,' Cobe said, his eyes falling to the floor.

She let out yet another derisive laugh. 'You knew, and *still* you wanted to save him! You really are more pathetic than I thought.' She started towards the door. Before she left, she turned back to him. 'I'll send in someone to clean up this mess and take Akhezo back to his cell.'

'What about me?' asked Cobe. 'Aren't you going to kill me now you know the truth?'

Ember smiled. 'Of course. But first, we have one last assignment for you.'

33

The Assassin's Wife

'I thought I'd find you two here.'

Silver and Butterfly were in the room Silver had woken in earlier that day. They lay on the bed, Silver curled up to Butterfly's side, having spent the whole night alternating between fits of restless sleep and long discussions over Joza's revelation the previous day. Silver felt unbearably conflicted by her feelings for Joza. Sometimes she thought she'd burst from the anger she felt at her brother for what he had done. Other times she remembered the pain she'd seen in his eyes as he'd told her why he'd left the city and how he'd been defending people in the Outside for years against the Purges, and she knew that he was acting with the best intentions.

They had been left alone by everyone in the building until now. They sat up as a young Mainland woman with piercing grey eyes and long blonde hair looked into the room. A deep scar ran down her right cheek, puckering the skin around it and distorting the corner of her lip. Despite the scar, the woman was very pretty.

'Butterfly,' she said, nodding at him. 'I need both of you to come with me. There's urgent business to discuss.' She disappeared, leaving the door ajar.

'Who's that?' Silver asked.

'Percie,' Butterfly said, smiling grimly. 'I met her earlier, while you were still knocked out. She's Joza's wife.'

Silver looked at him in surprise. 'Joza's married?'

'Why is that such a surprise?'

She shrugged, getting off the bed and smoothing down her clothes. 'Just that it's a wonder he found someone to marry him since he's *such* a delight.'

But Silver's surprise had not been at how Joza had found someone to marry him. No, what had surprised her was that Percie – a Mainlander – had married her brother, a Red.

Percie led them to a room off the main hall. A large circular table took up most of the space, the rest of it filled with chairs and machines crawling with wires. Strips of harsh white light lined the walls. As the door shut behind them, the noise of the activity in the hall muffled slightly, but it still pressed against the door, an endless tide of shouts and crashes and metallic screeches.

Percie motioned to the table. 'Sit.'

Silver and Butterfly took seats opposite her. Tablet screens of various sizes were embedded into the table's surface. Though many were blank, some blinked with lights and moving lines of text that seemed to be in a strange code Silver didn't understand.

'This is our surveillance and communications room,' said Percie. 'We've not got access to as much technology as we like, but over the years we've managed to work with our contacts within Neo and those in other settlements to build an adequate system. It's run by energy siphoned from Neo's wireless grid and a couple of our own solar generators.'

So Yasir was right about the energy leeches, Silver thought.

'Joza said you work with the Pigeons,' said Butterfly, watching Percie carefully.

She nodded. 'We also have contacts in the Industrial District – that's really helped us with getting all the equipment we need. And we have contacts within the police. Even the Council itself. Then of course there are those contacts outside Neo. Let me show you.' She leant across the table and touched a large tablet screen in the middle. It lit up instantly with a map. She pointed to a red dot near the centre. 'This is us,' she explained. 'Iarassi. The green dots are settlements that are sympathetic to our cause. The yellow ones are ones that are not.' She moved her finger to a black dot. 'That's Neo. Although we get a lot of resources from the city, we'd never have been able to even consider attacking the Council without help from the settlements nearby.'

'Why do you need us, then?' asked Silver.

Percie sat back in her chair, her grey eyes expressionless. Silver was starting to wonder whether she ever smiled. Had what had happened to give Percie that scar made her this way, so serious and detached?

'We initially wanted you here so that the Council would track you and send their soldiers here, to Iarassi,' Percie explained. 'We'd planned to be gone by the time they arrived, and then we'd have much less resistance while attacking the Council back in Neo. Less casualties all around, and a swifter takeover. It would have minimised the damage to Neo and its people.' She folded her hands on the table, her eyes on Butterfly. 'We are sorry for how that plan turned out. But now we need your help with something else – destroying the DNA Holding Towers.'

Whatever Silver was expecting, that hadn't been it. Her eyes widened. 'The Bee-Hives?' she breathed. The Bee-Hives was the nickname everyone used for the Holding Towers, where the records of every Neo-Babel citizen's DNA were stored. She shook her head. 'But you're already bringing down the Council. Why bother destroying the DNA records?'

'We want a free Neo,' Percie answered. 'Whatever new government comes into power, the records of DNA cannot be around for them to use. It's too easy to fall into the same patterns. We cannot leave this until after the attack. It must be done during it.'

'And you need us,' said Butterfly, glancing quickly at Silver, 'because you can't get to the Bee-Hives without the highest level of authority.'

Percie nodded. 'Exactly. Our contacts in the Council have been unable to get anywhere near enough to the Holding Towers to even formulate a plan to break in, and we don't have enough explosives both to force our way in *and* destroy the records inside.' She tilted her head, looking across the table at them. 'But Elites have access to the Holding Towers.'

Butterfly pushed back his chair and stood up. 'I'm sorry to disappoint you, but Silver and I are pretty much outcasts now. Our birthchips will have been invalidated.

We won't be able to get anywhere near the Bee-Hives.'
He moved towards the door and Silver joined him
quickly, keen to get out of the room.

'We know that, Butterfly,' Percie said behind them.

They turned.

'Silver's parents said there is an Elite still in Neo who
might be willing to help us,' she continued, standing up
and walking towards them. She looked at Butterfly.
'Apparently he helped your family once.'

'Cobe,' Silver whispered, touching Butterfly's arm.

'We need you to call him and ask for his help. Take
some time to think about it, by all means, but we'll need
your response within an hour.'

'That's not long,' said Silver.

Percie nodded. 'We don't *have* long. The Council
will know you're alive after what happened at the
Purge. They might not know you're with us, but they
have their suspicions about the Pigeons working with
a group outside Neo. We can't risk them heightening
security.' Her eyes narrowed. 'The Ghosts leave for
Neo tonight.'

As soon as they left the room, Butterfly and Silver were
swallowed up in the frenzy of the main hall. They found
a space by a wall and leant against it, looking out at the
Ghosts preparing for their attack. Their pace hadn't let
up all day. Silver felt exhausted just watching them.

'I don't like this,' she said.

Butterfly looked away, his mouth set in a tight line.
'It's not ideal, getting Cobe involved.'

'No, I meant . . .' Silver raised her eyebrows. 'You mean you're actually *considering* this?'

He nodded. 'Aren't you?'

She turned away from him. 'I can't get over what Joza did,' she said quietly. 'Even though he didn't mean to, he still brought the Council to Yasir's village.'

Butterfly was silent for a while. When he next spoke, his blue eyes were fierce, but his voice was steady. 'I think that's just the way life is. Everything starts with good intentions. People fighting for what they believe in, thinking it's the right thing to do. But somewhere along the way, the Council have lost themselves. They've gone too far. It doesn't mean I support Joza and the Ghosts. But I'll fight alongside them if it means bringing down the Council and stopping them hurting any more families the way they have done mine.'

Silver thought back to the Purge. For the last few days, she'd wanted nothing more than to forget about it. It was too painful, too raw. But now she realised she could never let herself forget. She *had* to remember it, to give herself the courage to fight against the Council. She made herself remember the smell of smoke in Leanor and Emeli's house, the bits of bodies strewn across the ground, fire still licking some of them. Yasir's body piled on top of others.

For some reason, the Council's motto entered Silver's mind then; *A Place for Everyone.* She shook her head. *How far they've come from that,* she thought.

'You're right,' she said eventually, taking Butterfly's hands. 'Let's fight. Not for Joza or the Ghosts, but for Yasir. For Emeli and Leanor. For ourselves.'

275

34

The Story Behind the Scar

Butterfly and Silver stepped out of the building, stopping at the top of the steps that led down from the grand front doors. They still had an hour until meeting Percie again. The city was eerily still, its silent, empty buildings and streets in complete contrast to the busyness of the building they had just left. Butterfly had forgotten how depressing and unsettling Iarassi was. Here, the whole world seemed to have turned grey. Grey buildings, grey streets, grey sky, grey air.

Butterfly looked at Silver beside him, her hand warm in his. She met his eyes for a second, giving him a quick smile, and his chest tightened. There was nothing grey about Silver. Her eyes, her face, her whole body and presence were bright and fierce and beautiful and alive. He was remembering the heat of her lips against his when they kissed, the two times he had truly forgotten about everything else in the world, when the door opened behind them.

'Mind if I join you?' asked Joza, stepping out. 'I have something I'd like to say.'

Butterfly shrugged. He didn't like Joza, and not just because Joza had unintentionally caused the death of his mother and sister. The problem was, Joza reminded him too much of the Council, of people like Senior Surrey who were prepared to sacrifice others to get what they wanted. But Joza was Silver's brother. Now more than ever, Butterfly knew how important family was. He wouldn't be the one to create a divide between them.

They followed Joza down the steps of the building and along the street to a bench. Silver and Butterfly sat down, while Joza stood in front of them, his hands in his pockets.

'Well?' asked Silver.

Joza cleared his throat. 'I wanted to apologise,' he began, shifting uncomfortably. 'Before we leave for Neo and gods know what happens. I wanted to make sure you both understood why I did what I did.' He pulled his hands from his pockets, holding them out, and Butterfly could see that he was shaking slightly. 'This wasn't easy for me. Please don't think it was. If I had known what would happen, I would've tried to find another way. But there isn't any other way now. The Purges keep happening despite everything we've been doing to stop them. That's why I needed you to help me. I thought that if you led the Council to Iarassi, we'd have a real shot at bringing them down.' Joza fell silent and turned away from them.

He looked so defeated that Butterfly felt a rush of pity for him. 'He's trying,' Butterfly whispered to Silver.

She nodded. Getting off the bench, she walked over

to Joza and touched his shoulder hesitantly. 'I'm not saying I forgive you,' she said as he turned to look at her. 'But I think I understand why you did it.'

His face brightened in an instant. 'Thank you. And I'm sorry that you won't be able to see Mum and Dad until after all of this is done, but they'll be right behind us when we enter Neo.'

'They'll be fighting too?' Silver asked uneasily.

He nodded. 'I've been training them personally. They'll be fine, don't worry. Mum's a bit of a firecracker when it comes to shooting.' He grinned. 'Seems it runs in the family.'

Just then, a loud beeping sounded. The electronic sound was harsh in the stillness of the city, and Joza and Silver spun round to look at where it was coming from.

'Your comms cuff!' gasped Silver. 'It must be Cobe!'

Butterfly stared at the device on his wrist, his heart beating faster. He nodded. It was the only person it could be; they'd blocked their calls from other numbers. Cobe's name on the screen confirmed it.

'Is that him?' Joza asked, looking nervous. 'The Elite my parents said would help us?'

'It's him.' Butterfly met Silver's gaze. 'Ready?'

She took a deep breath, then nodded.

Butterfly touched his comms cuff to answer the call. 'Cobe?' he said tentatively, his head lowered towards the speaker.

There was silence.

'Cobe?' he repeated.

Cobe's voice came from the speaker. 'Butterfly.' He sounded tired. Strained. 'I just . . . just wanted to check in. It's been a while.'

'What's wrong?' Butterfly asked. 'You sound –'

'Nothing's wrong,' said Cobe quickly. 'It's just . . . I don't want them tracking this. Let's make this short. Have you found Silver's parents?'

'Yes,' said Butterfly. 'But I can't say any more. Look, Cobe – there's something we need from you.'

A pause. 'Yes?'

'We're heading back to Neo tonight. We'll be there by daybreak tomorrow. Are you able to meet us?'

Another pause. 'Where?'

'The Stacks,' said Butterfly. 'I'll call tomorrow to set a meeting place. I'm sorry, that's all I can tell you right now. See you tomorrow, Cobe. And thank you.'

As soon as Butterfly ended the call, Joza let out a long, deep breath. 'It's happening,' he said quietly, as though barely daring to believe it. He grinned at Butterfly and Silver, taking a step back, his hands grasping his head. His voice grew louder. 'It's really happening!'

Silver threw her arms around Butterfly, squeezing him tightly. When she pulled away, her eyes were bright and fierce. 'This is it,' she breathed. 'This is the end of the Council.'

There was so much hope and determination and excitement in her eyes that it almost broke Butterfly's heart. Though he returned her smile, he couldn't shake the feeling that something was going to go terribly wrong.

* * *

'Listen up, everyone!'

It was an hour till they left for Neo-Babel. The Ghosts were gathered in the main hall. Some looked down from the balconies lining its sides, while others crowded the hall floor itself, a few standing on the tables and benches in the cafeteria and on top of machines. Butterfly and Silver were at the back of the hall. They watched as Joza climbed atop the roof of a crane's control box. He was wearing his usual grin, but there was a hardness to it, a grim determination that was reflected in his small, sharp eyes.

'There's so much I want to say to you all,' he said, his voice raised for everyone to hear. 'But I know you all know it anyway, so I'll keep it short. Whether you've been with us for the whole five years –' there were cheers and stomping feet at this – 'or have only recently joined us here in Iarassi –' a smaller number of cheers and shouts – 'you're all Ghosts through and through. Every one of you is integral to our cause. What we're about to do won't be easy. It's likely not all of us will make it through to the other side. But whatever happens, each and every one of us can know that we risked our lives to take down the Council. To fight for a new Neo!'

The room thundered with cheers. A chorus of 'New Neo!' rose. Butterfly could feel the electricity of the crowd like a charge in the air, powerful and dangerous and irresistible.

'Tomorrow,' continued Joza, his voice loud to be heard over the rising noise of the crowd, 'we fight for the future! A future in which Neo opens its doors to the rest of the world and helps rebuild the world that once built *it*. A future in which people have the right to determine their own lives and no one is held back by what their DNA says they can or can't do. A future in which people may come and go as they please, and not be confined to either inside Neo's walls or outside them. So, Ghosts!' He punched both hands into the air. 'Let's take those Council bastards *down*!'

The room erupted once more in a deafening chorus of cheers, shouts and stomping feet.

Before Butterfly knew what was happening, Silver had grabbed his shoulders and pushed him against the wall. She pressed her body against him, kissing him so hard on the lips, their teeth bumped.

'What was that!' he gasped as she pulled back, laughing nervously.

'Did you mean what you said to Leanor?' she asked, not quite meeting his eyes. 'About . . . about loving me?'

Butterfly smiled. He curled an arm round her back, pulling her against him. With his other hand he cupped her face. 'I did,' he said quietly.

Silver blushed, looking down. She pressed one hand to his heart. 'It's true for me, too.' She glanced up at him. 'I just wanted you to know. Before.'

He nodded. He understood what she meant, but he didn't want to think about it. They kissed again then, more gently this time, and Butterfly was just starting to forget where they were – the world had shrunk to just him and Silver, the places where their bodies touched,

281

their lips on each other's – when they heard a loud laugh from nearby. They pulled apart quickly.

Joza was watching them, the grin on his face even wider than usual. 'Still a bit young for that, aren't you, little sis? Anyway, if you two can stop kissing each other for just a few minutes, we're getting everything moved into the trucks ready to leave in half an hour. We could use your help.'

Even with all the Ghosts moving at top speed, it still took an hour to transport everything from the hall into the dozen or so trucks that had been driven outside onto the street. Night had fallen fast across the city. A few portable lights had been set up along the road. As the Ghosts hurried around, their shadows stretched across the ground like watery flames.

Butterfly and Silver were helping a male Ghost carry a large box to one of the trucks. They had changed back into their Elite uniforms, ready for the battle. Butterfly felt strange wearing it again. He hadn't touched his uniform since the Purge. He couldn't help associating it with that day, and he felt every betrayal the Council had done to him pressing against his skin with the fabric.

'Why are we bringing so many things?' asked Silver as they lifted the box into the truck.

'It's not just for us,' said the Ghost. 'We'd be pretty useless trying to lug all this around *and* fight the Council at the same time! Nah, we've got to bring supplies to the Pigeons too since they're fighting with us. We've been doing some of it in small instalments over time, but it was best not to store too much in the Limpets in case the Council found it. Anyway, thanks for your help. And good luck!'

After saying goodbye to the Ghost, Silver kissed Butterfly. 'I'm just going to get our backpacks from the room,' she said. 'See you in a minute.'

As soon as she'd left, a hand clapped Butterfly's back. 'Looking good,' said Joza. 'We're almost ready to go.'

'I still don't understand how we're getting in to Neo,' said Butterfly. 'These trucks are going to have a hard time fitting through the Limpets' tunnel.'

Joza grinned. His teeth looked bone-white in the stark lights. 'Don't you want to have any surprises?'

He turned to walk away but Butterfly grabbed him, slamming him against the side of the truck. 'This isn't a joke,' Butterfly growled.

The grin disappeared from Joza's face. He pushed Butterfly off him, brushing himself down and straightening his clothes. 'I know that,' he said coldly, before walking away.

Butterfly glared after Joza. After a few moments, he noticed Percie watching him from nearby. He couldn't read her expression; her pretty face was as impassive as always.

She stepped towards him, pulling back her long hair, and pointed to the ugly scar that ran down her cheek. 'Do you know how I got this?'

He shrugged.

'I came to the Outside with my parents when I was a

teenager,' Percie said. As she spoke, she traced the scar with a finger. 'We made our home in one of the nearby villages – much like the one your family lived in. We lived there happily for years, until one night soldiers came from Neo. They killed everyone.' She glanced away for a second, her eyes shivering in the darkening light. 'This was right at the start of Joza's defence of the Purges, so he was inexperienced and ill-prepared. By the time he arrived with a few others, I was the only one in the village left alive. Only because a couple of the soldiers had decided to . . . to keep me. For a bit of fun, I think they called it. I have no doubt they were planning to kill me after. Joza found us just outside the village. I'll never forget how he looked when he killed them.'

Butterfly shook his head. 'I didn't know.'

'Joza smiles and laughs and jokes,' she continued, 'because that's the only way he can bear it. But don't ever think he is not serious about this. There is *nothing* more important to him. He –'

Her voice was drowned by a blaring beep, long and deep. It came from the nearby truck, cutting through the chatter and noise of the Ghosts that crowded the street. Another low beep joined it, and another, until all the trucks were making the same noise, and the Ghosts joined them, cheering and whooping and punching the air.

Percie smiled stiffly. 'Looks like it's time to go.' She gestured at the nearby truck. 'You and Silver are travelling in this one.'

Butterfly nodded. As he turned to leave, she placed a hand on his arm, stopping him.

'I'm sorry,' she said. Her face had softened, and her voice had lost its crispness. 'About your family, I mean.'

After what she had told him, Butterfly realised he might have more in common with Joza's wife than he had originally thought.

Percie squeezed his arm. 'Do this for them, Butterfly. Take down the Council for them. I'm doing it for my family,' she added quietly before walking away, her hair shimmering like a blonde waterfall down her back.

Part III
NEO-BABEL

35

The Air-tram Ambush

Akhezo was running. Running through endless grey corridors, the only sounds the drumming of his heart and the pounding of his feet. He didn't know where he was running to, or even why he was running, but he felt darkness at his back like some monstrous creature's wide open mouth waiting to swallow him whole.

He turned a corner and found that he couldn't move properly. It was heavy to lift his feet. He saw that the floor had turned to mud – Limpets mud – and he was stuck in it.

'Stupid rat,' hissed a hoarse old voice.

Akhezo looked up to see Domino standing in the corridor. No, not standing; Domino was *hanging*, a rope attached to the ceiling tight around his wrinkled neck.

'Get here and help me down, useless boy,' he wheezed.

But Akhezo couldn't move. The mud was rising. It was up to his waist now. As he looked round for help, he saw a beautiful woman with flame-red hair standing above him.

'Pathetic,' she sneered. 'You're going to die in the mud just like the Limpets rat you are.'

He tried to speak but no words came out. He could

feel the darkness behind him closer now, heavy and cold and immense, a pressure that squeezed the breath out of his lungs.

'Useless boy.'

'Limpets scum.'

'Filthy little rat.'

The corridor was suddenly filled with people, all looking at Akhezo and laughing, sneering, their lips twisted with wicked smiles. He struggled, trying to pull himself out of the mud, but it just dragged him down deeper.

The mud rose to his chest.

Neve appeared in the middle of the crowd. Her brains were dribbling down her face, smearing it red and purple and grey. The juices dripped into her mouth as she opened it to speak. 'Squeak, you little rat,' she said. 'Let me hear you *squeak*.'

Akhezo tried to shout out to her, but the mud had risen so high it lapped over his head and filled his open mouth, sour and rotting and –

'Get up.'

He felt someone shaking him awake. His mind struggled to push through the dream clinging to him, and it took him a while to focus on the huge Afrikan man bending over him. Akhezo remembered his name from yesterday as Allum.

The man's eyes were expressionless as he straightened. 'Come with me.'

Akhezo scrambled to his feet. He was still in the same room he and Neve had been taken to after that red-haired witch had tricked them, though he had no idea how long ago that was. All the hours had bled together into one long grey lifetime spent in this room, until Neve –

Until Neve had been shot.

Akhezo felt the hours after *that*, each one slow and sharp and piercing, straight into his heart, like needles, like daggers, like the red-haired witch's fingernails tearing into his flesh to reach his pulsing insides.

'Neve?' he whispered as Allum grabbed his shoulder, pushing him towards the door. It still surprised him every time he opened his eyes and she wasn't there.

Allum led Akhezo down sterile grey corridors like the ones in his dream to a lift. 'I am sorry about what happened to your friend,' he said as the lift slid upwards. 'I did not know Ember was planning that. If you co-operate, I ensure you will not come to the same fate.'

'Cooperate with what?' Akhezo croaked. His voice was hoarse. He must have been screaming in his sleep.

Allum didn't look at him. 'It is time for you to take us to your anti-birthchip group's new hideout.'

It was not a question, and Akhezo knew he had no choice but to go along with it, or he'd be the next to receive a bullet in the head.

When they arrived at Achebe Bridge Station, Allum's hand still clutching Akhezo's shoulder, there were three people already waiting at the platform. One was a tired-looking station guard, but the other two were policemen. Liquid black shadows slid across their masks.

The station guard bowed as they entered. 'Good morning, sirs.'

Allum inclined his head. 'Good morning.' He turned to the policemen. 'You are here to accompany us?'

The taller of the two nodded. 'Senior Surrey thought it would be good for you to have, er . . . *assistance.*' There was a mocking tone to his voice, which was thick with a Northern Mainland accent.

Akhezo felt Allum's hand squeeze tighter on his shoulder. He wondered what had happened to make this Senior Surrey person not trust Allum to take Akhezo to the Limpets alone.

'Senior Surrey should know I do not need babysitting,' Allum said, his voice cool.

The policeman shrugged. 'Orders are orders.'

An air-tram that had been approaching slid into the station. It made an electric humming noise as it waited, its sliding doors open. Cables creaked overhead. The station guard quickly ushered them towards the first-class carriage at the end of the air-tram, perhaps sensing the tension in the group.

Akhezo had never been on an air-tram before. It didn't feel safe. It seemed much too small to be rushing through the air hundreds of feet above the ground. Once they had sat down on the padded seats that lined the windows – Allum and Akhezo on one side, the two policeman opposite them on the other – the air-tram began to move. It was surprisingly fast. As the carriage tilted back, the air-tram making its ascent to its high route through the inner city, Akhezo gripped the armrests of his seat. The carriage shivered, every now and then bumping or jolting slightly, sending a fresh slice of panic through him, and he stared at the floor, not daring to look outside.

They stopped at a new station every few minutes, but no one boarded their first-class carriage. Akhezo heard people climbing into the other carriages though. He guessed from the grey-blue light that had started to filter through the windows that the city was beginning to wake up with the new day, people going to their jobs, oblivious of what was happening in the carriage next to them.

'Remind me,' said the policeman with the drawling Northern Mainland accent as the carriage slid away from another station. 'Why are we going to the Limpets in an air-tram? At least in a rickshaw I can smoke –'

A loud *crack* snapped through the hushed morning air. Then a squealing of brakes. Akhezo felt the air-tram slowing to a halt.

The policemen were on their feet in a second. 'What is it?' asked the Northern Mainland one, drawing his gun. There was a twist of panic in his voice.

There was another thud on the carriage roof, then another, and another. The carriage bounced on its cables. Akhezo clung to his seat as the policemen ran to one side of the carriage, while Allum moved to the window above Akhezo.

Allum let out a loud curse. 'Get down.'

'But –'

'*Now!*'

Akhezo threw himself to the floor, throwing his hands over his head as a shudder rocked through the air-tram.

The windows smashed inwards. Shards of plastiglass flew down, filling the carriage with their hard, glittering petals, and suddenly the carriage was tilting as a metallic screeching filled the air, and he slid hard into the row of seats on the other side.

Akhezo couldn't tell what was going on. The carriage was a blur. He could see someone climbing in through a broken window, one of the policemen struggling to free his foot where it was trapped beneath a seat. Then someone grabbed his arm, dragging him to his feet.

'You're not getting away that easily,' snarled the policeman with the Northern Mainland accent.

The air-tram made another ear-shredding screech. It dipped again, swinging wildly on its cables, and Akhezo and the policeman were thrown to the far end of the carriage. They smashed into the emergency door in the far wall, and with a sickening feeling in the pit of his stomach, Akhezo felt the door give way beneath them.

He only just managed to grab the edge of the doorway as it swung open. He and the policeman fell through it, and then cold wind was rushing around him, his body dangling in the empty air. He clung on tightly, his fingers burning with pain at the effort, but he forced himself to hold on as the scream of the policeman falling to the ground below snapped off suddenly. *Don't look down!* Akhezo told himself, but he had never been one to follow order. Even his own.

He looked down.

At once, his stomach lurched. There was nothing between him and the ground but air. The inner-city street hundreds of feet below was busy with tiny figures and rickshaws, flickering in and out of view as an early morning mist weaved round them. Yawning up on both sides of the air-tram were tall inner-city buildings. People crowded the balconies studding their facades, pointing and staring at him.

'Help!' he shouted. 'Help!'

And as if hearing his plea, two hands grabbed his wrists, and he looked up into a face with bright green eyes and golden-brown hair –

'Cambridge!' Akhezo cried.

The leader of the Pigeons pulled him up into the carriage. They fell against the wall, Akhezo gulping for breath, flexing his hurting fingers.

'How did you find me?' he gasped.

'Your birthchip,' Cambridge said, pulling Akhezo to his feet. His face was tight and serious. 'Come on, we need to go.'

The carriage was hanging from one end, the cables having ripped off their fastenings at the other side. They started up the length of the carriage, using the armrests of the seats to climb up towards the higher end of the carriage. Bullets whizzed past them; Allum and the other policeman were still fighting off their attackers.

When they reached the top end of the carriage, Cambridge leant out of the window. 'We're ready!' he shouted, looking up.

Akhezo didn't hear a reply. He'd barely heard what Cambridge had said over the bullet-studded air and the hissing of the wind through the empty windows, the creaking cables and metallic screeches that made it sound as though the air-tram was screaming in pain. But a second later Cambridge nodded and looked back at Akhezo.

Cambridge held out a hand. 'Go on. Don't worry, I'll be right behind you.'

Akhezo's was shaking. He'd thought that years of living in the skylung had accustomed him to heights, but there was something different about being in a tiny metal box hanging from a cable hundreds of feet in the air that nothing prepared you for. He hesitated. He glanced around, half expecting to see Neve, her mouth twisted in a smirk, saying, 'What is it, Akhezo? A little bit of height has got you weeing your pants?'

But she wasn't there.

The memory of her death gave him the courage he needed. Akhezo nodded and Cambridge grabbed him, lifting him out the window. As soon as he was out, another hand caught his. He looked up into the face of a Red man he dimly recognised as a Pigeons member.

'Gotchya!' the man said, yanking Akhezo up. 'Now take this and swing.' He thrust a thick cord into Akhezo's hand, the other end of which was attached to a balcony a few metres above the air-tram.

For a second time, Akhezo hesitated. He felt everything as though each inch of his body had become alert and alive. The roof of the carriage vibrating under his feet. The funnelled wind whipping past his ears. The hard, rubbery cord clutched between his fingers. For a moment, he was sure he wouldn't be able to do it. Then the air-tram lurched beneath his feet and, without thinking, he pushed himself off its roof, clinging to the cord as it swung through the air.

He slammed hard into the wall of the building opposite and dropped onto a small balcony below. Gasping for air, he got to his feet and stumbled to the edge of the balcony.

The air-tram looked as though it was about to break free from its cables. It was tilted at such a ridiculous angle it almost looked like a toy, and the people waving at him on its roof just plastic figures waiting for a huge hand to come and pick them up. Akhezo had no idea why they were waving. He started to raise a hand to wave back when there was a voice behind him.

'The cord, you idiot!' A woman rushed past, grabbing the cord from him and throwing it towards the carriage.

Cambridge swung gracefully across to the balcony in an instant. He pulled out a gun, handing it to Akhezo. 'Just in case.'

'But –'

Cambridge ignored him, turning back to the air-tram. He threw the cord. The man who had helped Akhezo onto the carriage roof was next to swing over. 'One more,' Cambridge said, taking the cord from him and throwing it back again.

The next things seemed to happen in slow motion. As the cord reached the air-tram there was a deafening screech. The last few cables holding the carriages snapped. The Pigeon member on the roof reached out and his fingers just brushed the tip of the cord when he was knocked sideways as – Akhezo had almost forgotten about him – Allum's outstretched hand closed around the cord instead. There was an awful, strangled shout. Then the air-tram dropped.

Akhezo only had time to watch its fall for a second before Allum landed on the balcony. The man's face was contorted in – *In what?* Akhezo thought. *Anger? Determination? Pain?* – but there was still something steady and almost peaceful about him as he straightened up, lifted an arm, and pressed a gun to Cambridge's forehead.

36

Home Sweet Home

'Wake up. We're here.'

Silver felt a hand on her shoulder shaking her awake. She opened her eyes to see Butterfly crouched in front of her. His outline was dark, silhouetted against the square of light of the open door of the truck.

When they'd first boarded it back in Iarassi, Silver hadn't thought she'd be able to sleep, but after just a few minutes lying in Butterfly's arms she fell swiftly away. Dreamless sleep had been empty and forgiving. Now, as Butterfly helped her to her feet and they followed the rest of the Ghosts into the weak, bluish morning light, she felt a slow dread return as the thought of what they were about to do wrapped itself around her, squeezing her insides.

The Ghosts were uncharacteristically quiet as they filed out of the trucks and gathered on the shoulder of hill they'd stopped on. Wind hissed through leaf-feathered trees, fog clinging to their trunks like discarded dreams. The trees were in a line on the ridge top, obscuring the view, but as Silver drew closer, she could see between the trunks to the wastelands. Beyond was the curving black shell of Neo-Babel's walls.

She stared at the city, remembering how it had felt

to look at it from the Outside a few days ago, when they'd exited the tunnel. She had been amazed at how different it had seemed then, how unrecognisable it was from beyond the walls. Now, she saw it for exactly what it was; a cage, a prison.

A lie.

'Home sweet home,' muttered Butterfly beside her.

Joza's voice sounded from the back of the crowd, and they turned with the Ghosts in his direction. 'The Pigeons will be creating the way into the city for us in eight minutes,' he said. 'Get into your groups now. Those going to Central Police Command with Wei Lei –'

A booming sound burst apart the air, drowning his words. Every Ghost jumped, spinning round in the direction of the noise, and they began shouting and whooping at the sight. Silver stared in amazement at the billowing sail of smoke which covered a large part of the wall that she guessed had just been blown apart.

'They're early!' cried Joza. 'All right, Ghosts. Ghosts!' he shouted louder and they fell silent. 'Form into your groups and get into the trucks. We're going in!'

The Ghosts scattered. In the rush, Joza pushed his way towards Silver and Butterfly, his mouth set in a tight line. 'You two are with me.'

They followed him to one of the trucks and squeezed into the front seats, Silver sitting on Butterfly's lap in the small space. Just as Joza started the engine, there was a frantic rapping of knuckles on the window next to him. He pushed the door open.

Percie's face was flushed as she leant inside, her usual

cool demeanour gone. 'Joza,' she breathed. 'If we don't –'

He raised a finger to her lips, stopping her. 'We will,' he said firmly.

Silver watched out of the corner of her eyes as her brother cupped his wife's face in his hands and kissed her. He whispered something Silver couldn't hear, but she could guess what it might have been. They pulled apart. Percie nodded, kissed Joza fiercely one final time, and then stood back, shutting the door.

They sped off straight away. Joza's truck led the group. Butterfly held Silver round the waist with one arm but she still had to press a hand against the dashboard, the truck was bumping so violently. They hurtled down the leeward side of the slope before speeding across the wasteland, their spinning wheels throwing up a cloud of dust that wreathed the truck, filling the air with a sound like rain as grit and dirt flung against the windscreen.

'The Pigeons *bombed* a part of the wall?' Silver shouted above the noise. She couldn't believe it. She'd always thought of Neo-Babel's wall as indestructible.

Joza nodded. His knuckles were white on the steering wheel.

'But where did they get the explosives?'

'Your friends at the Council made a kind donation,' he said, and grinned for the first time that day.

Joza drove so quickly they were soon approaching the exploded part of the wall. The cloud of smoke billowing from the gap was thick, opaque, turning the world into a swirling, white-grey ashscape.

'Hold on!' he cried.

Silver grabbed the dashboard just in time as the truck began to buck and bump even more than before, hitting the debris of the destroyed wall. There were metallic crashes and tearing sounds as the truck collided with unseen obstacles, just looming shadows out of the clouds that were too close to avoid.

'Be careful!' Silver screamed as they narrowly missed a chunk of wall that lay across the ground, the truck swerving madly, throwing them sideways in their seats.

Joza's grin was more of a grimace. 'Just be thankful you're not in the back of the truck.'

After a minute, the ash and smoke started to clear, and Silver could make out the blocky shapes of buildings beyond. The truck began to slow.

'We have to wait here,' Joza explained. 'Just a couple of minutes to meet up with the Pigeons, and then the four of us will head to the tunnel in the hydroponics that'll get us into the Council District.'

'Four of us?' asked Butterfly.

Joza nodded. 'Cambridge is coming with us. He's the leader of the Pigeons.'

Silver shifted uneasily as the truck crawled to a stop, still cloaked in a veil of shifting smoke and ash. 'Is it really a good idea to be stopping here?' It felt strange to be still after hurtling along at such high speed, and the poor visibility was making her feel uneasy. Anything could be hiding behind the clouds of smoke.

'We were actually meant to meet the Pigeons on that ridge outside the city,' said Joza. 'But something happened that meant Cambridge had to stay in Neo.' He opened the door to leave the truck and noise rushed in; the wailings of alarms, screams and shouts, a low rumble as debris from the explosion shifted. Joza had to shout to be heard over it all as he added, 'I think he said something about retrieving a lost Pigeon.'

At the same time, up on a windswept balcony high above an inner-city street –

'Hello again, Allum.'

Even with a gun pressed to his forehead, Cambridge was polite. Akhezo had to admire him for that.

Allum didn't respond.

The other two Pigeons drew their guns, but before they'd even aimed them at Allum, he flicked his gun at both of them in turn. The gunshots were so loud Akhezo felt them in his heart. Two hard pulses, and then nothing.

His breath came out in ragged drags. He was certain Allum would turn the gun on him next, but the man did not even look in his direction, and with an almost gentle carefulness, Allum returned the gun to Cambridge's forehead.

'Ah, of course you wouldn't kill the boy,' said Cambridge, and Akhezo was amazed to see a smile on the Pigeons leader's face. 'How is Taiyo doing?'

'Don't you *dare* ask about her.'

Cambridge clasped his hands together. 'I apologise. Will you at least tell her I said hello?'

Akhezo had no idea what was going on. He stared at the two men, his mouth hanging open.

'She does not need your pity, Cambridge,' said Allum. '*None* of us do.'

'When we met that time –'

Allum growled. 'You had no right to ask us to leave the Council and join you and the Pigeons. To try and turn us against our own family.'

'Family?'

'Yes. Family. That is what the Council is to us. To *me*. Even to Ember, who behind all her tough act I know to be just a girl fighting for what she believes in. That is why she would not leave with you, even if you *are* her father.'

Akhezo felt his stomach drop. The daughter Cambridge was so distraught over losing to the Council was *Ember*? He shook his head. It couldn't be true. How could a witch like her be related to the man who had given him everything?

'How is Ember?' whispered Cambridge, his voice broken.

'Well,' said Allum.

'Good.' There were tears in Cambridge's eyes now. 'You're not going to leave the Council, are you, Allum? No matter what I say.'

Allum shook his head. 'I will defend them to the grave.'

Cambridge looked hurt. He said softly, 'That might be sooner than you think.'

Allum replied by pulling the trigger.

Akhezo screamed. He screamed, but he didn't hear it. He just felt his mouth open and his lungs burn and his throat scrape raw. He made a jerking, lunging movement towards Cambridge's body but Allum grabbed him and twisted him round, pushing him towards the door leading off the balcony.

'I *hate* you!' cried Akhezo, thrashing under Allum's grasp. He hit out, his punches falling softly on the man's muscular bulk. 'All of you Council snobs! You and that red-haired witch and everyone else!'

Allum didn't say anything. He just dragged Akhezo off the balcony, his face set back in its expressionless mask.

Those two minutes waiting for the Pigeons to arrive were the longest two minutes of Silver's life. She, Butterfly and Joza stood in the drifting, wind-churned clouds of ash and smoke, their backs pressed against the truck, guns ready in their hands. They waited in tense silence for shapes to move towards them out of the grey cloud.

None came.

'Let's get the motorbike,' said Joza, glancing at his watch and tucking his gun away. 'We can't wait for Cambridge any longer.' He slid open the side of the truck, lifting out a large motorbike. One of the Ghosts left the truck too, and Joza grasped his hand as he opened the door to get into the driver's seat.

'For a New Neo,' the man said, pulling the door shut.

Joza sat down at the front of the motorbike, a grim smile on his face. Silver climbed on behind him. Butterfly linked his arms round her waist from behind. They pulled away quickly with a growl of the engine, and Silver heard the trucks begin to follow.

'Are we going to be all right without the Pigeons?' she yelled over the roar of noise in Joza's ear.

'They know the plan. I'm sure that once they've dealt with whatever's held them up, they'll join us.'

She was about to ask for more details about the plan when the wind shifted. The smoke that had been enveloping them since they'd entered the city cleared, and Neo-Babel was suddenly in front of them. For a few seconds, she couldn't breathe. Her eyes roamed over the squat shapes of the factories of the Industrial District they were travelling through, people standing around or leaning out of their rickshaws, staring at the motorbike and the trucks behind it as they passed, their faces dumb with surprise. Beyond, the buildings of the inner city rose, dark against the cloudy sky.

It was strange coming back. Though nothing had physically altered, everything looked different to Silver. Buildings and landmarks she was used to seeing on a daily basis – the skylungs lining the eastern stretch of the Outer Circle, Storm Point Tower, the tallest building in the inner city – had changed somehow.

No. *She* was the one who had changed.

The motorbike twisted through the morning traffic, Joza driving so quickly she was amazed they didn't crash. They crossed a bridge over the Outer Circle of the river, heading westwards.

Silver leant in close to his ear. 'Why're we going through the tunnel in the hydroponics?' she shouted. 'Surely we could just attack the police directly to get into the Council District? They'll know we're here now.'

'We need to divert attention away from the Council District,' he explained, his gaze still trained ahead on the busy street. 'We need them to focus on the other locations we've sent the Ghosts and Pigeons to. And if we storm the Council District, it'll be too difficult to get to the Bee-Hives. The Council might block access to them, and then even with your friend Cobe's help we won't be able to get in.'

As they drove, the trucks behind them swerved away one by one, heading to create the diversions Joza talked about. By the time they were alone, the motorbike moving slower now, they were passing along a pretty street in the Mediterranean Quarter lining a part of the river Silver knew as the Tuscan Intersect. Residents crowded the ornamental balconies pocketing the pastel-coloured facades of the buildings. They stared at the bike as it squealed to a stop. With the engine off, everything fell unnervingly silent.

'The entrance to the tunnel is just a couple of minutes from here,' said Joza. He pulled out his gun, Silver and Butterfly following suit. 'We can't take the bike in case they follow us – we'll be as good as dead if they corner us in the tunnel.' He nodded, mouth set tight. 'Let's go.'

They scrambled off the motorbike and started running, Joza leading the way. Silver didn't even hear the cries and shouts of the people they passed. All she could hear was the blood pounding in her ears – a tribal drumbeat, hard and intoxicating – and the burn of her feet as they slapped against the floor. At the end of the street they turned left. Ran down another street. Turned right, left, left again.

'Here!' hissed Joza, swerving off into a narrow alley between two buildings.

Silver and Butterfly followed. They slowed as they approached Joza bent over something on the floor.

'This is it?' asked Silver, catching her breath.

He nodded. He stepped back to reveal a square hole in the ground. She peered into it, seeing nothing but murky blackness.

There was the sound of running footsteps in the street behind them. Silver noticed now the wailing siren of police bikes, drawing closer.

'Come on!' urged Joza.

Butterfly went down the hole first, then Silver, who discovered in the darkness a ladder attached to one side of the shaft. Joza went last. He pulled the heavy grate overhead back into place just as shouts came from the alley entrance.

'Alley's clear,' said a gruff male voice. 'They must have gone up here.'

Silver didn't breathe until she heard their footsteps grow faint. 'Now?' she asked after silence fell.

'Now we go down,' said Joza.

37

Into the Stacks

After descending in total darkness for ten minutes, a watery blue light appeared at the bottom of the shaft, glowing brighter as they drew closer. Silver had only been to the underground hydroponic farms a handful of times. The thing she remembered most about it was its eerie twilight glow that gave the whole place a dream-like, underwater feel.

At the end of the ladder, they stepped down into a narrow tunnel, so low-ceilinged that Butterfly and Joza had to bend their heads. Beneath their feet the metal was grated. They caught glimpses of the farm-chamber below; water boxes in neat parallel rows, hydroponic workers moving around, tending the plants. The whole place was filled with the low humming of the farm-chambers' filtration system.

'They haven't used this ventilation system for years,' Joza said. 'We should be able to follow this tunnel all the way to the Council District without any problems.'

'How do you think it's going up there?' Silver whispered to Butterfly as they started down the tunnel.

He didn't meet her eyes. 'We know better than anyone what the Ghosts and Pigeons are up against.'

She thought of her parents in the city above. It was strange how she'd left Neo-Babel to find them, and now here they all were again, back inside the city walls, and she still hadn't been reunited with them. She knew Joza would have prepared them well for battle, but she still felt anxious. She wished she could have met with them before they left Iarassi. Not knowing how they were was making Silver even more nervous, and the minutes passing by felt like years. She couldn't wait for this all to be over, and she could finally see her parents, finally hold them in her arms, and know that the danger was gone.

It felt like it had only just begun.

They'd been walking for an hour before Joza finally stopped. They were below an opening which led to what looked like a shaft identical to the one they'd climbed down.

'We're here?' asked Silver, peering up into the murky darkness.

He nodded. 'This leads to the workers' dormitories round the back of the Stacks. Once we get out, things are going to get hectic. You ready?'

Without hesitating, Silver and Butterfly nodded.

'Then call Cobe,' Joza said. 'Tell him we're coming.'

Allum had dragged Akhezo off the balcony where Cambridge's body lay, through the abandoned apartment it led into and halfway down the stairs before pushing him against the wall and saying, 'If you are not quiet, I will have to knock you out.'

Akhezo was silent after that.

He was silent when they walked out of the building and into the street they'd both been high above just minutes ago. The air-tram they'd been riding in was now a twisted lump of metal on the floor. The street was packed with people and rickshaws, police surrounding the crash site. A body hung from one of the broken air-tram windows. The man's arms hung limply down, as though waiting for someone to grab his hands and pull him free.

Akhezo continued to be silent all the way back to the Council District in the rickshaw. He was silent as it stopped outside the Stacks and they stepped out, Allum tossing the driver a few coins. And he was silent when, before Allum could place his hand back on his shoulder, Akhezo pulled out the gun Cambridge had given him, aimed it with shaking hands at Allum, and pulled the trigger.

The kickback of the gun threw Akhezo's aim off. Rather than hitting Allum's chest, the bullet shot into his thigh. Swearing, the man pressed a hand to his leg, blood spurting between his fingers.

Before Allum could recover, Akhezo ran for it. He sprinted up the wide steps towards the glass front of the Stacks, a mad grin on his face; all his running work had finally come in useful. Before he knew it, he was outside the atrium. He raised the gun to shoot the glass of the tall doors blocking his way, but just then they slid open. A crowd of people streamed out. They rushed past him, a stream of colour and anxious faces. None of them noticed the small Afronese boy moving through them in the opposite direction.

Butterfly and Silver were running through the Stacks. They'd lost Joza in the chaos after emerging from the ventilation shaft, somewhere between the workers' dormitories and the east wing where they were now, but there was no time to stop and look for him. Joza had told them that if they got separated, they were to continue to where they were meeting Cobe on a floor above the Bee-Hives. They could regroup there.

They ran out into a large hall. One of its walls was completely clear, and through it Silver could see the manicured trees and bushes of the senior Council members' private ornamental gardens. On the adjacent wall were the lifts they needed to travel to where they were meeting Cobe. She barely had time to feel relief at reaching their destination before a group of masked soldiers ran at them, gunshots studding the air.

Silver ducked, returning fire. She hit two soldiers in their arms, forcing them to drop their guns, but missed the others. Out of the corner of her eye, she noticed that Butterfly didn't seem to be shooting, though his gun was in his hand. A bullet clipped past her left ear. She swerved to avoid more as the soldiers fired, gaining on them. The lift Silver and Butterfly needed was just metres away. If they could just –

Something knocked into Silver, throwing her to the side. Her body slid across the varnished floor. She twisted round and moved to sit up when a foot slammed down on her chest, a masked face leering towards her as the soldier raised his gun –

Bang!

The soldier swung sideways off her. Blood spurted from one side of his neck.

'Come on!' Joza cried, grabbing Silver's hand to help her up, and they sprinted to the lift.

Butterfly was waiting inside. He had an arm locked round the neck of a struggling soldier. 'Need to use him for his birthchip to pass the scanners,' he said as they ran inside. The next moment the doors slid shut, the lift moving downwards. 'His authority level will get us to the floor one above the Bee-Hives, where we're meeting Cobe. From there, Cobe's birthchip should see us through.'

'Then why is he still alive?' Joza raised his gun, aiming it at the soldier.

Butterfly smacked it down. 'We don't have to kill him.'

Joza shrugged. Then he jerked forward, hitting the soldier round the side of the head with the hilt of his gun. The soldier slumped to the floor.

'Can't have him telling anyone where we're going,' Joza said in response to Butterfly's accusatory stare.

The lift stopped at a long, narrow corridor. Both of its ends curved out of view. After the chaos of their run through the floors above, the silence was unnerving. Silver could hear her own heartbeat thudding hard in her chest.

'Where's Cobe?' she asked.

Joza turned to the left. 'I'll check down here. You two search that end.'

Butterfly and Silver nodded. They started down the right-hand path of the corridor, moving slowly with their guns raised. Silver could see Butterfly's arms were shaking.

'Are you all right?' she whispered.

'What?'

She stopped walking and touched his arm. 'Back there in the hall. You didn't shoot.'

'The masks,' he said in a strained voice. 'They remind me . . .'

'The Purge?'

He nodded.

Silver took one of his hands and squeezed it. Before she could say anything, they heard running footsteps, and a voice rang out in the corridor.

'Butterfly!' A slim, shaven-haired boy half ran, half fell round the corner of the corridor. His eyes were wide, his face white.

Silver's heart jumped. 'Cobe!' she cried.

Butterfly ran forward. Cobe slammed into him and they staggered back, clutching at each other, Cobe's face buried in Butterfly's neck.

'I'm so sorry,' Cobe sobbed. He pulled back and his eyes roamed over Butterfly's face. 'Ember told me they'd turn your birthchip blockers off, that they'd find you and torture you unless I called and pretended everything was fine to find out when you were coming. I thought this way you had a chance. I thought –'

'Ember knows we're coming?' Silver interjected, a shiver of fear in her voice.

Cobe didn't even glance in her direction. 'I'm so sorry, Butterfly.'

Butterfly shook his head. 'Don't be.' He gripped Cobe's arms. 'You've done more than enough for us.'

Cobe shut his eyes. When he next spoke, his voice was a whisper. 'I never told you why I helped you and Silver,' he said. 'It was all for you. I . . . I love you.'

There was silence in the corridor. Silver stared at them, and everything suddenly made sense. Cobe's coldness towards her, his determination in helping Butterfly with whatever he wanted, even if that meant Butterfly leaving Neo-Babel; leaving *him*. She wondered if she should feel jealous, but all she felt was an aching in her chest and a strange desire to go to Cobe, to hug him and say, 'I know. I love him too.'

When Butterfly spoke, his voice was soft. 'You're my senior, Cobe. I'd do anything for you.'

'And I you,' Cobe said, smiling faintly.

Bang!

The sound of the gunshot was horribly loud in the corridor. Cobe fell forward, slumping into Butterfly's arms. There was a bloody bullet hole in the back of his head.

'My little junior,' Ember said, appearing round the corner of the corridor. She opened her arms wide, her lips curled in their usual sneer. 'It's been *so* long.'

38

The Bee-Hives

Silver stared at her Elite senior, too appalled to speak. Out of the corner of her eye, she saw Butterfly laying Cobe down at the side of the corridor, but she couldn't look away from Ember. She didn't think she'd ever hated anyone as much as she hated Ember right then. Even the anger she'd felt during the Purge was nothing compared to this. Her whole body shook with a raw, desparate fury. She felt as though it were ripping her apart, tearing her in two.

Ember raised an eyebrow. 'What's wrong? I thought you'd thank me for killing the competition for your boyfriend's affections.'

'One more word, Ember,' Butterfly said, 'and I swear I'll put a bullet through your face.'

She smirked. 'I'm not afraid of filthy, Red-loving Mainlanders like *you* –'

Butterfly lunged at her, raising his gun. Ember stepped forward and raised her own, a cruel laugh twisted across her lips. But it was Joza – who must have heard the gunshot and came looking for them – who fired first.

His bullet hit Ember's shoulder. She twisted from the impact, a hiss escaping her lips. It was only a second of lost composure, and then she turned back and raised her gun again, but by now Silver had darted forward. She grabbed Ember's arm, twisting it behind her back, wrapping her other arm round Ember's neck.

Joza touched Butterfly's shoulder. 'I'm sorry, but now Cobe's gone, we need Ember alive to get into the Bee-Hives.'

Butterfly didn't say anything. He was still staring at Ember, the arm holding his gun shaking. His blue eyes had turned a dark, ocean colour, and Silver could feel the anger emanating from him in cold waves.

'She's not worth it,' she said, looking at him over Ember's head. 'Remember what you told me after I'd fallen in the river? Ember's not the one to blame.'

'You're right,' said Butterfly. 'But I know who is.'

'Senior Surrey?'

He nodded.

Beneath Silver's grip, Ember struggled. 'Leave him out of it,' she hissed. 'Don't –'

Silver squeezed her arm tighter round Ember's neck until she fell silent.

'Where do you think he is?' Butterfly asked Silver.

'Try his office. He'll probably be there waiting for Ember to bring our heads back to him.'

Joza stepped forward. 'Now, hang on. Is this a good idea?'

'Yes,' Silver answered firmly. She knew exactly how Butterfly was feeling. She had felt it that day back at Yasir's village when the soldiers arrived, and she felt it now, squeezing her arm round Ember's neck. 'Go get him,' she said. 'Make him pay.'

Butterfly nodded. Then he was off, running back down the corridor. When he was out of sight, Silver and Joza started down the hallway towards the lift that would take them to the Bee-Hives. Using Ember's birthchip to get them through the scanners, they travelled down to the lowest level of the Stacks and crossed a hallway to the observatory deck lining the front of the cavern which housed Neo-Babel's DNA store.

The name DNA Holding Towers was misleading. Rather than being built upwards, the DNA stores went the opposite way, hanging down from supports in a funnel shape which had gained them the nickname Bee-Hives. From the observatory deck, the huge hanging masses of the Bee-Hives were not fully visible, but there was still a sense of awe from the vast space of the rocky cavern, the wide, flat discs from which they hung, connected by tubular chains to the immense support structure that covered the cavern ceiling. A swirling mist wreathed the Bee-Hives, keeping the DNA at the cold temperature needed for preservation.

'Incredible,' Joza breathed, placing both hands on the slanting glass.

Silver moved to the door at the far end of the observatory deck, gripping Ember tighter. 'Come on, Joza.'

'Don't want to destroy it now, do you?' said Ember, a gurgling laugh catching in her throat. 'Now you've seen its power.'

'Its power?' Joza hissed. With a snarl of rage, he grabbed Ember out of Silver's hold and slammed her against the door. 'Oh, I've *seen* its power, you bitch – out there, beyond the walls. I know what it does to people. How it drives them to kill to keep the power to themselves.'

Ember laughed, and seeing what she was about to do a second before it happened, Silver lunged forward and grabbed her shoulder. She dug her fingernails into the bleeding bullet wound. Ember screamed with pain but still pushed forward to attack Joza, but now he'd realised what was happening. He slammed into Ember, knocking her back.

None of them heard the hiss as the door to the Bee-Hives slid open, but Ember must have slid over the birthchip scanner, for the next moment the three of them fell onto the circular staircase that led down into the cavern. Still wrestling to keep hold of each other, they tumbled down the stairs. They slid to a stop on the floor of the walkway lining the cavern.

Silver sprang up, sitting on top of Ember's struggling body. 'The Bee-Hives!' she cried at Joza. 'Destroy them!'

He stood up slowly. He stared out over the railing at the flat disc-tops of the DNA towers. 'It's just . . .'

'Just *what?*' It was taking all Silver's energy to keep Ember down. She wished she could kill her, put a bullet in her head. But they needed her alive to get back out.

'We could punish them,' said Joza, staring out at the Bee-Hives. 'With all this information, we could punish them *all*. Every single policeman and Council member who helped with the Purges, every man and woman who maimed and raped and killed –'

'And then you'll be just as bad as them!' Silver was

struggling to keep Ember down. 'Joza – destroy them. Now!'

But he just continued to stare.

Ember laughed so loudly it echoed throughout the cavern. 'Well,' she said, lying still under Silver. 'Now the Bee-Hives aren't going to be destroyed because your stupid brother has realised just how important they are, maybe you'd like to go take a look at your *own* DNA store. Surrey told me something very interesting a few days ago. I can't believe he'd kept it from me this long.'

'Why don't *you* just tell me and save me the bother?' snapped Silver, barely listening to what Ember was saying. She wished she knew how to get through to Joza. They had to destroy the Bee-Hives *now*.

'All right,' said Ember. 'If you insist. See, I'd always known you were useless, Silver. You *are* a Red, after all. That was enough for me to despise you. But I couldn't understand how someone like you had been streamed into the Elites programme. So you can imagine how delighted I was when Surrey finally explained it to me.'

Silver looked down at Ember. 'Explained what?' she asked, a sense of dread trickling down her spine.

Ember smiled nastily. 'That your useless Red blood is worthless. The only reason you became an Elite was because Surrey organised the DNA hacking himself. He wanted to get payback for what your brother did, forming a resistance outside Neo. He wanted to turn you into the very thing Joza hates most.' Her smile grew wider. 'You see, Silver? You're not an Elite. Your DNA is worthless. You're *nothing*.'

39

The Limpets Rat and the Witch

Silver felt a dizzying sensation at Ember's words. She thought for a moment she was about to wake up in the back of the truck outside Neo-Babel and discover this had all been a dream. 'I'm not . . . *what*?' she whispered.

'Not an Elite, no,' said Ember silkily. 'It explains it all. Why Surrey paired you with me as your senior. Why he covered for you after discovering your mistake the day of the parade. He's been trying to hide the fact that despite his best efforts, you really *have* turned out to be as redundant as your DNA.'

Silver stared at her. 'I don't believe you.'

Ember's laugh was so loud Silver flinched. 'You don't? Surely you know better than anyone else what a pitiful Elite you've turned out to be? How do you think you got your name? Silver – the colour of the dollar notes Surrey had to pay to hack your DNA. His little joke.'

Silver shook he head. 'I don't believe you,' she said again. It *couldn't* be true.

Ember shrugged. 'Why don't you check your DNA store, then?'

Silver looked up at the disc-tops of the Bee-Hives in the chamber beyond. The answer was waiting for her in one of the softly glowing blue vials. If Joza destroyed the birthchips, she'd never know the truth. She hesitated for a second, loosening her grip on Ember –

'Look out!'

Ember had freed one of her arms while Silver was distracted, grabbing the gun from the belt around her jumpsuit. At Joza's shout, Silver twisted off Ember just in time. A bullet screamed past her ear. She rolled back, expecting another shot, but Ember was running to the circular staircase now, her red hair flying behind her. With a surge of panic, Silver realised that if Ember left, she and Joza would be trapped.

'Joza!' Silver shouted, pushing herself up and running after Ember. 'The Bee-Hives!'

Whatever spell had taken over him, it seemed to have been broken by the desperation in his sister's voice. Joza ran in the opposite direction towards the huge clasps in the disc-tops where support chains connected to the Bee-Hives, while Silver hurtled up the stairs.

Ember was not as fast as Silver. Just as she reached the top of the stairs, Silver grabbed her foot. They fell. The edge of the steps jutted into Silver's chest, winding her, but she ignored the pain, pulling herself up Ember's body.

Ember kicked back. She pushed Silver off and darted for the door to the observatory deck.

'No!' Silver cried. Desperation swelled inside her. She couldn't let Ember leave without them.

But Ember did not leave. Instead, she stopped still as the door slid open, revealing a figure standing there.

It was a young Afronese boy. He wore dirty, blood-stained

clothes, and his cheeks were hollow. Silver had no idea who he was, but Ember's eyes widened at the sight of him.

'Akhezo,' Ember growled, raising her gun –

Silver threw herself at Ember. They crashed to the floor, Ember's cheekbone cracking sickeningly as the side of her head smacked into the ground. Silver wrestled the gun from her hands. She was just about to shoot Ember in the leg to stop her from running away again when a hand grabbed her wrist.

It was the Afronese boy. 'Please leave the witch to me,' he said quietly.

Perhaps it was the surprise of seeing what looked like a Limpets boy here in the Bee-Hives, or perhaps it was her own anger at Ember, but for some reason Silver found herself looking back into the boy's dark, serious eyes, and nodding.

As soon as Silver stood up, Ember started to her feet, but the boy shot her in her leg and she fell down. He shot her again in her other leg.

Ember's scream was a horrible, animal sound. Horror rose in Silver's throat like a great black wave. She knew she had no part in whatever was happening here, and after the way Ember had treated her her whole life, she shouldn't feel bad for her. But she still felt pity for her senior Elite. Feeling sick, she turned away, and noticed the boy had jammed the doors into and out of the observatory deck open. If he'd done the same for the lift, then she and Joza could get out of here.

Silver looked back out into the cavern. Ember had slid

down a few steps, leaving a trail of blood that Akhezo was standing in. Beyond, Joza ran back across the disctops of the Bee-Hives. *He's done it then*, she thought, but there was no relief or happiness. Not even satisfaction.

Ember's screams curdled the air.

Joza was at the staircase now. At the top, he stopped abruptly at the sight of Ember and the Afronese boy. 'What in the gods . . .?'

'Leave it,' said Silver.

Joza met her eyes. He nodded. Then the two of them were running out along the observatory deck, down the curving corridor and towards the lift to take them back up into the Stacks.

As Ember stared up at Akhezo from the circular steps, her body screaming with pain, she dissolved inside herself. She disappeared, falling back through her years to a night from her childhood.

She was thirteen years old. She'd just moved into the new bedroom she would be sharing with her Elite senior. Ember remembered meeting him earlier that day; a big Afrikan boy, all muscles and grisly stubble. He smelt of wood and sweat.

'Hello, Ember.'

His grip was strong as he took her hand.

'Hello, Quoma.'

Ember had not been able to meet his eyes.

Now it was night. Ember was lying in her bedpod. She lay straight, her arms at her sides, staring up at the shadowy metal casing that curved around her. Tears slid down her face. She wanted her mother. She wanted her big brother. Despite everything, she wanted her father.

There was the sound of footsteps outside the bedpod. A sliver of moonlight sliced across her blankets as the shutters opened, and Quoma's face came into view. Ember sat up, wondering what was wrong, but before she could say anything he'd reached in and grabbed her neck, pulling her out of the bedpod.

Quoma threw her so hard to the ground that she bit her tongue. 'This is how Elites must be,' he said, crouching over her. His breath stank of alcohol. 'They must be numb to pain. Numb to *giving* pain.' He kicked her in the stomach and she doubled over, curling into a ball. 'When you kill for the first time, don't let yourself feel it. You can't be like me. You can't let them haunt you.' In the moonlight, his eyes shivered. 'Do you understand, Ember?' he asked. 'Do you understand how to be an Elite?'

She nodded, trying desperately to hold back the sobs that were choking in her throat. Quoma straightened. Then he kicked her again, and again, and he kept kicking her until she fell unconscious from the pain.

'I hate you!' Akhezo's voice reached Ember as though from far away. 'You killed Neve, and Cambridge died because of you and Allum! I *hate* you!'

There was another gunshot. Ember felt her chest exploding with pain, but she had folded herself away, deep inside herself, just as Quoma's abuse had taught her to, and she didn't acknowledge it. She felt herself falling again, her years fluttering by her like a warm wind.

It was another night. Ember was eighteen. She was lying on a thick, furry rug on the floor of an elegant room, a slender acer tree standing in its corner by a long glass window. Moonlight slid across her naked body.

'I love you,' said Surrey. He kissed her ear.

Ember smiled. 'I bet you say that to all the girls.' She hesitated, adding quietly, 'I haven't seen Quoma around.'

'You won't be seeing him around.'

'You did it?'

'Yes.'

'For me?'

'Always for you.'

The room twisted and shrank and Ember was swimming amid her memories once more, snatches of them passing just out of reach. She fell right through them and back into the present. She felt calmer now, almost peaceful as she lay on the floor looking up at Akhezo.

His face swam, turning into Surrey's.

'I love you,' she whispered, and then a hard blackness slammed into her, knocking everything away.

When Butterfly reached Senior Surrey's office, he saw that Silver's guess had been right. Senior Surrey was standing over the acer tree in the corner of his room. The pale light of the dying day washed in through the glass wall, lighting up the mottled grey-red leaves of the tree so that they glowed, making them look almost as though they were on fire.

Senior Surrey turned as Butterfly entered the room,

an expectant look on his face, but it fell away as soon as he saw who it was. 'Butterfly,' he said stiffly.

'I need you to come with me.'

'Why?' Senior Surrey's hand moved behind his back. It was just a fleeting gesture, but Butterfly knew that he'd taken hold of a gun by the tightness in his arm.

Butterfly lifted his own gun. 'There's something I want you to see.'

'I'm afraid I can't go with you. I'm waiting for somebody.'

'Ember? She won't be coming.'

Something flickered in Senior Surrey's eyes. 'You have her?'

Butterfly nodded.

'Will she be coming back?' Senior Surrey didn't add what Butterfly knew he meant; will she be coming back *alive?*

'I doubt it,' Butterfly answered quietly.

Senior Surrey glanced away. Butterfly moved forward, ready for a fight, but when Senior Surrey looked back at him there was such sad defeat in his eyes that Butterfly faltered.

'If I come with you,' Senior Surrey said, taking the gun from behind his back and handing it to Butterfly, 'will you spare her?'

And just like that, Butterfly realised suddenly what was going on; Senior Surrey *loved* Ember. For some reason, the realisation made Butterfly hate him even more. How could anyone who knew what it felt like to love do the things he had done?

'Will you spare her?' Senior Surrey asked again.

'Yes,' Butterfly lied.

Silver and Joza ran out of the Stacks into murky afternoon light. They crouched down behind a line of trees at the side of the road to catch their breath. The sky was glaringly grey, the fierce whiteness of the hidden sun threatening at the paint-like edges of the clouds, and Silver could smell oncoming rain in the air.

The Council District was almost empty now. Some of the buildings looked as though they had been bombed, fire flickering from their empty windows, smoke curling from their tops. From far away came the deep chugging thud of smallbombs, muted but still strong even at this distance. Silver felt their impact in her bones. A slow, rolling shudder that made her sick with worry.

'Where are our parents?' she asked Joza.

'They're with Percie's team,' he said, touching her shoulder. 'Don't worry. They'll be safe with her.'

Silver flinched as what sounded like a grenade went off nearby. Shouts rose up, a few cries. She craned her head to look round the trees at the source of the noise. Smoke billowed up the broad avenue of Noda Parkway, rolling slowly towards them.

'The fight's coming this way,' he said. 'Everyone has orders to come here after they've finished with their diversions. We're going to secure the Council District. Do you –'

There was a sudden flash of brilliant, blinding white. Silver felt the ground lift beneath her as she was thrown into the air, crashing down amid a cloud of smoke. For a few moments, her mind struggled to grasp what was happening. Lights danced and whirled in front of her eyes. She gasped for breath, winded by the fall. Then, through the whirling grey smoke and ash, she saw masked soldiers running towards her, and her brain clicked back into place.

She scrambled up, pulling the gun from her belt. The soldiers fell as her bullets hit their legs, but more were coming, too many for her to overcome, and she turned, running back up the steps towards the Stacks.

The tall atrium was deserted. Silver ducked behind the reception desk, her breathing so loud she pressed a hand over her mouth, terrified someone would hear her. The noises of battle reached her from outside. She thought about Joza out there, and Butterfly, and her mother and father, and even Taiyo and Allum, who had been her friends once. She wasn't sure what they were now.

Crouching there in the dark space behind the desk, she thought about staying hidden, about waiting here for the battle to be over. Immediately, she felt disgusted at herself. After everything she had seen, after everything she had been through, how could she be a coward now? Silver's own parents were out there fighting. Her mother, who usually spent her job as a nurse healing people. Her father, who couldn't even bring himself to kill a fly. And there were hundreds of Ghosts and Pigeons out there risking their lives for the futures of others.

She could hear Ember's voice sneering, *You see, Silver? You're not an Elite. Your DNA is worthless. You're nothing.*

'I'm *not* nothing,' she said loudly.

Silver knew she wasn't an Elite now, but what she'd realised was that didn't make her worse than an Elite. It made her *better* than one. She was just a normal Red girl whose blood was filled with a fierce fire to protect the people she loved and save her city from the cruelness of others. She might be ordinary, but right now that was the most empowering thing in the world.

She remembered feeling ashamed of her ethnicity back in Leanor and Emeli's house the night before the Purge, and being surprised at how a Mainlander like Percie had married her Red brother. How stupid she had been. The Council had got it wrong. No, Neo-Babel's *founders* had got it wrong all those years ago when the city was first created. A person's DNA shouldn't dictate their lives. Skin-tone, genetics; how could any of those things decide what a person could become? That sort of thinking only bred hatred and created people like Ember who thought science had proven that their races were superior, and Reds like Silver weren't worth a thing.

But science had done nothing of the sort; it was *people* who had used science to turn their prejudices into justifications. And it was time those people were stopped.

Silver knew what she had to do. Raising her gun, she stepped out from behind the desk and ran back outside into the roar of gunshots.

40

A New Neo

The far western edge of the city was quiet. Not silent; noises from the battle drifted across on the smoke-tinted air, and there were soft rumbling tremors through the ground. But it was quiet all the same. The battle seemed to be concentrated in the Council District and eastern half of the inner city, leaving the western side clear of fighting. Some people had gathered on the streets to watch the battle from afar, but most took cover inside their homes, so when Butterfly slowed the motorbike to a halt, stepping off it with a gun aimed at Senior Surrey's head, no one confronted them.

'Get off,' Butterfly ordered.

He had stolen the motorbike from a street in the Council District, and he'd used it to bring Senior Surrey to the waterfall at the edge of the city. He'd get back to the battle as soon as he could, but there was something he had to do first.

Without a word, Senior Surrey dismounted the bike and walked forward as Butterfly motioned down the street. It was broad and straight, lined with neatly trimmed trees at its riverside edge. At its end was a platform overlooking the waterfall where the city's river tumbled out to join its course back in the Outside. They walked along the edge of the street. Wind lifted spray at them, sprinkling their clothes and skin with small droplets. Down to the right, the waterfall disappeared under the heavy lid of the city walls, half hidden by a curtain of fine mist.

'This is what you wanted me to see?' asked Senior Surrey when they stopped at the platform at the end of the street. Water roared beneath them. 'I'm sorry to disappoint you, but I've been here before.'

Butterfly shook his head. He motioned to the towering grey-black wall in front of them. '*That* is what I wanted you to see.'

Senior Surrey raised his eyebrows. 'The city walls? Again, I've seen those plenty of times.'

'No,' Butterfly said, his voice tight with anger. 'I want you to see what is *beyond* them.'

Senior Surrey did not respond to that.

Butterfly pressed the gun to the back of his head, pushing him forward until he was against the railing lining the platform. 'You made me come here once on a boat,' Butterfly said, shouting to be heard over the roar of the water. 'Following what I thought were the dead bodies of my parents and baby sister. For ten years, I thought they were dead. *Ten years*. Do you have any idea what that's like?'

Senior Surrey said nothing.

'I learnt to think of them as dead,' Butterfly continued. 'Even when I actually met my mother and sister in the Outside a week ago, I thought they were ghosts. But I

332

started to believe in them again. And then guess what happened.' He pressed the gun harder against Senior Surrey's head. 'You took them from me *again*.'

Water dripped into Butterfly's eyes. His hair, which lay across his forehead, was slick with river-spray. The feeling reminded him of something, and he hesitated for a moment as he cast his mind back, searching for the memory. It came to him like a hand reaching out to take his; kissing Silver in the woods outside Yasir's village. He remembered the feeling of her lips, water running down their faces. The hope he had felt blooming inside their mouths. The feeling of coming home, the feeling of *rightness*.

And he remembered what came after.

Butterfly blinked, bringing himself back to the mist-filled platform at the edge of the city. 'Climb,' he said, motioning at the railing.

Senior Surrey was as composed as ever. 'As you wish.' He climbed over the railing, holding himself in place, and craned his head back to look at Butterfly. 'If you want to kill me,' he said, 'there are more effective ways to do it.'

Butterfly shook his head. 'I'm not going to have your death on my conscience. This way, you leave Neo which-ever way. You might live. You might be killed. But I'm not going to be the one that makes that decision. I'll leave it up to them.' He nodded up at the sky.

Senior Surrey smiled. 'You're sounding rather like a Red.'

'Good,' Butterfly said. 'Some of the best people I know are Reds.'

Senior Surrey turned back to the water. He squared his shoulders, took a deep breath, and then jumped.

Butterfly looked away from the churning water that had swallowed Senior Surrey's body. He wasn't sure what he'd expected to feel, but as he walked back to the motorbike, he felt his body sagging with relief. Warm tears clouded his eyes, and he knew that it was over.

Back in the Council District, Silver was fighting alongside a group of Pigeons and Ghosts who were storming Council House.

It was a small building on a street parallel to Noda Parkway. A large number of Council members were being protected inside it, and the Pigeons and Ghosts were outside, attempting to break through the barrier of soldiers. Bullets sprayed the air like metal raindrops. They tore through the city with high-pitched screams that almost deafened Silver as she and the group advanced on the building. She let her Elite instincts take over. Her hand moved as of its own accord, as though her gun was a magnet that pulled only towards soldiers. She was one of the most skilful shooters there, and although the group were making good headway, more and more of their number were falling as enemy fire found their mark.

'Fall back!' cried the female Ghost leading the group.

Silver didn't know who the woman was or where Joza had gone, but she wanted to help where she could, and these were the first people she'd run into after leaving the Stacks.

The group fell back behind a building to the left, pressing themselves up against the wall, panting.

'We need to place a smallbomb,' said the female Ghost. 'To clear our way through.'

'I'll do it.' A young Red man stepped forward. From the look of his clothes, Silver guessed he was a member of the Pigeons.

The female Ghost nodded. She turned to Silver, her eyes sharp. 'You cover him – your aim is excellent. Shoot the bomb when it's placed, then move across to the right of the building. We'll come from the left, ready to enter after the explosion.'

'Understood,' said Silver.

At once, the female Ghost passed the small explosive to the Red and he darted from out from behind the wall. Silver followed close behind. She barely thought as she ran, shooting swiftly at the masked soldiers that fired at them.

They were just at the steps to the front of the building when the Red tripped. He straightened quickly, but a round of bullets had already found him. His body fell still. The soldiers turned their attention to Silver but she dodged their fire, running to the man's body and grabbing the smallbomb from his hand.

Bullets flicked off the ground around her as she darted up the steps. At the doors to the building, one of the soldiers guarding them moved and she slammed into him, her knee connecting with his stomach. Silver turned to take down the others when hands grabbed her round the waist, lifting her up.

'Hold your fire!' a deep voice commanded the soldiers. It was Allum.

He twisted Silver round and slammed her against the wall of the building. His dark eyes were cold. He held her up by her neck, and Silver could almost feel her bones being crushed beneath his hands.

'I *defended* you,' he said. There was no booming laugh now, no affectionate cry of 'Baby Silver!' Hardness and anger had replaced all of that. 'When Ember and Senior Surrey thought you and Butterfly were working for an anti-birthchip group, I defended you both. I didn't believe them until they showed me the evidence – your birthchip records, the Limpets boy's testimony. I didn't believe them,' he said again, as though saying it would make it true.

Silver was still clutching the smallbomb in her left hand. With the other – her gun had dropped to the floor when Allum had got hold of her – she clawed at his fingers round her neck. A pulsing red light had crept into her vision. 'Please,' she gasped. 'Let me explain –'

'They are making Taiyo fight!' Allum roared. 'Even if she is an Elite, she is still just a child. She isn't ready for battle. But because of the destruction you brought to the city, they are sending her out to her death!'

There was a flicker of movement from behind his head. Silver saw the female Ghost running for cover to a statue at the side of the street, and then she leant out, signalling to Silver. None of the soldiers seemed to have seen her; they were too intent on Silver and Allum's confrontation. The female Ghost made a throwing motion with her hand, and Silver knew in an instant what she wanted her to do.

'What was so important to you to risk your Elite family's lives?' Allum squeezed Silver's neck harder. '*Our* lives?'

Tears filled her eyes. 'I'm sorry, Allum,' she whispered. She wished she could explain it all to him. She wished she could open her mind and take her memories into her hands, giving them to him to look at so he could understand. But there was not enough time and not enough words, and she only had that one second to look into her friend's eyes before –

Smash!

The glass doors to the building shattered as bullets whipped through them. Allum loosened his grip just enough for Silver to swing her arm round, and she threw the smallbomb as hard as she could through the broken doors. Then the female Ghost was running up the steps, her gun searching for the bomb.

Butterfly was walking towards the Council District. He'd taken the motorbike back from the waterfall on the city's eastern edge as far as he could before having to walk. He could have flown, but it seemed a perverse thing to do when there were bodies lying still on the ground.

The ruined streets smelt of gunpowder and burnt things. Shattered glass crunched beneath his boots. Ash and debris drifted down from above like a ghostly rain, and walking through it he felt as though it was the dead whispering to him. Once Butterfly would have gone to them, would have given up his body to the promises of darkness. But now the thought of Silver was like a glowing thread, holding him to the world of the living.

He stopped when he reached the river's Inner Circle. Flames burned wetly in the water, charred bits of debris puncturing the reflections flickering in its surface. The fire of the buildings behind him bloomed across the water. It was like looking into someone else's dream. Beyond the water were the darkly shining buildings of the Council District.

Butterfly felt a stab of anger at the sight of the place that had taken almost everything from him. He took out his gun, crossing the bridge. Soldiers were clustered round Council House, and he saw with a sudden clenching feeling in his gut that Silver was there too, right at the centre of it all, Allum holding her against the front of the building.

Butterfly began to run. He reached behind him to pull down the zip in his jumpsuit that ran between his shoulderblades. At once, his wings burst out and he pushed off the ground, launching himself into the air and speeding towards Silver.

Below, Ghosts and Pigeons moved out from a side street, running towards Council House. Their bullets shattered its wide glass doors. Butterfly saw Silver swing her arm round, throwing something into the building.

He forced himself to fly faster. He was almost at Council House now, its steps a blur beneath him. Wind screamed past his ears, the roar of the battle swelling as he gave a final hard beat of his wings, reaching out his hands –

Butterfly grabbed Allum, throwing him off Silver and picking her up in his arms. He pushed off the wall of the building to swerve round, flying away from Council House as quickly as he could, even though his whole body burnt with pain at the effort of carrying her.

An instant later, there was a deafening roar as the bomb exploded. The world burst open. Butterfly was thrown, riding the furious wave of the blast, but he forced himself to hold onto Silver, to keep her close to his chest, and the last thing he thought was how he'd been just seconds away from failing to save her from the explosion, from losing her forever, when an iron fist of pain burst its way into his skull and his mind snapped off into darkness.

The explosion was over in a heartbeat. Silver sat up slowly where the blast had thrown her. She felt the heat of the explosion at her back and heard the frenzied shouts of the Pigeons and Ghosts as they ran past her towards Council House, but they sounded distant, and she felt disconnected from it all. A thick cloud of smoke swirled around her, obscuring her view. She didn't understand how just a minute ago Allum had been pressing her against the wall. Butterfly seemed to have come from nowhere. She hadn't even had time to feel relieved that he'd saved her before the explosion had brought them crashing back to the ground.

'Butterfly?' she whispered.

The smoke shifted, and she saw his body lying face down a little way away from her, unmoving. Silver crawled over to him, hardly daring to breathe. She felt a terror then unlike anything before in her life. Fear so strong it made her heart ache. As she pressed her fingers to his neck, her fingers were shaking so much that she almost didn't feel his heartbeat, but it was there beneath his skin, strong and steady. Tears filled her eyes. She was about to lie down next to him – just a moment's rest, just a minute of peace – when she remembered Allum.

Silver scrambled to her feet. She moved slowly, carefully, trying to avoid the bodies that littered the steps of Council House. Halfway up the steps in front of the building, she found Allum.

'No,' she breathed.

A shard of metal pierced his abdomen, and the lower half of his body was crushed beneath a broken slab of wall. Silver didn't need to feel for a pulse. It was clear he was dead.

'No,' she said again.

Silver sat down next to his body and cried. She looked at Allum through her tears, not seeing his mangled body at all, but instead remembering his great booming laugh, his infectious grin. She couldn't imagine how someone that *alive* could now be dead. He hadn't deserved this end. Allum had been good. Always. He was like Butterfly, kind and honest and loyal, and Silver had no doubt that if Allum had learnt what they had about the Council, then he'd have been fighting alongside them instead of against them.

She raised a hand to close his eyelids. As she got up to go back to Butterfly, shouts and whooping noises erupted from Council House behind her, Ghosts and Pigeons streaming suddenly out of the building. They touched hands to her back. 'It's over! We did it!' they cried joyously. 'A New Neo!' Silver tried to return their smiles, but she couldn't. Not yet.

The smoke was clearing as she returned to where Butterfly lay. It trailed along the ground in thick clouds, a chill wind lifting it into the air like sails billowing open, and she saw Joza crouching over Butterfly's body.

He stood as she approached. 'Butterfly will be fine, I think. But we should get a medic to see to him.' His face softened as he noticed the tears streaming down her face. 'Silver, I'm so sorry,' he said, opening his arms.

She went to him, realising that it was the first time she'd hugged her brother since their reunion. She closed her eyes, feeling his arms around her, and her tears fell faster at the realisation that she'd never feel another pair of strong arms – Allum's – holding her ever again.

'Are you all right?' Joza asked, rocking her gently.

'No,' Silver whispered. 'But I will be.'

41

Second Lives

Surrey emerged into his second life out of fire and water. Memories bore him; he struggled through them, trying to break free of their smothering hold. But they wouldn't leave. Ember's face hung in his mind, a pale echo of his past. He longed to see her in the flesh, to make sure she was all right – she *had* to be all right – but of course he could not go back. They'd kill her, too.

Surrey struggled to stand but fell straight down onto wet, grainy earth. A riverbank. His body felt as though it had been pummelled half to death, but as he looked up at the dark sky, the fiery silhouette of Neo-Babel high above him beyond the waterfall, he knew he was alive. He felt a deep rage at that. *If only Butterfly had had the guts to kill me*, he thought, for surely death would be better than a life like this? And there it was, along with the anger –

Fear.

Fear and anger, always hand in hand for him, just as it was for Ember. Lying on the riverbank then, Surrey felt as terrified as he used to get when he was just a boy and his father came home stinking of beer and perfume that was not his mother's. He'd not been able to imagine loving someone as ferociously as he'd loved his mother that night, when he'd picked up the carving knife from the kitchen and plunged it once, twice, into the arm his father had locked round his mother's neck. But Surrey had met Ember, his flame-haired girl who knew what it was like to hate and love so deeply at the same time.

Half drowning in his memories, Surrey watched Neo-Babel burn. He stared at the flames and the fire crawled into him, entering his body and filling him with its heat until he could taste the bitterness of burnt metal in his mouth and feel the screams of the dying scratch across his tongue. He imagined he could hear Ember's screams as she blackened under the touch of flames.

She's alive, she's alive. Surrey made himself think it over and over until he believed it was true. Then he closed his eyes, drifting away into the forgiving emptiness of sleep.

Akhezo began his second life running, which he would later think of as some god's weak idea of a joke.

He'd only just made it out of the Bee-Hives before the earth had given a huge shudder, a moment later exploding with a sound as though the world was bursting open. He was thrown forward by a wall of flame and broken glass. Scrambling to his feet, he'd done the only thing he knew how to –

Run.

Akhezo had found his way back to the deserted centre of the Stacks. He ran through the smashed doors at the entrance into gunfire and smoke. He didn't know what got him through it. Luck? His small size? Speed? Whatever it was, he found himself untouched as he had dashed across the Council District, following the promise of the tall inner-city buildings beyond. He barely noticed the rhythm and flashes of guns, while below his feet the ground replied with shudders and deep, low grumbles that seemed to rock it like an angry sea. His brain only registered glimpses of the city around him. Air-trams hanging from their supports like roosting bats. Broken tendrils of wire dangling overhead, their ripped ends sparking.

When he wasn't able to run any more, Akhezo had done something else he was used to from a lifetime in the skylung; he'd climbed. He was deep in the inner city by then, the buildings tall and tight around him. He went through a building's smashed entrance doors and climbed up the staircase – its lift was not working – right to the top. Later, he would wonder where he got the energy to climb all those stairs. But then, all he knew was that he had to keep moving or the ghost of Ember would catch up with him and clasp her long, perfect fingernails around his neck.

It took hours for Akhezo to reach the top. When he finally stepped out onto the solar-panelled rooftop, night had fallen. The sky was dark and starless. He didn't know where the hours had gone. It felt both like a few minutes and a whole lifetime ago that he had been down in the Bee-Hives.

Up on the roof the wind was strong, bringing with it the stink of ash. A fine mist hung in the air. It prickled

344

Akhezo's skin with drops of moisture. He climbed up onto the parapet that lined the roof and sat, dangling his legs over the edge. For the first time since Neve died, tears fell down his face. Akhezo liked to think of himself as strong, all hard edges and corners. But there, huddling amid the drifting dust and ashes and flame-flecked wind, feeling the unfamiliar wetness of tears pouring down his face and blurring his vision, he had a sudden urge to call out for his mother, forgetting for a moment that he'd never had one, that he didn't even know her face.

He was so lost in thoughts that he didn't hear the roof door open and close behind him. He only turned when he heard a girl's voice say, 'Hey. Are you all right?'

She was a Japanean girl, short, with jet-black hair cropped into a bob.

He didn't answer.

The girl stepped forward. 'I'm Taiyo.'

'Akhezo.'

She joined him on the edge of the roof, crossing her legs under her and sitting facing out at the city. She was wearing a black jumpsuit, the hilt of what looked like a gun protruding from a belt round her hips.

'You look like one of them Elites,' he said.

She nodded. 'I am one.' She hesitated. 'At least, I was. I'm not sure what I am now.' She glanced at him. 'I followed you from the Stacks. What were you doing there?'

Akhezo thought about Ember. How she'd broken Cambridge: her father. *His* father. How she'd taken Neve away from him. She'd killed the only two people in the world he'd ever loved.

345

'There was something I had to do,' he said simply. 'What 'bout you? Why are you here?'

Taiyo nodded at the city. 'I was meant to be out there. But I got scared.'

Akhezo realised that he hadn't wiped his face. He raised a hand and rubbed his tears away. 'I'm not scared,' he said.

She took one of his hands. 'Of course you're not.'

They sat like that for what felt like hours. Akhezo stared out at the city, thinking about the last time he had been looking at Neo-Babel, imagining it all for himself. Now he didn't want any part of it. He wanted nothing to do with this horrible place that had taken Neve and Cambridge away from him. He was finally at the top of the world, but suddenly the world didn't look so good.

Eventually, Taiyo spoke. 'I'm hungry. Let's go get some food, maybe a couple of bedpods to sleep in. What do you say, Akhezo?'

He nodded, and the two of them made their way off the rooftop, still hand in hand.

The main hall of the Stacks was crowded with people. It had been hours since the Pigeons and Ghosts had won the battle. Outside, flames flickered across the city in the dark of the night, lighting the hall with an orange glow. They'd not yet been able to get all the injured to hospital, so for now everyone was gathering in the Stacks. Joza and Percie were giving instructions to anyone not too badly injured to help, setting them to care for others or

346

gather water and food supplies to distribute among the crowd.

Silver watched her brother and his wife move through the hall. They stopped every now and then to listen to the worries of Ghosts, Pigeons and Neo-Babel residents alike. When they reached a group of Council members, Joza and Percie didn't change their behaviour. Joza even wrapped a blanket around a Council member who was shivering badly, the two of them grasping hands for a moment, seeming to share a wordless exchange. Silver felt a rush of affection for Joza then. For the first time she felt proud to call him her brother.

She turned her attention back to Butterfly. He was huddled with her against the wall to one side of the hall, in a private spot behind the reception desk. His hair was messy and caked with dirt. Across his chest a large gash ripped open his jumpsuit from where it had dragged across the ground in the explosion. Silver was changing the bandage on his broken arm; the fabric was already soaked through with blood.

Nurses from Neo-Babel's hospitals had been bringing spare medical supplies to the Stacks all night, and a number of medics worked to check people's injuries. Butterfly had not been as badly damaged in the explosion as Silver had feared. Apart from his arm – which alongside broken bones had a deep gouge from where it had dragged along the ground – the medic had diagnosed him with mild concussion, suspecting a few broken ribs as well.

The hospitals were too full to admit Butterfly yet for tests to confirm the diagnosis. That made Silver anxious.

If they're full with people seriously injured from the battle, she thought, *are my parents among them?*

'Hey,' said Butterfly, raising his healthy arm to touch her cheek. 'You're thinking about them, aren't you?'

She avoided his eyes. 'I can't help it.'

'If your parents are anywhere near as strong as you, they'll be fine.'

She finished changing the bandage and set his arm carefully down onto his lap before curling up against him.

Butterfly wrapped his good arm round her and kissed the top of her head. 'I love you,' he said quietly.

Silver looked up at him. Though scratches and cuts ran across the skin of his face, his blue eyes were gentle, calm. Looking into them she felt as though she could ride away on their wave. 'I love you too,' she said, smiling softly, and she didn't think that she'd ever meant anything more truly in all her life.

They sat like that for the rest of the night, holding on to each other as the busyness of the hall continued around them. Silver's head rested against Butterfly's chest. She listened to his heartbeat loud in her ear, and it helped calm her, helped push away thoughts and images of the death and destruction she had seen over the past few weeks. It made her think of the millions of people out there in the city and beyond, each one with a heart beating just like Butterfly's.

It made her think of life.

People arrived in the Stacks all through the night. The place was noisy with the sounds of frantic conversations, hurried footsteps crossing the plastimarble floor. There were happy cries as friends and family were reunited, their voices bright with the joy of having found each other whole and alive.

Will that be me and my parents, soon? Silver wondered. She could tell Butterfly's injuries were affecting him; he winced every time he moved. Although she was desperate to look for her parents, she couldn't leave him just yet. Besides, she had just remembered something her father had once told her when she was five, after she'd woken from a nightmare in which she had become separated from her parents in a floating arcade. She didn't know why it only came to her then, but she held on to the memory of it, turning it over and over in her mind, his words giving her the strength to wait. To hope.

'I thought I'd never see you again!' Silver had cried, clinging to her father, and he had smiled, squeezing his arms round her.

'*Never* think that, my *mei li*,' he had said. 'We are family. We will always find our way back to each other, no matter what might stand in our way.'

42

The Break in the Wall

Silver and Butterfly were walking through the city. It was late afternoon. Overhead, sunshine blossomed between thin, watercolour clouds, filling the day with soft, amber light. It was not enough to hide the horrors of the city in its devastated state. But it was a start.

They were walking to the eastern edge where the Pigeons had blasted the gap in the wall at the start of the battle. People had been arriving from the Outside all day, bringing food and medical supplies. Many of the Ghosts and Pigeons – and Neo-Babel citizens who'd offered to help – had already gone to meet them, and Silver and Butterfly were also on their way.

Silver hadn't wanted Butterfly to come. 'You need to rest,' she had told him. She'd been trying to sneak away that morning when he'd woken and demanded he go with her.

'I'll rest later,' he'd said, with a hard look in his eyes that she knew meant he wouldn't take no for an answer. 'Once we find them.'

Silver hadn't needed to ask who he was talking about; she'd been thinking about her parents all night.

* * *

They walked steadily, stopping every now and then to help people as they passed. There had been two enormous women in hysterics, trying desperately to repair the damaged hull of their ornately carved boat to save it from sinking, and then a wrinkled old man had batted Butterfly away when he'd tried to take a look at the deep cut on the man's forehead.

'Imbecile!' the man had croaked. 'I have no time for that. I need to find him.'

Who? Silver had wanted to ask, but they'd moved on quickly, the man's search making her desperate to get back to her own. Joza thought their parents might be at the broken section of the wall helping the newcomers. She had to try looking for them there.

Walking in silence, Silver was lost in her thoughts. She looked round at the city that had once been her home. Now it felt as though it belonged to someone else. As they passed through Little New India, she realised that overseeing the information transaction in the chai bar on Brick Lane had been her last assignment. It was strange to think she'd never work for the Council again. What would she do now? What would her job be? Joza and Percie would establish a new government soon. Would they want to involve her? Silver didn't know whether she wanted to help or not.

She thought of the Outside, of the rolling hills, of lying in the grass when she and Butterfly had left the tunnel out of the city and feeling, just for one moment, invincible. Perhaps she'd go back and explore the world beyond the walls. Silver remembered Yasir telling her that once he'd known about the Outside, he couldn't stay in Neo-Babel. She finally knew how he felt.

Every place in the city held memories of her old life. The jamon and brandy bar where Allum had got drunk and danced on the table. The floating arcade on New York Strip where Silver had brought Taiyo to cheer her up after her bad results in the first-year Elite tests. The beach where Silver and her friends had spent their last day together before their worlds were turned upside down. The thought of leaving the place where memories like these lived was unbearable, and yet it was also unbearable to stay.

It took Silver and Butterfly half the day to walk to the eastern edge of the city. As they approached the part of the wall the Pigeons had destroyed, Silver could see a large crowd of people gathered round it. The trucks they'd travelled in were parked nearby. Along with motorised rickshaws, they were being loaded with supplies people from the Outside were bringing.

'Go on ahead,' Butterfly said, stopping suddenly.

Silver turned to him. 'Why?'

He nodded to their left. The explosion that had blasted through a part of the wall had also destroyed the stretch of the Limpets that had been built against it, creating a ragged gap in the slums. The jagged edges of the Limpets' upper floors were exposed, bits of broken wood and metal sheets hanging down from their supports. Singed tarpaulin and canvas flapped in the wind. Silver noticed with relief that there weren't any bodies. The Pigeons must have evacuated this section before the explosion.

People clustered to one side of the gap in the Limpets, talking and sharing food. As she scanned the crowd, Silver's eyes fell on a Japanean boy sitting against a wooden pillar that had broken in two. Something about the stiff way in which he was propped up seemed strangely familiar to her.

'Is that . . . Sauro?' she gasped, grabbing Butterfly's arm. 'The boy in the Limpets who'd been paralysed by a birthchip operation?'

Butterfly nodded. 'Someone must have helped him out.' He leant in and kissed her, his lips hot against hers, before backing away towards the Limpets. 'Find your parents. I'm going to help Sauro. He doesn't need to be a slave in the Limpets any more.'

Silver watched Butterfly go, feeling such a strong rush of love for him that it took her breath away. Then she turned, walking again towards the break in the wall. Beyond, past the vast stretch of dehydrated wasteland, she could just make out the green of grassy hills and forests. The sight filled her with hope. Hope for the future of the city, for its people. For her. She was sure now her and Butterfly's lives were never meant to be confined to Neo-Babel's walls. Before she could find out what those lives would be like though, she had to focus on finding her parents. Plans for the future could come later.

Silver forced herself to look away from the view past the broken wall and to the crowd in front of it. There must have been hundreds of people gathered there, and the place was chaotic with activity as vehicles came and went. She didn't know how she'd ever manage to find her parents. She looked frantically around at the crowd, searching for them.

They didn't appear to be there.

Fear started to well up in Silver's throat. What if after everything she had been through, after doing everything to find them, she'd find out it had all been for nothing, and the only reunion she'd have was with the bodies of two of the people she loved the most in the world?

No, she thought. *I'm not going to think like that. Remember what Dad said – we are family. We will always find our way back to each other, no matter what might stand in our way.* And as she moved through the crowd, forcing herself to believe that any second now she'd see them, the cluster of people in front of her parted, and there they were, just a few feet away –

Her parents.

They were standing close together, heads lowered as they talked to each other. Silver's father's left leg was bandaged, and her mother had one arm in a sling, but apart from that they looked healthy. Her father was saying something to her mother. As he turned, his eyes fell on Silver. He stopped speaking. Silver's mother looked up, following his gaze, and clutched a hand to her chest as she spotted her.

It was as though time had slowed suddenly, slowed right down to just a crawl, and Silver was staring forever at the glorious sight of her parents standing there; her mother's small, bright eyes, her father's gentle face trembling. For one, wonderful moment, Silver looked at them, hardly daring to believe her eyes.

And then the moment was broken. Silver broke into a run, her feet slamming across the ground, her heart pounding in her throat, and she slammed so hard into her father that they staggered back, clutching at each other. In a second her mother was there too, her face buried in Silver's neck. Her mother was laughing, and Silver felt tears spring to her eyes at the sheer beauty of the sound.

She held onto her parents as tightly as she could. All the heartache and pain she'd felt over the last few weeks seemed to melt away as a warmth radiated through her body, bright and exuberant, and she knew that it had all been worth it just to hear her parents' laughter again.

They're alive, she thought, tears streaming down her face. *They're alive.* No word had ever sounded so wonderful in all her life. Whatever happened in the future, Silver knew that if she thought of this moment and remembered how it felt to have her parents' arms round her after weeks of not even knowing if they were alive, she'd have the courage to face anything life could possibly throw at her. It was proof that she'd fought – *bled* – for what she'd believed in.

Silver had heard the rumours about the Elites. That they were superhuman. That they didn't bleed. But of course they did. They were no more or less human than anyone else. And what some people didn't understand was that bleeding wasn't a sign of weakness; it was a sign of *strength*. It demonstrated to the world that you were vulnerable and ordinary, but when you wanted something enough, and fought hard enough for it, you were capable of doing extraordinary things.

'Silver,' her parents kept saying over and over as they held onto her, 'Oh, Silver,' and she heard her name then for what it really meant. Not the money Senior Surrey had paid to get her birthchip hacked. Not the Council's ownership over her as an Elite. But the actual *substance* silver –

Something bright.

Something strong.

Something precious.